The Bottle Conjuror

BOOK ONE: STEFAN

JOHN KACHUBA | JACK GAGLIARDO

BECK AND BRANCH PUBLISHERS

THE BOTTLE CONJUROR BOOK ONE: STEFAN
Copyright©2023 John Kachuba and Jack Gagliardo
ISBN 979-8-9866069-8-9

Beck and Branch Publishers
New York, NY 10024

ADVANCE ACCLAIM FOR THE BOTTLE CONJUROR

"Deftly combining adventure, humor, and romance, the authors bring a centuries-old tale of mystery and magic to life for a modern audience."
~ D. Felton, *author of* Haunted Greece and Rome *and* Monsters and Monarchs: Serial Killers in Classical Myth and History

"Gripping and engrossing. A rollercoaster trip of intellectual delight that weaves history, magic, romance, intrigue, mystery and good-natured humour."
~ Aparajita Hazra, The Gothique: Myriad Manifestations

"How to fit Romani magic, beautiful pickpockets, shifty nobles, bare-knuckle boxers and wicked eighteenth-century London into one ripping yarn? John Kachuba and Jack Gagliardo, able sorcerers both, aren't telling. Jump in and see for yourself."
~ Charlie Haas, *screenwriter and author of* The Enthusiast

The Bottle Conjuror is a work of literary magic. With an illusionist's flourish, the book transforms an arcane historical event into a captivating tale of intrigue, romance, and the dark arts of the Romani culture.
R. A. Moss, *author of* King Robin

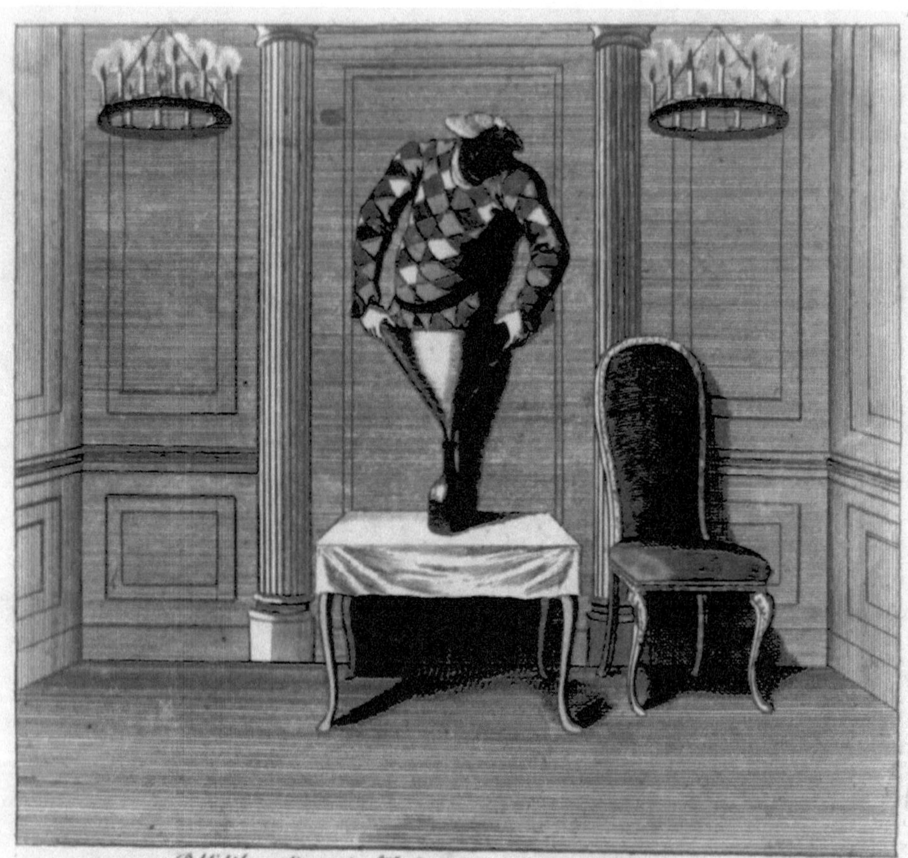

An APOLOGY to the Town, for HIMSELF and the BOTTLE,
By J. * NICK-ALL.

Bedford Coffee-House, Covent-Garden, Feb. the 6th.   * N. B. Mr. P——TT——R was mistaken in the Name.

YE English Sages grave and wise,
  Who Apes of Foreign Lands despise;
Ye Foplings, Flatterers and Smarts,
Who first abroad to shew your Parts,
Ye conqu'ring Heroes and Commanders,
Return'd with Glory Home from Flanders,
Who your own Skill and Talents boast,
And think your Neighbours wholly lost;
Say, cou'd a better Thing be shewn
To make ye all your Folly own?
Let modish Names for tricking cease,
The Bow, the Hen, or what you please:
No Dupes cou'd e'er be better work'd,
Than bottled thus and closely cork'd.

Henceforth be that the leading Phrase,
When one his Ignorance displays.
  French Policy's too much you find
For the weak Species of Mankind,
Your English Beef makes Bodies fat,
But dulls the Head and makes it flat;
Keep to your Province, nor divine
That you can feed on lighter Wine:
An Ox hath often piece-meal crept
Into your Guts with Porter steept;
And cou'd you idly thence infer,
A Man cou'd in a Bottle flit?
  Oft have your Follies known no Bound,
And been a Laugh to Nations round;

But none, like this, cou'd nicer hit
Your reigning Taste and Want of Wit;
Your Taste that still 'gainst Reason flies
To grasp Impossibilities:
And, void of Sense, to all that's new
Impatient flies, or false or true;
Each foreign Gazette now compleat
With Pride reveals the glorious Cheat.
  But still amongst Ye, some there are
Who others Dulness can repair;
What was meant Jest and form'd in Sport
To draw the City, Mob, and Court,
Is nicely manag'd neatly done,
The Bottle was referv'd for LUN.

The above Print is an exact Representation of HARLEQUIN's Escape into the BOTTLE; introduc'd in the Pantomine Entertainment of APOLLO and DAPHNE, or the BURGO-MASTER Trick'd, acted at the Theatre Royal in Covent-Garden, to crouded and polite Audiences.

The Character of HARLEQUIN by Mr. PHILLIPS.

LONDON: Printed for B. DICKINSON, the Corner of the Bell Savage Inn, on Ludgate-Hill. (Price Six-Pence.)

Eighteenth-century map of London around Haymarket Street

*For
Mary and Terri*

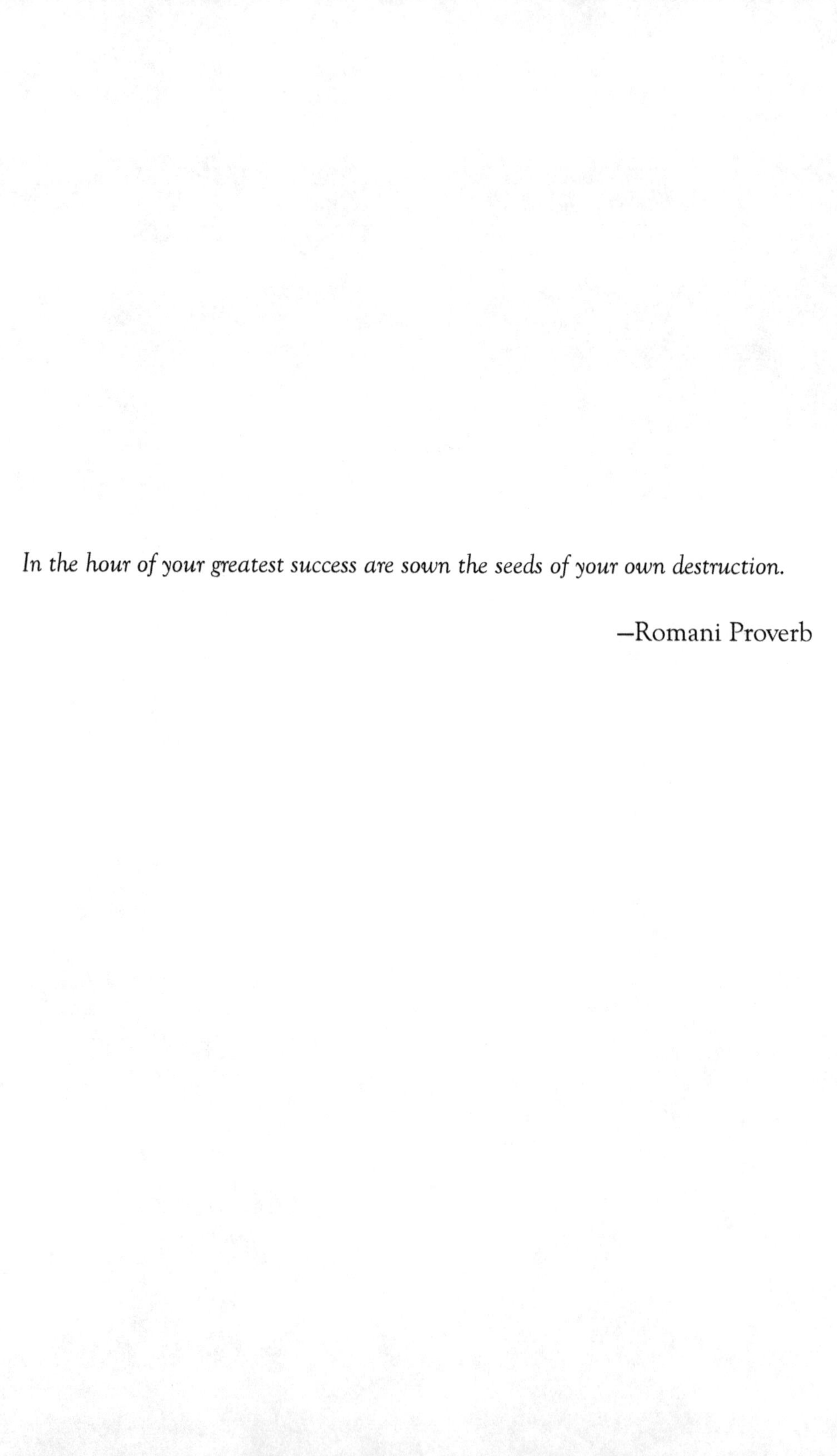

In the hour of your greatest success are sown the seeds of your own destruction.

—Romani Proverb

Prologue: 1729

WISE T⊕ THE ways of the night, Cassandra slipped unafraid through the forest, basket in hand. Moonlight filtered through the dark trees, the mist glowing like ghosts as they floated above the forest floor. Bent over, her worn shawl wrapped around her to ward off the night chill, Cassandra crept slowly between the trees.

"Where are you?" she whispered. She stopped and with a slow wave of her hand parted the mist as though it was solid. "Ah, there you are. So lovely."

She knelt to pick the white mushrooms and place them in her basket. Then, murmuring words known only to herself, she carefully dragged a finger in a circle around the spot where the mushrooms had been. In only a few minutes little caps of white began to poke through the mossy ground, reaching up until a cluster of new mushrooms stood gleaming in the moonlight. Her brother Belasco's favorites. She picked them and put them in the basket. She'd cook them for him when she returned to camp. Looking up to the night sky, she said, "Thank you."

She eased herself up, realizing with a pang that she was beginning to age and was not as spry as she had once been. She picked up the basket and continued her search.

An owl hooted, startling her with its ominous portent of impending death; she blessed herself with the sign of the cross. She started back for camp but then froze, her head cocked to one side, listening. *What was that?* From somewhere far off, she heard a wolf howl but that wasn't what had stopped her. No, something else.

There! A plaintive cry. Human. *The Shaitaan!* And again. No, a woman's cry of pain.

She dropped the basket, the precious mushrooms spilling onto the ground, and ran toward the sound. She heard the woman call out in agony just as she reached her. On the banks of a creek a young woman lay on her side, her water bucket overturned in the grass. Her eyes were wide with fright, her breathing labored.

"Anna!" Cassandra dropped to the ground beside her and rolled the woman onto her back.

"Get . . . Belasco," the woman said, fighting for breath.

"No time, Anna," Cassandra said. She pushed up the woman's skirts. *Oh, merciful angels! So much blood!*

"Please . . . my baby!"

"Be strong. I'm here for you," Cassandra said, even as the baby's head began to crown. Her hands slick with blood, she guided the baby as Anna screamed.

"Hold fast, Anna!"

Suddenly, the baby dropped into Cassandra's hands, squealing like a banshee. She grabbed the knife from her belt, cut the umbilical cord and tied it off. She placed the baby on the grass and turned her attention back to the mother. *But the blood, the blood!* How could she stop it?

Anna's eyelids fluttered, then closed. Cassandra shook the woman by her shoulders. "Don't you go away on me, Anna! Your baby needs you!" No response. She pressed her fingers against the woman's throat, just below her ear and felt a feeble pulse. Once. Twice. Then, nothing. "No!" Cassandra sat back on her heels, staring mutely at the young woman's face turned marble-like in the cold moonlight. She wiped the tears from her face with her bloodied hand, feeling the warm blood leaving a sticky trail on her skin.

The squalling baby brought her back to her senses. She picked up the baby. She wrapped it in her shawl and noticed the leg cocked at an odd angle. A tear fell from her eye, anointing the baby's forehead. "Ah, poor little boy! The Fates have played you false." She slowly pushed herself up, the baby a burden in her arms, and walked toward the camp.

In a forest clearing, over forty Romani wagons nestled in a fortress-like circle. Belasco, a tall, handsome Roma with hair dark as a raven's wing, sat on a stump. He took a deep breath, the sweet night air reminding him that nothing in this world could stop him from enjoying his magic, performing his juggling, and being rewarded for his talents. How easy it was to have *gorgers* toss their coins in appreciation of his talents!

He laughed loudly, catching his friend, Rafael, by surprise. Belasco looked at his stout friend and took a long, cool drink from a bottle with a crude label portraying a juggler entering a similar wine bottle. He placed the near-empty bottle on the ground.

Rafael picked it up for yet another swig and slurred, "You know Belasco, the more I drink, the more the juggler on this bottle reminds me of you."

Belasco smiled, took back the bottle and wiped the neck with his billowy sleeve, He took a drink. Somewhere, the distant cry of a wolf split the quiet night, worrying Rafael. "It's just a love-crazed wolf. Not to worry, my old friend. Here," said Belasco, handing him a coin. "Tell me, what is on the coin?"

Rafael held the coin up to the light from the campfire. "It's the face of the king, the bastard that he is."

"And on the other side?"

Rafael turned the coin over. "Britannia sitting on a throne."

"Now," said Belasco, "give me back the coin." Rafael handed the coin to Belasco, who flipped it high into the air. "Catch it, Rafael!"

His friend stumbled from his seat but caught the coin before it hit the ground.

"Take a look, Rafael. What do you see?"

Rafael looked at the coin resting in his hand. "Why, it's the image of a coiled snake!" Curious, he turned the coin over. "And it's the same on both sides!"

Belasco sat back and grinned. His astonished friend grabbed the wine bottle and took another drink. Belasco was about to reach for the bottle, but something stopped him. He looked around the camp. The fire burned brightly, making it difficult to see into the surrounding woods. He heard twigs snapping in the darkness, as if a large animal was rapidly approaching.

Rafael jumped up. "Did you hear that?"

Belasco felt a cold breeze, turned, and stared into the dark forest. "Hush, my friend, something is in the wind this way."

A silhouette of a woman emerged from the dark and was illuminated by the campfire. For a moment, the woman neither moved nor spoke as she struggled to catch her breath.

"Cassandra? Is that you?" Belasco said.

She walked toward him, carrying something bundled and twitching in her tattered shawl. He saw the distraught expression on her face. Now, only a few feet away she held out the bundled baby.

"Cassandra! What . . .?" Looking at the baby, he felt the hairs on the back of his neck rise. "Where's Anna? What's happened?" She sadly shook her head, fighting back tears, and held the baby out to him. At that moment he understood. "No! That can't be! She can't . . ."

Cassandra again attempted to place the child in his arms. "It's a boy, Belasco. My dear brother, you're all he has now. Here, take him." As she moved closer to him, holding out the child, her shawl fell away, revealing the baby's deformed leg.

Belasco backed away, horrified. He looked to Rafael, who didn't understand what was happening. Belasco turned back to his sister and stared at the child's left leg, crooked and bent to the side. "No," he said, almost whispering, "I can't."

"He's your son!"

"And born with the Devil's mark! No, I won't care for him. I won't!" The anguished father suddenly grabbed the wine bottle from Rafael, shoving him out of the way, and ran out of the camp. The darkness of the forest swallowed him up.

Tears slid down her cheek. Cassandra called after him, "Belasco! Come back!" Her cry became an echo. The wolves howled in reply.

Chapter One

. . . .

TWENTY YEARS LATER

CASSANDRA STOOD IN the shade of the trees, contentedly smoking her pipe. Surrounding her, gaily painted Romani wagons stood like a wall, circumscribing a ring in the forest clearing. Several Romanies gathered around a cooking fire in the center of the camp, singing and passing a bottle around. Someone was playing a hammer dulcimer, the bright notes of the "Fire Dance" lifting into the sky like colorful butterflies. That tune always brought back memories for Cassandra. Some beautiful, others not so. Her attention drifted to her nephew, Stefan, sitting with the others on a log around the fire, his walking stick lying beside him. The young man was always up to some prank, or busy practicing his magic. Apparently, today was not to be an exception.

"Ah, a four-legged assistant," Stefan said. He grabbed a black cat that had rubbed up against his boots by the scruff of its neck before it could run off. As the others laughed, he stuffed the struggling cat into a leather bag. "In you go, my friend."

Stefan held the bag aloft. The bag pulsed and jerked in his grasp as the screeching cat tried to claw its way out.

"Careful, Stefan!" a woman called out.

He smiled, shook the bag hard one time and suddenly, the bag went limp. Deflated. He opened it, turned it upside down, crumpled it in his hands and threw the empty bag on the ground.

Cries of astonishment rose among the group. "What devilry is this?" a man said, making the sign to ward off the evil eye.

Twenty feet away, the black cat glared at Stefan, hissing, then turned tail and ran off into the woods. Stefan beamed. He had their attention now and played it up for all he was worth. Picking up his walking stick, he held it to his lips as though he were playing a flute. By now, the dulcimer music had stopped, suspended in mid-note by the antics around the fire.

All was quiet. Stefan took a breath, placed his fingers along invisible holes on the stick, and blew. The same tune that only moments ago had echoed through the camp, now emanated from the walking stick turned flute. Dulcet tones, clear and lovely.

The people were mesmerized, listening raptly to Stefan's music, but suddenly they were on their feet, scrambling to get away as they noticed simultaneously with the musician that the stick-flute was now neither stick nor flute, but had morphed into a writhing black snake. Stefan shrieked and threw the snake down, falling off the log, his lame leg preventing him from running away.

"Damnation!"

The coiled snake bared its fangs at him. The others huddled a safe distance away. Stefan, wide-eyed with fright, could not move.

From the shade of the trees, Cassandra calmly walked to the fire, her pipe still clenched between her teeth. The snake turned its head to her, hissing, its forked tongue flicking. She raised her right arm, reared back, then made a violent throwing motion toward the snake, as though hurling a stone at it.

The snake froze.

She approached it but the snake did not move. She grabbed it by the head and picked it up, the body still coiled. The snake had turned to wood. She tossed it to the onlookers, scattering them like wind-blown leaves. She chuckled and reached down to where Stefan lay sprawled on the ground. She helped him up.

"How . . . how did you do that?" the shaken young man asked.

She removed the pipe and smiled coyly. "Do what?"

"You know what I mean. The snake."

"You assume much, nephew." She tapped the ash from the pipe onto the ground. "Come, walk with me."

Stefan leaned on her as she led him to her vardo. They sat on the steps. "I certainly didn't conjure up that snake, Cassandra. It scared the daylights out of me."

"Maybe you didn't but your skills are escalating. You have the makings of becoming truly great," she said. "You could do that."

He sighed. "Do you really think so? I want to be, great," he said, looking down at his deformed leg, "but I have the Devil's mark."

"No! You have the mark of the conjuror."

He looked across the camp to where the others were still marveling over the wooden snake. "What more must I do? What more is there to learn?" He turned to her. "I'm bored with simple sleight of hand tricks.

Any fool can do those. I want something that will make me famous. I want people to say, 'There goes Stefan, the world's greatest conjuror.'"

She looked into his dark eyes and saw traces of her brother Belasco in their depths. Stefan had the same good looks, the same dark hair, the same longing for something beyond his grasp. She hoped, no, she prayed Stefan would not end up like his father.

"It will happen, Stefan."

"When? I'm twenty years old, practically an old man!" She laughed. "I'm serious, Cassandra."

"Yes, I know. I can see that you are. You're ambitious. I've seen that in men before. It's not always a good thing. But you are who you are, for good or ill. I have always looked after you, haven't I?" He nodded. "I will always do so."

"So, tell me," Stefan said, "what must I do to learn real magic? There must be something no one has ever done before."

She looked away, peering into the gathering shadows in the forest, seeing again all that had transpired twenty years ago, all that had brought them to this time, this place. She knew that it had always been fated.

"There is . . ."

"Yes?" Stefan said, leaning closer to her.

"It's . . . no. I can't tell you. There are so many other astonishing things you can learn. And I don't mean parlor tricks. I speak of wondrous feats. True magic!"

He looked at her silently, searching her face for deception, but not finding it. "Like what?" he finally asked.

She smiled. "I'll show you." She pushed herself up from the step and entered her vardo. Stefan heard her rustling around inside. She returned and sat down beside him. She held something wrapped in a shawl on her lap.

"What I'm about to show you must never be trifled with. I've long debated even showing it to you but think that now may be the time."

She unwrapped the shawl, revealing a small, worn leather book, *Liber Umbrarum* inscribed in gold. She gazed at it with reverence and, Stefan thought, sadness.

"*The Book of Shadows*," she said, softly. "What you may learn in these ancient pages, Stefan, could truly make you the world's greatest conjuror."

His eyes burned with excitement. "Please! May I see it?"

She held the book out to him, but a twinge of doubt unsettled her. He almost had to tug the book from her hand. His fingers moved quickly but carefully through the parchment-thin pages. He saw strange drawings and symbols, chants, and invocations in Latin and other languages he didn't recognize. So many chapters with beguiling titles promising truly wondrous magic: *How To Draw A Fountain From A Stone*; *Walk On Water And Not Drown*; and *The India Mango Tree*. He had no idea what these were about, but he could feel in his bones that they promised greatness. A chill coursed through him when he came to a section titled *Revenants*. He paused; his eyes riveted on something at the bottom of the page. "What's this? *The Bottle Conjuration*? It looks fascinating."

"Oh, Stefan, forget that one. Put it out of your mind!" She had to lure him away from that conjuration, turn his thoughts elsewhere.

He looked up, confused. "What's the matter?"

She looked at him as if seeing him for the first time. He was no longer a child. Fate is fate, she thought. It cannot be denied. She sighed. "Many people have tried to do the Bottle Conjuration. It's dangerous. Life threatening. How could anyone ever fit inside a wine bottle?"

Stefan's eyes opened wide. "Fit inside a wine bottle!"

"Yes. Imagine the endurance, the excruciating pain it would take to do such a thing. The sound of bones crunching. The sight of a man disappearing before your eyes!"

"I would surely become the greatest conjuror of all time," he said, his eyes glowing. "That would be spectacular!"

"No. That would be suicide."

He heard the sadness in her voice, and saw it written on her face. There was a mystery there, he could see that, but could not fathom what it may be. As Cassandra sat lost in her thoughts, his eyes drifted. He saw as if for the first time, the magnum wine bottle tucked beneath a stool in her wagon. The bottle whose label depicted a harlequin half-descended into a wine bottle. His voice low, he said, "You say it can't be done, I say I can do it."

Fear swept through her. How could she prevent him from trying the conjuration? She snatched the book from his fingers.

"What the . . .?" he said.

"No, it's too dangerous!"

Slowly, he pushed himself up from the step. He stood, clutching the side of the wagon. "I vow to learn this magic."

She shook her head as he started limping across the clearing. "Stefan!"

He stopped and turned, swaying unsteadily. "Don't worry, Cassandra." He noticed the snake, alive once again, slithering out of the brush. He stood his ground, then made the same throwing motion he had seen Cassandra make. Instantly, the snake transformed back into his walking stick. "I'm not afraid."

"Maybe you should be afraid," she said. "Remember, the borderline between good and evil magic is as fine as a spider's web."

Chapter Two

. . . .

THE PIG'S HEAD was a smoke-filled London taphouse where the pints flowed as freely as the women who worked the floor. Henry Roberts, a stocky brute of a man with a stubbly red beard resembling the bristles of a paintbrush, owned the tavern. He wiped the sweat from his brow while simultaneously filling a large mug of ale from a cask. He momentarily took his eyes off the mug when he saw that Lucinda, an attractive young brunette was resting her arm on the bar as if she didn't have a care in the world.

"Look lively, girl! The gypsy girls will be here soon. Best get your mark before the competition strikes." Lucinda half-smiled and half-sneered back at him. He scowled. "Get a move on! And don't gyp me on my cut of the take."

"Believe me, they are no competition to me," she said. "And by the way, you're spilling the ale."

"Bloody hell!" Foam spilled over Henry's hand and puddled on the floor.

Lucinda's deep blue eyes scanned the room. Some bootnecks from the Royal Navy filled the taphouse that night, a bit rowdy and not worth the risk. A table or two of the usual loud riffraff, half-drunk, were knocking back their ale, spilling much of it on themselves and the floor.

A gentleman sat by a window. He looked to be every inch an aristocrat. By the way he tilted in his seat, it looked like he had imbibed far too much grog. Lucinda smiled. An easy mark. She spied a bulging vest pocket under his purple jacket. The gentleman was trying to keep himself upright in the rickety pine chair which seemed determined to toss him to the floor. He looked up, delighted to behold the comely Lucinda.

"My, my," he said.

His chair suddenly took a precipitous dip backward. She quickly reached out to steady it, while fingering his jacket, deftly removing a few coins from his vest.

"Tell me my lord, is this coat lined in silk?" she asked.

The gentleman could only slur a response. Realizing he was not making himself clear to her, his hopeful intention being to bed her, he reluctantly waved her away.

Within view of her encounter with the gentleman sat a short, balding cigar smoker who had been watching the little dance between Lucinda and the gentleman with interest. William Haymarket owned the theatre that bore his name directly across the street. At one time, the Haymarket Theatre had a reputation as the cultural epicenter of London, but now it functioned more as a venue for song and dance troupes, a few plays, and an occasional night of opera. William knew talent when he saw it and recognized Lucinda's thievery as talent, indeed.

As she walked by, heading for the bar, he grabbed her arm, pulling her close. Before she could react, he whispered in her ear, "You, my dolly, are not only beautiful but talented." He pried open her fist, revealing two silver coins.

Without causing a scene, she struggled to free herself from his grasp and keep hold of the stolen money.

"This can be our little secret," William whispered. "Please, come sit with me."

She struggled harder but was surprised how strong this little man was. She looked back to make sure Henry hadn't noticed this confrontation, but as usual, his attentions were behind the bar, filling more mugs of ale.

William let her close her fist, retaining her coins. "I mean you no harm, lass," he said, smiling. "I have a proposition that will reward your, uh, natural ability. It will make these two coins seem a pittance. I own the Haymarket Theatre. Come with me. I have someone you should meet."

Before she could reply, the double doors of the Pig's Head burst open. A raucous troupe of gypsies entered, ready to entertain the patrons. They were led by Sophia, a beautiful olive-skinned woman who wore one large silver hoop earring in her left ear. Her colorful skirt, adorned with stars and moons, swirled as she walked. The other women started tapping their tambourines, adding to the cheers of the happy crowd.

William pulled Lucinda closer, trying to make himself heard over the din. "Come with me," he repeated. "You won't regret it."

The last of the gypsies to arrive was Stefan who had been the girls' cart driver and escort. He limped toward the bar.

"Hey!" shouted Henry from behind the bar, "You best turn around and get out. This is a respectable establishment!"

Stefan stopped in his tracks. Everyone was looking at him. He gripped his walking stick tightly.

"I said, NO gypsies!" The girls stopped dancing. The crowd looked at Henry. "Well, I mean, no gypsy MEN!" and with that, the crowd cheered.

Stefan inched closer to the bar.

Red-faced, Henry yelled, "Are you crippled *and* deaf? Get out!"

"It's been a long hot ride from our camp," said Stefan. "Could you not spare a cool cup of water? I'll gladly drink it outside where I can perform my street conjuring."

Henry bulled around from behind the bar and grasped him by the collar. "You're a damn trickster!"

Stefan clutched his walking stick tighter. He smelled Henry's foul breath on his face. "No, actually I'm a conjuror," he said, "so please, some water?"

Henry pushed him backward toward the door. "If you want water you can conjure up a glass." He gave Stefan a final shove, pushing him stumbling into the street. "Or you can drink from the horse trough for all I care!"

Stefan fell into the street. Henry slammed the door shut, the "Always Welcome" sign swaying from the vibration.

William had been watching the scuffle. "Well, now, that was entertaining, but I really need you to come with me." Lucinda pushed herself away, grabbed a pitcher of water from a table, and headed for the door.

Outside, Stefan wiped the dust from his pants and tried to straighten his rumpled jacket. He limped to his walking stick lying a few feet away. As he retrieved it, the tavern doors opened. Lucinda stood framed in the light from the doorway. She looked like an apparition, with smoke from the tavern streaming around her. She held a tall pitcher of water. She didn't say anything at first, as Stefan looked embarrassed. "No one should go thirsty on a hot night like this," she finally said. She looked into his eyes and held out the vessel to him.

Even in the dark night he noticed the soft glow in her deep blue eyes. Taken aback by her kindness and her beauty, he happily accepted the water. His right hand holding the stick, he clumsily reached for the pitcher with his left hand. His walking stick began to vibrate, causing him to stagger. As he juggled the pitcher, his stick fell away. The pitcher lurched forward, dowsing Lucinda with its contents, soaking her head to toe. The pitcher lay shattered on the ground. The awkwardness of the moment was broken by William who, exiting the tavern, took her by the arm.

"My dear, drenched or not, we have unfinished business to discuss," he said. He noticed a constable approaching on his rounds. He tipped his hat to the constable as if to say, *nothing to be seen here.* He tugged gently on Lucinda's arm and said quietly, "I need you to meet the famous magician, the Soho Swami."

Puzzled, she asked, "Who? Why?"

With a wry smile, William proceeded to guide Lucinda across the street. "Fortune knocks, lass. I can hear her."

Stefan seemed enchanted as he watched her walk away, but the constable interrupted the spell by pulling out his baton and motioning for him to move along.

THERE WERE NO performances that evening so the Haymarket Theatre was dark except for the ghost light burning on the stage and a lamp by the manager's office. In that weak light, Lucinda's eyes gradually took in the ornate majesty of the stately theatre. Even as William led her down a side aisle toward the stage, she stopped, staring up at the gilded balconies, the winged cherubs flying above the proscenium, the velvet curtains.

"I've never been inside before, it's right lovely!"

"As are you," William said, leading her closer to the stage. "With your orbs and bod, you can be much more than the assistant the Swami needs. Why, I think we can . . ."

A tall, cadaverous man wearing a shabby dressing gown stumbled onto the stage from the room at the rear. The sight of William and a drenched woman whose dress clung to her like tissue paper startled him.

"Ah, I'm glad to see you're awake, Swami," said William. "Meet your new assistant." He pushed Lucinda forward.

The Soho Swami stared at her, his eyes traveling up and down her water-soaked body as he tried to puzzle out who she was, why she was there, and why in the hell she looked like she had just been dredged up from the Thames. His gin-fogged brain could not find an answer.

"She's not only beautiful," William said, "but also very talented."

"In the art of magic?" the Swami asked.

"Not a wink. I see you're confused. This lass can float like a butterfly but can strike quickly as a cobra when she deftly plucks a gentleman's pocket. We can all benefit if you two combine your talents."

The magician fished a pocket watch out of his dressing gown and frowned at it, as if he had someplace to go and was already late. With a sigh, he returned the watch to his pocket. "Hmmm, a man of my talents should have an assistant. That's certain. What did you say your name was, girl?"

"Lucinda," she replied.

"Alright then, Lucy, come up here."

She lifted her skirts as she walked up the steps to the stage.

"Why are you sopping wet?" the Swami asked. He gestured as if swatting away a fly. "No matter, I'm sure there's a story there if I really wanted to hear it, but I don't."

The Swami drew himself up theatrically, trying to suppress the effects of his dressing-room gin. "Lend me your ears, Lucy. All you would have to do is bring my props when I call for them and look beautiful for the audience. I do close-up work so you would escort some fine mark, I mean *gentleman*, on stage for me to perform my magic."

He reached into his dressing gown. "Let's see what we have here." He retrieved a red ball and passed it back and forth in his hands as Lucinda looked on.

"Alright, my dear, which hand holds the ball?"

"The right one," she said, but did not seem surprised when the Swami opened his right hand, revealing it to be empty. Nor was she surprised when the ball did not show up in his left hand either.

"Now, Lucy, you would turn to the audience and show that you are as confused as our fine gentleman. Where has the ball gone? I will ask you in which of my pockets is the ball secreted and you . . ."

She slowly walked to the Swami, her eyes fixed on his, a coy smile on her lips. Perspiration gathered on the magician's face as she drew closer. Lucinda took hold of his hand. "Neither," she said, softly.

"No. Actually, I will need you to point to my right pocket and . . ." He reached into the pocket of his dressing gown, but the ball was not there. "Huh?"

He rummaged in the pocket but then gave up, turning his attention to the left pocket. Nothing doing. That pocket was empty as well. The Swami began turning both pockets inside out, vainly searching for the ball. "Where in tarnation . . .?

Beneath the stage, William snickered. "Check your stockings, Swami!"

Lucinda grinned. "Are you looking for these?" she asked, holding out the red ball and the magician's pocket watch.

Stunned, the Swami snatched his watch from her hand. "You're hired!"

Chapter Three

SEVERAL WEEKS HAD passed since Stefan journeyed into London. The night was warm, and without trace of a breeze. The air hung heavy as he hobbled down Fleet Street. He was anticipating a prosperous evening. Besides his loosely fitted and ragged coat, he had a small knapsack draped over his shoulder filled with his essential props. He turned the corner onto Suffolk Street where the Haymarket Theatre and the Pig's Head Tavern were located.

A large group of bloodybacks had arrived home from overseas and, together with the usual bootnecks on shore-leave, Stefan knew the street corner by the tavern would be the perfect location for his conjuring. Once he found his spot, he dropped the knapsack and pulled out a small woven cloth adorned with images of the Sun, Moon, and stars. He placed wooden props of the three astronomical items on the cloth and hid a pair of painted wooden eyes in his coat pocket. He finished setting up his performance area by carefully placing his wide-brimmed leather hat face-up to collect the coins he hoped would be tossed into it by the appreciative crowd.

A woman wearing a light summer dress with a white silk scarf, and accompanied by her gentleman, walked by his makeshift stage.

"Excuse me, my lady," Stefan said, "but I think this belongs to you." The couple stopped as he reached up into thin air. He opened his hand to reveal a deep purple ribbon. The woman smiled. Her gentleman friend wore a more dubious look.

Holding the ribbon in her hand, she said, "Why it's lovely, but it's not mine."

Stefan smiled and acted as though he had made a mistake. "Sorry about that, my lady, but I think you like the purple color, do you not?"

The lady returned his smile and politely replied, "Well, actually purple is my favorite color."

"If you please, madam, may I borrow your scarf?"

She hesitated and looked to her gentleman friend. He nodded his consent. She removed her white scarf and handed it to Stefan. He formed the cloth into a ball in his hand and closed it in his fist. "Maybe this is yours?" he said. Slowly, a hint of purple material emerged from his fist. He pulled and pulled some more, revealing a beautiful purple silk scarf.

Looking down, she exclaimed, "Where did my scarf go?"

He took the purple scarf and draped it over her bare shoulders.

The woman was mystified but had enjoyed the moment. The gentleman took her hand and started to walk away. She nodded and smiled back at Stefan while giving her gentleman a look that told him he needed to toss a few coins into the conjuror's hat.

A small crowd formed before Stefan. Bending down, he took the golden painted suns and began tossing them in the air. Balancing on his good leg, he used his stick to kick up the two moons from the ground. The crowd applauded as he kept the five objects simultaneously circling around him. He called out to the crowd, "May I have a bit of assistance, please?"

Gesturing with his twisted left leg toward the three stars still lying on the cloth, he said, "Would you please, kind sir, grab the stars and toss them to me?" A man from the crowd grabbed the silver-painted stars and held them out to him. "As you can see, I have my hands full," Stefan said. The crowd laughed. "Just toss them up to me one at a time."

The man shook his head in disbelief as he tossed up the stars. They blurred into the circle of objects orbiting around Stefan. The crowd applauded. As all objects were at their apogee, he yelled, "Begone!" As if the night had swallowed them, they disappeared. The crowd cheered. More spectators walked over.

Noticing the crowd, John Montagu, the Duke of Montagu, wove his way through the people for a better view. Tall and dashingly handsome, he was fashionably dressed in a light blue summer coat of the style worn by those of title, although if one were to look carefully at his sleeves, one would notice some fraying around the cuffs. The skill and magical elements of the performer impressed him. He turned to a man next to him and asked, "Who is that man?"

"Don't rightly know, gov'nor. A gypsy looks like. But he's magic alright."

Stefan concluded his performance and walked among the crowd, collecting donations in his hat. In a loud voice to the dwindling crowd he said, "Thank you, friends, but the best is yet to come. Soon, I'll be here to perform the greatest feat the world has ever seen . . . Imagine a man disappearing inside a wine bottle!"

The crowd reacted in wonder and disbelief. An old woman cried out, "Poppycock, it can't be done!"

"Can't it? Come see for yourself, madam. Very soon."

Stefan approached the Duke who tossed a coin into the hat.

"You're quite a capable trickster," the Duke said.

"Conjuror, sir."

Montagu smiled. "Conjuror, then. You can attract quite a mob. Gullible fools, but judging by the silver in your hat, they are willing to pay handsomely to be gulled."

"Begging your pardon, sir, but they are not gulled."

"Oh?" replied the Duke, "Do you expect me to believe you can disappear yourself into a wine bottle?"

Stefan said, "There are stranger things in the world." With that he turned his hat toward the Duke, revealing his earnings had vanished and had been replaced by two wooden eyes.

The Duke looked at the hat and sighed. "Perhaps, but none that I have ever seen. No matter. It's of no concern of mine how you do your trickery . . . excuse me, your conjuring, but I spy an opportunity here."

He pulled Stefan aside as the crowd dispersed. "You deserve a better audience, a richer audience. What would you say if I told you, I could guarantee you a performance . . .?" He turned Stefan toward the theatre. "There. At the Haymarket Theatre where you could earn real money. No passing of the hat. I know the owner of the theatre well. Think of me as your mentor, your financial advisor. As such, I would only charge you a pittance of the harvest. You can rest assured your hat will always be filled with silver, so to speak.

"You could do that?"

"My young friend, the Duke of Montagu is a conjuror in his own right."

Chapter Four

THE PIG'S HEAD was its usual rowdy, rambunctious and smoke-filled den of inebriation the night the Duke of Cumberland, the third son of King George II, and his bewigged and perfumed sycophants sat at a table drinking and playing Whist.

Gypsy women in their colorful rags competed with the regular tavern bawds for the attention of the gentlemen whose purses bulged almost as much as their paunches, but Cumberland's party ignored them. At least for the nonce.

One of the party, the Earl of Peterborough, grumbled, "Leave me be, trollop!" pushing away the searching hands of a particularly ravishing gypsy beauty. The others laughed.

"Ha!" Cumberland suddenly yelled, throwing a card down on the table and taking the last trick. "Come now, gentlemen, you make it so easy. I almost hesitate to take your money." Leaning over the table and greedily raking in the silver coins, he said, "Almost." He beamed at his partner. "Well played, Jeppson."

A sudden commotion at the tavern door diverted Cumberland's attention and caused the women to fly to the door like startled partridges. The Duke of Montagu strode into the tavern as if he owned it. Judging by the fawning reaction of the women swarming around him, bees to nectar, it would seem that, indeed, he was the proprietor or better, for he was a man as known for his skill in bed as he was for his skill at the gambling tables. His black hair, lightly streaked with silver, was tied back with a black ribbon. A thin braid draped by his left ear danced like a windchime as he walked.

He had hardly taken two steps when the bawds surrounded him. He smiled at the women, his gray eyes penetrating their hearts, and politely steered a path through them, stopping only briefly when accosted by Sophia.

The beautiful gypsy clung to him, pressing her body close to his like a cat rubbing against its master's boots. She lifted her face and whispered in his ear, "Tonight, my stallion, my quick talons shall score another mark on your back, if it so pleases you."

"A delightful offer, Sophia," he said, kissing her cheek softly, "but I'm afraid I have other obligations tonight."

As if on cue, Cumberland called from across the room, "Montagu!"

Montagu gently pushed the disappointed woman away. "Another time, love. I promise."

He walked to Cumberland's table, removed his tricorn, and bowed. "Your Grace."

"Come, draw up a chair," Cumberland said. "Make room, gentlemen, for my old comrade in arms." Montagu sat. "We haven't seen your rogue's face in quite some time, Monty. Where have you been hiding?"

"In a hayloft with some frisky milkmaid, no doubt?" Jeppson said, peering over his spectacles.

The men laughed but Montagu did not share in their laughter.

"Just like the battle of the Netherlands Forest, eh, Montagu? You remember," said Cumberland.

Montagu did remember. He clearly remembered the boom of cannon that had spooked him from beneath the covers of the farmhouse bed where he was bravely engaged in swinking the loveliest Dutch blonde he had ever seen. A second volley shook the bed and he leapt to the window naked, the bed quilt trailing behind him. Smoke drifted above the trees in the distance. Below the window, British soldiers were quickly forming up.

The buxom blonde sat wide-eyed in bed, a pillow barely concealing her breasts. "My lord?"

There had been a loud knock on the door as his aide burst in, drawing up short at the sight of the naked woman and naked Duke. "Sir, I . . . uh. . . oh, my, beg your pardon, ma'am." Reluctantly turning his eyes back to the Duke, he said, "Sir, the battle has begun! We must reinforce Lord Cumberland at once!"

"Yes, of course," Montagu said, turning from the window, the quilt ensuring his modesty. "Go and see to my horse."

The aide hesitated, eyes again lingering on the blonde. Montagu took two quick steps to the door and slammed it in his face.

"Sorry, lass, but I must go." The quilt tangled in his feet, tripping him, sending him falling to the bed and the whole thing, naked lady and all, crashed to the floor.

Somehow, she had landed on top of him, her breasts at eye level. "Really?" she said, "I think not."

Oh, yes, he remembered that very well.

Cumberland interrupted his pleasant thoughts. "By the time you got your cavalry on the move, my men and I had won the day. The battle was over."

"There were extenuating circumstances," said Montagu.

"So, I hear. Falling off your horse, several times. Forgetting your sword. What was it, Monty? A little too much John Barleycorn, I'll wager."

"With all due respect, my lord," Montagu said, drawing himself up, "it was hardly a battle. More like a skirmish."

"Yet how would you know? Musket balls whizzing around my ears. Men dropping in their tracks like fallen trees. Does that sound like a *skirmish?*"

Montagu recalled finally arriving at the scene of battle and seeing, not a victorious British army, but instead, a small group of enemy soldiers laughing and firing their muskets in the air as the redcoats, led by the courageous Duke of Cumberland, scampered away. Realizing discretion to be the better part of valor, Montagu chose not to engage his men and retreated, as he now retreated from the conversation in the Pig's Head.

"And would the King . . ." Cumberland continued.

"Your father," Montagu said.

"I say, would the *King* have awarded me this . . ." Cumberland stood, and withdrew a jeweled dagger from his waistcoat. He waved it in the air, a bright red stone in the hilt sparkling in the candlelight, "for a mere *skirmish?*"

The answer was *yes*, but Montagu remained mum.

The room went quiet, the men staring at each other for a few moments before Cumberland laughed and broke the awkward silence saying, "Ah, but all's forgiven, Duke. We are what we are, eh?" He sat down. "And you're a hale fellow for a drink and game of chance." Calling to a serving girl, Cumberland said, "A tankard here for the Duke of Montagu!"

"No ale for me, lass," Montagu said. "Fetch me a bottle of port. Wait; not a bottle, but a magnum of your best."

The girl returned shortly, placing the magnum bottle on the table. She stood waiting, her tray held out, as Montagu fumbled in his waistcoat.

Seeing the duke's fingers were not going to emerge from his pockets anytime soon, Cumberland sighed. "I've got it, Monty. As usual." He dropped some coins in the girls' tray.

She smiled, curtseyed, and walked back to the bar, Montagu's eyes registering the sway of her hips.

As if he had purchased the wine, Montagu uncorked it and filled Cumberland's glass and his own. Peterborough grabbed the bottle and poured the wine for himself and the other two men.

Montagu stood. He raised his glass high. "To His Grace's health!"

The others stood and toasted Cumberland. Once reseated, the men passed the bottle around, drinking, joking, and talking. Women. Parliament. Women. Taxes. Women. The American colonies. Women. Montagu, however, was strangely quiet. While the men talked, he sat toying with the bottle, turning it in his hands, inspecting it closely as though he had never seen glass before.

"What is it, Montagu?" Cumberland asked. "What are you doing?"

"Huh? Oh . . . nothing... Just thinking."

"Well, there's a first time for everything. What were you thinking about?"

Montagu sat back, holding the bottle in two hands. "Your Grace, could you stick your little finger in the neck of this bottle?"

"What? Of course, I could. Are you daft?"

"Two fingers?"

Cumberland took the bottle and stuck two pudgy fingers into the neck. "Quite so."

"Could you put your entire hand inside?"

"A ridiculous question, Monty. What are you driving at?"

"I just met a street performer. Right outside the tavern. He asserts he can fit his entire body inside a wine bottle."

"Preposterous!"

Montagu nodded. "So, I said. Yet, he insists he can."

"Insisting doesn't make it so," interjected Peterborough.

"The man must be a lunatic," said Cumberland. "Has anyone checked Bedlam to see if they have an escapee?"

The men laughed.

"He seemed quite sane to me," Montagu said. "Moreover, he will perform that very trick at the Haymarket Theatre soon. Or at least attempt it."

"And he will fail," Cumberland said, draining the last of the wine from his glass and quickly refilling it.

"Will he?" asked Montagu.

"Most assuredly he will! Have you any doubts?"

Montagu thought for a moment. "I wonder. Would he really perform on stage if the trick could not be done? To what purpose? I propose we attend his performance."

Cumberland was silent and the others did not offer opinions until

Jeppson spoke. "It could be entertaining," he said.

"Hmm, we'll think on it," said Cumberland. "But now, I have other business to attend to." He stood and the others rose with him. "Gentlemen?"

The three men followed him out the door, leaving Montagu sitting at the table, turning the bottle in his hands. A sly smile played on his lips. He signaled to the serving girl. "Ale this time, lass!"

The Duke of Montagu sat at the table, his mind racing with thoughts of chicanery as he formulated a scheme so unlikely, so incredible, that it just might work. A serving girl brought a pitcher of ale and two tankards, setting them on the table.

"Two?" said Montagu, looking up.

With a turn of her head, she indicated Jeppson, who had come back into the tavern and was now headed for the duke's table. Without asking, Jeppson pulled out a chair and sat across from Montagu.

"Something on your mind, Andrew?"

"Not really," Jeppson said. He poured ale into a tankard, the sudsy foam spilling over the top, "I just needed to get away from that bag of wind."

Montagu laughed. "Our Lord Cumberland certainly is that. Drink up, then."

"He does have it in for you, though, doesn't he, Montagu?"

"Aye. He thinks his farts don't stink. They all think that."

"They?"

"Those nose-in-the-air, better than anyone else rich bastards. I'm fed up with their arrogant pomposity. Always thinking they're better, smarter than everyone else."

"But you're a duke, yourself, John."

Montagu wiped his lips on his sleeve. "You know me better than that, Andrew. A duke in name only. Penniless. Without property. I am the Duke of Nothing!" He took a long swig from the tankard. "I would love to knock them all down a peg or two, see them *hoisted with their own petards,* as the Bard would say."

"As would I," said Jeppson.

"You!" Montagu slammed his palm on the table. "If you stuck any closer to Cumberland, I'd think you were Siamese twins."

"Look, I know on which side my bread is buttered. His Grace is a great patron of my printshop. I'm happy to lift a tankard or two with him to keep his business. Even if he is a bloated oaf." Jeppson leaned across the table and lowered his voice. "But I have my reasons to tweak Cumberland's fat nose."

"Oh?"

"Ah, it's nothing," said Jeppson, taking a drink from his mug." I shouldn't . . ."

"Tell me, Andrew!"

"Fine." He lowered his voice. "Cumberland's a thief."

"No doubt," Montagu said.

"No, I mean he stole from me. I had my eye on a lovely piece of property out by Westminster, a place where I could build a second house away from all the muck of the city. I signed a contract with the owner but before I could blink my eyes, I found the contract null and void."

"Cumberland?"

Jeppson nodded. "He invented some legal impediment to 'lower classes,' as he called them, buying property so near to royal holdings."

"I assume you lost money through his machinations?"

"Indeed! The bastard! So, tell me, what are you thinking? I know you're up to something."

"I'm thinking of the Bottle Conjuror."

"What?" He sat back. "Oh, come now. It can't be done!"

"Of course not."

"Of course, not? But you said . . . "

Montagu gestured with his hand as if waving him off. "Listen, Andrew, we both know the trick can't be done. Cumberland and his toadies know the trick is impossible. But if we insist that it *can* be done, that a man *can* insert his entire body into a wine bottle, they will want to see it fail."

"I'm not following you. Perhaps too much wine and ale have muddled my brain. And yours."

"They would want to see *us* fail. They would pay good money just to have us completely humiliated."

"But you would not let that happen I presume."

"That is correct. It would not be you nor I who would become the laughingstock of all London. For once, we might have the last laugh."

The men hushed when the serving girl returned to their table. "Are you all done, then?" she asked.

"Aye, lass, take them away." She grabbed the empty pitcher and tankards with one hand and stood waiting, her other hand extended. "Of course," Montagu mumbled as he rummaged through his pockets.

"Never mind, Montagu," said Jeppson. "Here you go, dearie." He handed her a few coins.

"Must have a hole in my pockets," Montagu said.

"You might want to visit a tailor."

Ignoring the remark, the duke continued. "Not only would we make fools of all the *silver-spoons* of London, but we could also very well fatten our purses. If all goes right."

"If all goes right?"

"Never mind, all will be well."

Jeppson was silent, thinking. Montagu could almost hear the rusty cogs turning in his cranium. The printer nodded a few times as though mentally debating with himself. Apparently, he won the debate.

"I admit, I am intrigued, Montagu. I'd like to know where this is going."

Montagu smiled. "Wait until you hear the rest . . ."

Chapter Five

⊕LIVE ⊕IL C⊕⊕LED his battered fists, the golden liquid running through his fingers, splashing on the grass. This was Jack Broughton's second bare-knuckle boxing match that day. The oil helped to ease the bruises and cuts on his knuckles. He looked like a man who had battled his way through life. Born a farmer's son in Gloucestershire, he worked the fields by day and at night, his mother taught him to read by reciting the Holy Bible. He left home at seventeen and moved to the port city of Bristol. A bustling city, Bristol was infamous for its most lucrative cargo, transporting slaves to the Americas. He soon found a job working in the shipyards loading and unloading cargo.

He took what was once a white towel, now crimson from fresh bloodstains, dried his fists, then wiped the sweat from his thick neck and bald head. His benefactor, the Earl of Peterborough, stood by dressed in a yellow silk coat, his face powdered and adorned with a painted mole. He insisted Broughton complete two matches that day to help earn his keep and to be ready for a more important exhibit at James Figg's amphitheater near Oxford Street.

Jack had enjoyed working in the shipyard, lifting, and toting the cargo; it helped make him stronger. He developed quickness of foot, running down the planks lugging heavy bales across his shoulders. Soon, he grew from a farm boy to a bull-necked man.

He turned to see that a small crowd had gathered, most standing around the makeshift boxing ring, common ship rigging tied around four large posts. The withered grass comprised the floor. The crowd would wager on his opponent and himself as they battled like red-tailed roosters corralled in a cockfight. Larger crowds and money would come later at the various amphitheaters in London attended by those with titles and wealth.

His adversary, some bloke named Cabot, entered the ring. He strutted around, arms raised, egg-shaped head cocked to one side. Jack instantly disliked this fellow who spewed spit as he walked past, the spittle landing on Jack's feet.

A tall beanpole of a man entered the ring waving a red cloth and began to settle the crowd. His long awkward arms made him seem ten feet tall. Jack chuckled to himself; the man was a Duke of Limbs, to be sure.

Once the crowd settled, the Duke of Limbs glanced over at the Earl of Peterborough and announced the usual rules of the match. Basically, no rules. Each round would last five minutes. The fight would end when a fighter was knocked senseless or surrendered. If the fight continued for an hour, the fighters would take a break for water and food if so desired, then back into the ring. The Duke of Limbs threw down his red cloth. The fight was on.

Jack moved out of his corner and stood in the center of the ring; fists raised to his chin. He watched his opponent intently. Cabot raced around the ring once again, waving to the sparse audience for support. A few chirped in. He turned and stood face to face with Jack, quickly swinging his left hand at Jack's face. His punch never landed; Jack's left arm blocked it as his right hand powered into Cabot's stomach. The force, like a cannonball, pushed deep into the man's belly. His eyes widened in surprise. His breath flew from his lungs. He reared back in pain. Jack took a half-step forward and landed a solid blow to Cabot's jaw with his left. The man's head quivered like a soft-boiled egg. He fell backwards, crashing to the ground. His spittle mingled with the blood flowing from his mouth and pooled on the grass.

The Duke of Limbs rushed into the ring. He glanced down at the unconscious combatant. He looked to the Earl of Peterborough, who acknowledged the fight was over. The Duke of Limbs raised Jack's hand. Another quick victory for him.

Peterborough warmly greeted Jack as he exited the ring. "My dear boy, excellent form once again! Walk with me, I want to introduce you to the famous James Figg."

Jack saw Figg, the boxing champion of London, taking refuge in the shade of a large oak tree.

The earl introduced the men. They stood silently sizing up each other.

"Jack, Mister Figg and I have been discussing your skills and we both agree that with proper training you could become a valuable fighter," Peterborough said. Still, the two boxers stood in silence. "You probably know that Mister Figg is not only the Boxing Champion of London, but his sponsor is none other than His Grace, the Duke of Cumberland."

"Who's that?" Jack said, "And why the hell would I care? No disrespect,

Mister Figg."

The earl said, "Cumberland is the son of our majesty, King George! My, my, you are all brawn and no brains, aren't you? If Mister Figg approves, I will sell my ownership in you to the Duke of Cumberland, and you will train and fight under Mister Figg and his stable of boxers."

Figg said, "The earl has been telling me stories about you and has insisted that I come and see you box. I must admit, I never believe half of what he usually tells me. . ."

"Why Mister Figg," blushed Peterborough, "every word I speak, like honey, drips of truth."

"Be that as it may. When he told me how he chanced upon you in the back streets of Bristol, and that during a cheap brawl, you laid out five men, two of whom were twice your size, well, I had doubts about that. But, after seeing how you did away with that bacon-fed Cabot, I think you have merit. You would fit in well with Lord Cumberland's stable."

The Earl of Peterborough's smile shined brighter than his silk jacket as he grabbed Figg's hand and shook it. "Then we have an agreement. I will draw up the papers for the sale."

"Wait! Don't I have a say in this?" said Jack. "Am I just a load of cargo to you?" His face flushed and the back of his neck twitched.

"My dear fellow," replied Figg. "You will soon be a wealthy man as I intend to train you to become a champion. And, yes, you may call yourself cargo, but you are very valuable cargo."

Chapter Six

STEFAN STOOD IN the tall field-grass patiently waiting to spot fresh game. He took a long deep breath. Cassandra had taught him the power of using his breathing to calm his body and *feel* where prey was hiding. He slowly scanned the field and then, there it was, the slightest ripple of movement as a rabbit's ears poked up from the grass. The rabbit caught sight of him, froze for a moment, then darted out of the grass and ran toward the cover of the forest. Sensing where the rabbit would bolt, Stefan had already turned in the same direction. Though his maimed leg slowed his pursuit, Stefan paid no attention to the pain as he knew he could bring the rabbit down. He was already thinking: a stew? A roast?

The rabbit sprinted left, then right, and left again as it ran for the safety of a briar patch at the edge of the field. Stefan hefted his walking stick. Keeping a close eye on the rabbit, he whipped it into the air, sending it whirling toward his prey. The effort nearly toppled him, but he was satisfied to see that the stick had found its mark. He hobbled to the briar patch and awkwardly shifted his weight to his good leg as he leaned down to pick up the stick lying across the rabbit's body.

Yes, a roast.

CASSANDRA WAS IN her vardo, which had been home for as long as she could remember. It had been handed down to her from her mother. She, like Stefan, had lost her father, not by desertion, but through the whim of God who took so many souls away during the contagion that became known as the Spring of Death.

The aroma of roasted rabbit drifted into the wagon and interrupted her thoughts. She took her whale-bone pipe from her tin of tobacco and went out to find the lunch that would be waiting for her. She carefully stepped down the three rickety wooden steps and said to Stefan, "Do I smell fresh rabbit, or does my *cioc* deceive me?"

"Not just yet," he said. "I had to chase this quick one through the briar patch, so I'm roasting him a bit longer as punishment."

Cassandra laughed but stopped short. "Do you hear a rider coming this way?"

He immediately stood, knowing to trust her fabled hearing. The branches parted and true to Cassandra's ears, a rider came into view. Before Stefan could acknowledge the rider, Montagu had already dismounted and was leading his horse toward them. He hitched the horse to a wheel on Cassandra's vardo.

"Greetings, Stefan, I hope I'm not interrupting your repast?" He gestured to a stump by the fire. "May I?" He sat without acknowledging Cassandra who observed him with a wary eye from where she sat on a carved wooden chair always reserved for her.

"I was thinking," said Montagu, "about our conversation a few days ago and we have a few things to discuss."

Cassandra sat silently. She leaned forward with a piercing stare directed at this stranger. Her gaze fixated on a nearly threadbare patch on his silk shirt.

Stefan was confused. "How did you find me, sir?"

Montagu laughed. "Surely you jest. A band of gypsies camping in the woods is as easy to find as the nose on your face."

"That's true." Stefan smiled. "What's on your mind?"

"I told you I could get you onstage at the Haymarket Theatre. And I said I could fill the theatre with all the best people, the silver-spoons of London. The rich and powerful, the cream of society, including the King's son!"

"His son?" replied Stefan, astonished.

"Yes. Lord Cumberland himself. Would you like that?"

Excited, Stefan stood. "With such an audience, I would become famous!"

Cassandra knocked her pipe against the chair, shaking up the tobacco leaves.

Montagu, momentarily distracted, looked at the old woman, then turned his attention back to Stefan. "Well, yes, but only if you can perform. I'm not talking about simple parlor tricks like those of the Soho Swami. A child could do those, even though they enthrall the hoi polloi. No, none of that. You would have to show them the greatest trick any magician ever performed."

"Conjuror."

"What?"

Stefan, balancing on his good leg, raised his walking stick. "Conjuror, not magician!"

"Oh," replied Montagu, "Right. Conjuror. What about that bottle trick you talked about, *conjuror*? Can you do that?"

Cassandra finally broke her silence. "Be careful what you answer, Stefan!"

Montagu turned to her. "And who might this wench be?"

She gazed directly at him. "I'm hardly a wench, lad."

"And I'm hardly a lad. . . Madam."

"Excuse me, this is my *baba*, my aunt, Cassandra," Stefan interjected. "She's more like the mother I never had, than an aunt."

Montagu shined a smile toward her. "A pleasure to make your acquaintance."

She ignored him and turned her attention to Stefan. "Tell me you're not thinking of attempting the Bottle Conjuration."

"But I am."

Her face turned ashen. "Oh, Stefan, no! It's too dangerous."

"I've been practicing, Cassandra."

She rose from her chair and took a step toward him, deliberately turning her back to Montagu. She lowered her voice so only Stefan could hear. "I've suspected as much. Something's taken hold of you, hasn't it? "His eyes told her all she needed to know. She let out a sigh, heavy with sorrow. "Ah, it's your fate I suppose. Tell me, then, have you tried it?"

"I know I can do it!"

"That's not an answer," she said.

They stood silently looking at each other. There was nothing more to say. She knew the danger involved in attempting the trick and knew that others wanted to learn the secret. She had heard rumors over the years of the Shaitaan and their insatiable lust to master the conjuration. She didn't know why they wanted that knowledge, but she feared what would happen were they to be successful. Who knew what evil could happen to them all if the Shaitaan learned the mysteries of the conjuration?

Montagu broke the silence. "I say, might I get a word in? I asked if you could do the trick, lad. I repeat, can you?"

Leaning on his walking stick, Stefan turned to Montagu. "It's not a trick. And, yes, I can do it."

Montagu stood and smiled. "Excellent! Leave it to me, I'll make arrangements for you at the Haymarket."

Stefan was aglow with anticipation as he hobbled alongside Montagu to the duke's horse. Cassandra stepped forward, attempting to get between them. "Stefan, you've made your choice, my son, but listen to me and listen well. Should you be successful, you will not be the first to enter the bottle."

He did not understand what she meant and looked away from her to see that Montagu had mounted his horse.

"Don't turn your back on the knowledge of your heritage," she continued. "No one who has attempted the dark magic has ever returned. Do you hear me? No one!"

Montagu grasped the reins as his horse became restless. "Don't worry about that, madam. If the lad gets stuck, I'll just break him out with that damned walking stick."

"No! You won't!" she said, her face fierce with anger. "You *gajo* have so little understanding. No stick, no stone could break the bottle and free him. Only the power of the Blood Stone will do it!"

As she came closer, the horse reared up. Montagu attempted to regain control. "The Bloodstone?" he said.

She waved her hand and the horse settled. "Aye. An enchanted and powerful jewel."

Stefan whispered to her. "Don't worry, Cassandra, I will do it."

She placed her hand on his shoulder. Sadness flowed from her eyes as no words in Romani could express the fear she had at that moment.

Montagu pulled the reins tight to keep the horse in check. "I'll be at the theatre tonight. Join me there if you still think you can do it. If you don't show up, I'll know what that means."

Cassandra stepped back. "I fear this will not bode well for either of you. You're testing the Fates."

"I am a consummate gambler, madam. I'll take my chances." And with that, Montagu rode out of camp.

Chapter Seven

THE LAD WAS impetuous and headstrong, just like his father. Aware of how poorly those traits might serve him in the future, if Belasco was an example, she had done her best to shield him, to keep in check his more reckless nature. Still, Cassandra saw that Stefan was blessed with an ability beyond his understanding, a rare affinity for ancient powers that would help him become much more than a mere magician, a trickster. He had the makings of a true conjuror. A great conjuror.

She walked a tightrope between protecting him from harm and allowing him to develop his natural abilities. She knew the time would come when he would strike out on his own, no matter what she said or did to try to stop him. She feared that time might now be at hand as he insisted on performing the Bottle Conjuration. He did not know what she knew; that such a conjuring bordered on black magic and if he was not careful, he could lose himself entirely to the black arts. She also knew there were others that had willfully committed themselves to black magic, others that could pose a threat to him, if they knew of his abilities.

She remembered the night so many years ago when that knowledge came to her, suddenly and unwanted. At ten years of age, her understanding was only incomplete, but there was something in the commotion and raised voices outside her parents' vardo that gripped her heart and warned her all was not well.

She opened her eyes, seeing only her little brother, Belasco, still asleep, bundled beneath his blankets. She sat up in the dark, listening to the agitated voices outside. *Where was Mama? Papa?*

She threw off her blanket and crept to the door at the rear of the vardo and slowly pushed it open. She sat on the vardo steps and peered around the door.

The customary campfire was the only source of illumination in the dark, but she noticed the smoke was not streaming upward as it should. Instead, smoky clouds drifted across the campground, wrapping it in a shroud-like fog. Her mother, Maria, would say such smoke was a bad omen. A group of men near the campfire crowded around a figure lying on the ground. She recognized her father's broad back among the men blocking her view. Despite the cold seeping up through the wooden steps, chilling her bare feet, she crept down the steps to get a closer look.

The men were angry, swearing, making threatening gestures. It seemed everyone was talking at once, but in the babble, she heard words that chilled her.

Is he dead?

No, not yet anyway, but the wound is deep. He can't last.

Oh, God!

Who would stab . . .?

A Shaitaan hunter!

Then, her father's voice above all the others: "Silence! Don't ever utter that cursed name in this camp! Move aside!"

Cassandra saw him bend toward the figure on the ground and when another man stepped away, she saw the face of the supine man illuminated in the firelight. Long white hair and beard. She couldn't help herself and cried out when she recognized her grandfather, Ivan.

So transfixed was she by the horrible sight that Cassandra never noticed her mother standing aside with some weeping women, but her cry revealed her presence. Her mother rushed to her out of the haze like a banshee.

"Cassandra! This is no place for you! Go back to the vardo!"

Her mother's hair was wild, witchlike, her eyes wide. She stood wavering, her hands clenching and unclenching the air as though looking for something to hang on to or looking for some useful and healing purpose.

"But Mama . . ." Cassandra said, tears beginning to stream down her face.

"Go back!"

Maria was a strong woman. Cassandra thought nothing could scare her, so the anger and fear she saw written on her mother's face terrified her. *What was wrong?* She backed away toward the vardo, her mother glaring at her. There seemed to be a roaring in her ears, and she heard her father's voice once again but what he said made no sense.

"The book! He has the book in his coat! Blessed angels!"

Cassandra turned and ran the last few steps to the vardo, threw herself inside and burrowed deep beneath her blankets, sobbing and shaking with fear as she futilely tried to wipe from her mind the image of her grandfather dying in the firelight. *What was happening? And the book, what did that mean?*

As tormented as *she* was, Belasco dreamed on beside her, sleeping the sleep of the innocents.

And now, so many years later, Cassandra felt that fear again, jabbing her like a red-hot poker. *Why now?*

Stefan.

Chapter Eight

· · · · · · · · · · · · · · · · · · · ·

THE LAST PERFORMANCE of the night had ended an hour ago. It seemed like an eternity to Lucinda as she waited outside William's office to collect her wages and her share of the night's purse. Like most nights, the crowd was enthusiastic but small and mostly filled with the common folk of London, making the pickings sparse. She was pleased with an ornate pearl-handled knife that would be good to pawn, but when she plucked for coins, some of them turned out to be buttons.

She knew William was playing a game with her, hoping she would tire of waiting. The Swami had left a long time ago and now besides her, only a few of the stagehands remained.

Finally, she heard William calling her through the thin wooden door to come in. As soon as she saw that scrub of a man chewing on his ragged cigar, she knew she was to leave as unhappily as she had entered. He had a slew of papers strewn about his desk and several piles of coins.

"Have a seat, my pretty," he muttered, the words sounding as wet as the end of his cigar. "Here's your week's pay." He slid a few coins across the desk without looking up.

She glanced down but did not take them. All was silent. She broke the quiet with a cough. He looked up. "Oh, yes, yes indeed, here is your cutpurse for the week as well." He slid a smaller second pile toward her.

She grabbed both piles and looking at the smaller pile said, "How can this be?"

"Well, my dearie, the crowds have not been to our likin' have they?"

She glared at him. "But I know that several of the items I raised should do well at the pawn houses. Why should I be punished because of the riffraff that frequent this place? I spend most of my time in the audience slapping back their roving hands. I deserve more!"

He ceased his incessant chewing. "Look, the quantity of items has not been as good as we all hoped. Blame that on the bootnecks in port, pawning everything they bring in. I had hoped that acquiring the talents of the great Swami . . ."

"Oh, sure, he's only great at making his barleycorn disappear."

William sat back and smiled, showing his brown-stained teeth. "Indeed. Yet, with enough word of mouth I have confidence he can gain a following." He stood up to show her the door. "Lucy, you have added, shall we say, spice to his act and your lifting talents are splendid. That is why, my lovely, you were added to the program, but the dividends have not been what we all want."

He opened the door, reached into his pocket, and pulled out two shillings. "It's been a long week. I don't want you to go home with a frown. Here, consider this a bonus." He quickly shut the door on her.

She stood there for a moment. She felt her anger could melt the coins in her hand. But she knew there would be no remedy for her so she may as well go home. The walk to her common house, especially at that hour, only took a few minutes. She always saved time by cutting through a small park, keeping a watchful eye out as she did. No matter how short the walk, London at night was not a safe place for a woman alone.

Spring Garden did not accurately describe her neighborhood. It was, in fact, anything but a garden. A few warehouses, a fish market, and several common houses for men and a separate decrepit building for women lined the street. Her common house cost only five shillings per month and included one meal a day, although that one meal was not robust enough to ruin a lady's figure.

The rules of the Women's Spring Garden House were few: pay your rent on time, act like proper ladies--many were good actresses--and no men allowed. Break any rule and you would find yourself out on the street.

She quietly entered the front door, which was never locked, and careful not to disturb Edna, the tall and spidery house manager, she tip-toed up the stairs to the third floor. The house had twenty small rooms and each room slept three with single beds. A tin washtub on the first floor served for the rare times when Edna permitted bathing. If you had a special reason to bathe, an exception could be made for three pence.

She entered her room where her two roommates were fast asleep and was about to undress when she heard a slight tapping on the door. She opened it to find her only friend at Spring Garden House. Molly was short and full-figured, with dark red hair that brought out the freckles on her face. She worked by day selling nosegays to the shoppers at various streets in London and by night selling something more personal on the same thoroughfares.

Molly held up a bottle of wine. "Late night for you?"

Lucinda smiled, nodded, and entered the hallway, softly closing the door behind her. Being an old house that needed repairs, the door did not shut completely. It began to slowly swing back open.

Molly returned her smile. "I got me a bottle of wine. Not sure how good it is, but *wine is wine no matter the kind,* as me Auntie used to say. Let's go out on the porch and drain this poor one."

"Sounds, good. I'll meet you in a few minutes."

Molly nodded and started to leave but stopped to watch Lucinda enter her bedroom. From where she stood by the half-open door, she saw Lucinda sitting on her bed. She watched as Lucinda placed a handful of coins into one of her stockings and stashed it in the empty chamber pot under her bed. Molly smiled. If Lucinda were as tired as she looked, she'd soon be asleep after imbibing a bottle of wine, giving Molly the chance to sneak up to Lucinda's room and steal the coins. Of course, being a woman of honor, she would only take some of the money, figuring that, her head clouded with wine, Lucinda would not remember how many coins she had hidden.

There were several weather-beaten chairs on the front porch, all of them desperately in need of paint. Molly moved two chairs closer together. She had no glasses so they would have to share, sipping from the bottle. She looked upon Spring Garden Street, which at this hour was quiet. That would change once the fish mongers arrived at the nearby market.

"Not only has it been a long night waiting for that puff-guts William to finally pay me, but the entire week was also exhausting," Lucinda said, stepping out to the porch.

"Did you do well this week?" asked Molly.

Lucinda shook her head and reached for the bottle. "No glasses?"

"Didn't want the witch to catch me going through the cupboards."

"Well," replied Lucinda, "as I think about it, this week has been surprising to say the least. I went from serving ale at the Pig's Head, to performing at the Haymarket. Don't think even a fortune teller could have predicted that." She started to laugh but caught herself.

"What's so funny?" asked Molly.

"Nothing, just that the night I met that oaf, William Haymarket, I had an encounter with this shy man, almost a kid, who was thrown out of the Pig's Head. His only crime was asking for a glass of water. I brought a pitcher of water out to the man as an excuse to free myself from the clutches of Haymarket. The poor man stood outside, brushing the dirt off himself. There was something sweet about him."

"Sweet? Was he a man of means? Title?"

"Title?" she laughed again. "No, I think he's a gypsy."

Molly gasped, "A gypsy won't bring you wealth or the finer things in life. I'd steer away from him if I were you. Sweet or not, a damned gypsy is nothing but a scurrying rat."

"I guess you're right, and he nearly drowned me that night by spilling the water I brought to him all over me." Molly shook her head and took a long sip from the wine bottle. Lucinda looked out at the empty street and sighed. "Nice at this time of night. So, where did you get this fine vintage?" She laughed before taking a sip.

"I met a fine older gentleman this evening." Molly took the bottle back. "And a ripe one he was, a bit plump, probably just like your William. Before we shared our special time together, not only did he buy me some fish'n chips, but he also bought a bottle of wine from the street cart. We sat at one of those small outdoor tables set up on Market Lane where all the fancies take their wives to shop."

"Aren't you the lady, dinner with wine!"

"Actually, before the bottle was finished, I fluttered me eyelashes and twirled the top button on his blouse and asked if we could have another, especially for our special time."

Lucinda looked confused. "Somehow, I think there's more to this story."

Molly took a short pull on the bottle, then wiped her mouth with the back of her hand. "No, it's really a short story. As me gentleman's wife showed up and grabbed him by the collar and dragged him away, the entire time smacking his noggin with the bouquet of nosegays he bought from me. I was quick. Grabbed the bottle and ran home."

"That's all you absconded with?"

"Well, besides me virtue intact for the night I may have found a few quid in his vest pocket."

They laughed. "Well, mind you," Lucinda said, "I don't mind lifting a few items from those careless enough to make it so easy, but still, it's not what I want in life."

Handing the bottle back to Lucinda, Molly said, "Oh, tell me more."

Lucinda was starting to feel the effects of the long day and the cheap wine. "Just not much to tell. I have found it pleasing to be on stage with the Swami, looking into the audience and seeing all the faces, especially when they are smiling. I could do without the lewd comments and gropes, though."

"Groping is not so bad, dearie. Better than what I've endured with those jackanapeses who made me earn every half-pence with the bruises to prove it."

They sat silently watching the street as the night-soil men were making their rounds. "Maybe our lives have not turned out as we dreamt when we were children," said Lucinda. "But at least we're not cleaning out privies like them." She nodded toward the men in the street, toting noxious buckets of night soil. Again, she took another long sip from the bottle, almost dropping it when she handed it back to Molly.

Molly pretended to take a sip, and immediately returned the bottle. "Who can remember kids' dreams?"

Lucinda slurred her words. "Discs . . . I ever tell you I lost my mother to scarlet fisher . . . fever, when I was only a tike? Hardly remember her, this small locket is all I have from her." She pulled the locket from around her neck as if by stretching it towards Molly, it would make it easier to see. She took another sip and kept the bottle. "Then I was left with that bastard, my father, may his soul *never* rest in peace for every welt he gave me. I'll tell you a thing or two a-a- about men . . . never trust 'em."

Molly watched closely as Lucinda started to doze.

As she leaned towards Molly, Lucinda stirred and, bleary-eyed, took a long swig. "Why can't us girls find our Prince Charming? Hell, I'd even settle for a duke if he could take me away from here." She dropped the bottle of wine and what was left in it splashed across the porch.

Molly knew Edna would be angry about the stain. She took Lucinda's arm and started to help her walk up the stairs. "Methinks you've had your fill my friend. Let's get you to bed."

They entered Lucinda's bedroom. Molly gently helped her onto the bed. She folded the thin bedspread over her, then stood by, watching her drift off to sleep. She noticed one of the roommates peeking at her. Molly glared at her and made a motion as if a knife were cutting across her throat, a warning to look away or else. The roommate turned toward the wall and pulled the bedcover over her head. Molly stood by for a few more minutes until convinced Lucinda was truly asleep. She quietly reached under her bed and slid out the chamber pot, retrieved the stocking where Lucinda had buried her treasure, and took a few coins. She whispered, "Good night, my princess," and slipped out the door.

Chapter Nine

. . . .

WILLIAM HATED THE business of running a theatre. He
often envied the performers whose fear of failure was easily washed away
with applause from the audience. His day began with him having to respond to the letter he received from the Westminster Fire Office that his
insurance had lapsed due to non-payment.

He chewed his unlit cigar to a nub as he approached the office on
Kings Street. He questioned the need to carry insurance as he considered
it a form of blackmail. London insurance companies had devised a plan
to protect their assets by each of them forming fire brigades to battle fires.
They covered their costs by selling fire-marks, engraved metal plaques
with the insurance company name prominently displayed. The plaques
were attached to the building's facade. Firemen would only help an establishment or home that bore the fire-mark from their respective insurance
companies, so it was best to hire a company close to your business.

William had never met the owner, John Gray, as he had always dealt
with one of his employees, Samuel Marbray, a scruff of a man who not
only sold insurance but was the fire lead on the Westminster Fire Brigade.
He also had the curse of being a windbag; where one sentence ended,
another began without a breath in between. Over the past three months,
Marbray had become a nuisance, pestering him to keep current on his
insurance. And of course, the never-ending babbling annoyed William.

I may not be performing on the stage each night, William thought, but
I do have the talent of persuasion to my advantage. My words will sound
like a sad tune played on a sweet fiddle which should buy me more time.
Maybe with the extra time, Lady Luck could glance in his direction and
guide him to a winning bet on a boxing match or horse race. The gamble
would be worth the risk if it got Marbray off his back.

He neared the three-story brick building and its adjoining fire barn.
The large barn-like doors were open. William saw several horse-drawn
wagons, buckets, hand-held pumps, and ladders. Marbray stood just in-

side the open doors, carrying a brass-fitted water hose. William attempted to walk by, but Marbray recognized him and shouted out, "Mister Haymarket!"

William put on a warm smile almost as natural as the theatrical make-up the Swami applied to his pale skin. He removed the stub of a cigar from his clenched teeth. "Good morning to you Samuel."

Marbray fiddled with the fire hose so he could free his right hand in greeting his client.

William shook his hand; he had forgotten how powerful Samuel's grip was.

"Nice to see you, Mister Haymarket. How are things at the theatre? I've heard you have a wondrous Swami as your new headliner. Must take the time to see the show." He finished coiling the firehose. "I suspect you received the post about the status of your account?"

"Yes, and I am looking to meet with Mister Gray to discuss."

Samuel placed—with a thud—the coiled firehose over his left shoulder. "Best of luck to you with that, he's a hard man to barter with, if I may say so. You can go up to the top floor. You can't miss his office, the bloke's got a frosted glass door." Marbray pointed to the building next to the fire barn. "You know, the next big one, a fire to beat all, could come at any moment, so I'm glad you made it today as I was told to get over to the Haymarket theatre and remove your fire plaque. They are a pain to attach to a building, but it's a bigger pain in the arse to remove, if I say so. I said to myself, I sure hope Mister Haymarket can settle up and if not, well maybe after I remove the plaque, I'd stop in and see the Swami's show."

William smiled again as he started towards the office building. "I trust you will not need to remove the fire plaque. But do visit the theatre and tell the girl at the box office that you're a guest of Mister Haymarket."

That brought a wide smile to Samuel's face.

At the top of the third landing were several office doors. On the far left was a large, frosted glass door, and etched in black the simple title, Mr. Gray. William approached and before he could knock, the door opened. A petite woman exited carrying a bundle of papers. She left the door ajar as she brushed by him intently arranging the papers without even a nod and headed down the steps, her lilac perfume trailing behind her.

Through the door William could see into Gray's office; bookcases, paintings, maps, an enormous mahogany desk and two deep leather chairs. John Gray stood leaning over a large map on his desk, holding a magnifying glass. A distinguished looking man, probably in his fifth decade, he wore a short, curled, powdered wig over his grey hair. He was dressed in an expensive Lady Dunmore tweed jacket. His dark-rimmed glasses gave him the air of an Oxford don.

"Excuse me, Mister Gray, I presume?"

Gray looked up from his desk, noticed that his assistant, once again, had not closed his door and now some stranger had breached his privacy. "And who might you be?" he asked.

"Sorry to interrupt you, I'm William Haymarket. . ."

Gray quickly responded, "Ah, the owner of the Haymarket Theatre. I trust you came here to personally pay your late account. If so, go back down to the main floor. My assistant may not remember to close my door, but her memory is keen when it comes to ciphering. She can find your statement and take your payment."

"Actually, sir, I would like to speak to *you* about my account."

With a forlorn sigh, Gray motioned for him to enter. "Mister Haymarket, I'm not sure what there is to talk about as just the other day we reviewed your account and found you in arrears for at least seven months."

"Please, call me William. That is true, but once you hear the circumstances, I am sure we can come to a mutual agreement."

Gray placed his magnifying glass down. "Agreement? Listen my friend, it's all quite simple. You pay for our protection; we protect your property from fire. You don't pay, we remove our plaque, and you fend for yourself. Simple agreement, simple explanation."

William chewed on the remnants of his withered cigar. "Well, I can always find another company. . ."

Gray stood for a moment sizing up the man who had breached his office. He saw a balding figure, nervously standing before him. He almost wanted to take pity on him, but business was business. "Look Mister Haymarket, uh, William, I know that times can be hard on any business, and I would think even more so for a theatre. We are here to help you, probably more than you understand. Are you a scholar of history?"

"History? Not really."

"Look here at the map on my desk. It shows the areas that were destroyed during the Great Fire of sixty-six. William took a few paces closer to the desk and glanced down at the map. "You see, William, I studied history and mathematics at Oxford. Sounds unusual but it was perfect for owning an insurance company. I decided that to be successful in this business one had to learn from the past and calculate what future costs may arise if mistakes are repeated. Are you familiar with the Great Fire?"

"William stared at the map. "Of course. Your man, Marbray, who's tongue is enough for two sets of teeth, mentions it every time we meet, claiming that not only is the sky falling, but the next fire is around the corner." He looked up from the map. "Anyway, that was a long time ago."

"Well," said Gray, "as you know, it happened almost a century ago. People still talk about it as if it were yesterday. Marbray, for sure. The fire started on a cool Sunday night," he said, pointing to a street on the map. "A bakery on Pudding Lane erupted in flames. Back then there were no organized firefighters. When a fire could not be stopped, the only solution was to blow up the building with gunpowder and other nearby buildings to create firebreaks. Unfortunately, the winds changed that night and by Tuesday the fire roared throughout London. It was not until the following Sunday that the fire was extinguished. It was said that nearly a year later, coal cellars were still burning."

The actor inside William did not come front stage and perform a stirring soliloquy, but just stood speechless for the history lesson.

Seeing the blank expression on William's face, Gray pointed to another section of his map. "This is Haymarket Street. As you can see, the buildings are all built within mere feet of each other. If a fire broke out anywhere on the street, the buildings would fall like domino bones. All would be lost." He looked up to see if William was comprehending.

William raised his head. "You don't have to worry about my grand theatre, we take good care of the old lady. She's stood for nearly forty years and is as strong as the day the bricks were laid."

Gray sighed. "That may be true, but what about others near you? What if a fire broke out in the . . ."? He looked closer at the map. "Here, the mantua maker. That shop is filled with bolts of cloths, ribbons and who knows what else the lassies stitch in their shop to make their gowns? Once a flame was struck, that building would become an inferno and quickly shed flames."

William knew he could not win this argument and needed another approach.

Gray began to roll up the map. "Your plaque is not only to protect you from yourself, but from others. Simple, really." He placed the map on a high shelf. "I therefore advise you to go downstairs and pay your account."

Blackmail can be a two-way street. An idea began to smolder in William's mind; "You are correct, I do understand, and yes, times have been difficult this year, but I have acquired the talents of a great and powerful Swami who each week is drawing in larger crowds. If I could have just a few more weeks, I can begin to pay off my account."

Gray tapped his foot, a habit that had pestered him since his days at Oxford as he waited to see his posted grades. "Mister Haymarket, we have been very generous, but time has run out."

William paused then and spoke calmly, yet the timbre of his voice was strong. "Businessman to businessman, I understand your position. Let's say then you send your man Marbray over and rip out the fire plaque this afternoon. And soon thereafter, a fire does break out in the theatre. I will lose all. Not good for me. The gambler in me may want to take this risk. But are you?"

Gray's brow furrowed. "What are you saying?"

William grinned. "You know exactly what I'm saying, mate. As the Haymarket goes, so does Haymarket Street which, as the map shows, contains many assets that you would have to cover. Not good for you." He took out the shreds of his cigar and dumped them in the ashtray on Gray's desk. "So, are we agreed? Three more weeks' grace?"

Chapter Ten

JACK BROUGHTON SAT alone in the antechamber at Figg's Amphitheatre. The small room was used for a variety of purposes; to store supplies, tend to the wounded and for those boxers employed by the boxing champion of England, James Figg, and to use as a quiet waiting area before their matches. He shared the space on the long table with various piles of towels, bandage cloths, bowls of herbs and roots like foxglove and wood betony, a claret-red herb with an unpleasant smell that had often been applied to his bruises and cuts.

A month had passed since he began training with Figg. During that time, he had worked hard, improving his technique blocking blows, quickly striking back, and getting away before being struck. He fought harder and with powerful punches to his opponents' midsections had been victorious in ten fights.

The room was quiet and muffled the jeers, howls, and curses from those watching the preliminary fights. Tonight, Jack was the headliner. He shook his head in disbelief that a farmer's son, a waterman from the Bristol shipyards, was soon to emerge from this tiny space to be cheered by those who placed a bet on him and booed by those who bet he would end up a bloody and bruised body lying senseless on the floor.

Earlier in the day, Jack had noticed a flurry of activity as carpenters transformed a section of the gallery into a private box. King George himself would be attending that evening, having been invited by James Figg's benefactor, Lord Cumberland. A makeshift throne was constructed in the box along with a walnut wingback armchair reserved for Cumberland. On both sides of the royal box, the pine boards that served as seating were torn out and replaced by Windsor chairs. These were reserved for the various earls, dukes, viscounts, and their ladies who had been invited by Cumberland. Jack heard one of the carpenters shout out that a second row was now needed to seat more bollocks of title. With such an audience, the betting would be heavy. Figg always placed a wager on his fighters and be it large or small, split the winnings with them. Tonight, could be profitable for Jack.

He did not know much about his opponent, only his nickname, the Beast of Tiberias. Figg had trained him this past week to move to his left to avoid the Beast's large right hand that could topple a mule. The Beast was a huge man with a dark complexion who claimed to hail from the Holy Land. Figg believed he was merely a Scottish coal miner.

Jack heard cheers from outside. The last fight had ended. He still had a few more minutes, while the victor celebrated, and the footmen removed the bloodied victim before he had to leave the room. Jack always recited the Psalm his mother had taught him before every fight and he supposed tonight it was appropriate, knowing he was fighting the Beast from Tiberias, one of the four holy cities of Judaism. He bowed his head and whispered; *You are approaching battle against your enemies today. Do not be fainthearted. Do not be afraid, or panic, or tremble before them, for the Lord your God is the one who goes with you to fight for you against your enemies, to save you.* He whispered "amen," lifted his head, took a deep breath, and headed to the arena.

FIGG APPR⊕ACHED JACK as he entered the arena. "How are you feeling?" He wiped off some sweat from Jack's neck. The fighter did not reply, but focused on the ring, looking to spy the Beast. "As you know," Figg continued, "not only is my benefactor, Lord Cumberland here tonight, but he surprised us and invited His Majesty and the silver-spoons of London. Should be a grand purse!"

Jack continued to stare. "Where is he?"

"His Majesty and Lord Cumberland are in the royal box we constructed today."

"Not them, the Beast. Where is he?"

At that moment, the doorway to the alley opened and from the back bleacher seats a roar rose. The Beast emerged. The sound, like a rogue wave approaching the shore, grew louder as he walked confidently toward the ring. He truly was a giant of a man, with thick reddish-brown hair forming large clumps on his arms and back.

Figg looked deep into his boxer's eyes. "Tonight, is your night. If you win, I have decided, after fifteen years of being the champion, to retire from boxing. The years have caught up with me and I find it more profitable to manage the arena and train young bare-knuckle boxers like yourself. If you win tonight, no, *when* you win, I have discussed with Cumberland, that I will renounce my title as Champion and cede that title to you. Cumberland will become your benefactor."

At first, Jack did not comprehend what Figg had said. The crowd was becoming more active. Bettors were shouting out their wagers to the money-takers. Figg's words finally sunk in. Jack's eyes grew with determination as Figg led him to the ring.

WILLIAM HAD MISSED the preliminary fights and had to push his way through the cheering crowd. Finding a seat was not as important as finding a money-taker. He had heard the wager that would earn him the most was to bet on the Beast rather than Broughton. Broughton had yet to lose a fight, and in his last ten bouts had swiftly pounded his adversaries into submission. Faster-of-feet boxers, or colossal ones, he felled them all. The smart money was on Broughton, but the larger payout would be on the Beast.

Standing inside a circle of men waving pounds sterling in the air like tiny Union Jacks, William saw a money-taker and bulled his way through the circle. He shouted, "Thirty pounds on the Beast!"

The money-taker looked up and said with a wry smile, "Just to confirm, mate, you said thirty on the Beast?"

"Yes, hurry before the bout starts!" He pushed his money at the man.

"Pleased to oblige, but the odds are with Broughton, so with this kind of bet, you have to pay me a taker's fee of five pounds for my service."

William knew that was highway robbery, but because betting on blood sports was illegal, he knew he had no choice. He had seen the Bow Street Runners milling around the arena. The Runners were employed as unofficial constables by businesses to keep the peace and no doubt took a cut from the money-takers to look aside. His eyes burned as he handed the extra five pounds to the taker. If he lost, more than his eyes would be burning, especially if his wife, Rosalind, found out about his gambling.

MONTAGU DUSTED OFF the plank that was to be his seat. He was curious to see Jack Broughton. He had heard that Figg was impressed with the pugilist but knowing that Cumberland was Figg's benefactor gnawed at him, so he decided to place a small bet on the Beast. Once settled on the hard plank, he looked around and noticed the King sitting on a large throne and next to him, Lord Cumberland. Several lobster-backs with long muskets at their sides flanked the royal box. It irked him to know that Cumberland had invited mutual acquaintances such as the Earl of Peterborough, the Viscount of Daybrook, and several dukes, but not him. He noticed most of them were accompanied not by their wives, but by fashionable ladies that were probably the late-night entertainment for the men of title.

Several men entered the row where Montagu sat. One of them, reeking of fish, plunked himself down beside the duke. "Hey, there guv'nor, here to see our Broughton win again?" He flashed a crusted smile.

Montagu nodded and glanced back to the royal box.

His Majesty wore an ermine-cuffed coat and his blue silk jacket shimmered in the light of the oil lights. Several servants were at his side. One used an ostrich-feather fan to cool him, another held a golden goblet filled with a robust Port on a silver tray. A third servant offered various cheeses, blood sausages and grapes. Cumberland speared a sausage with his jeweled dagger and sliced it into several small sections, attacking the meat the same way he attacked the Jacobites in Scotland, earning him the sobriquet, the "Butcher of Culloden." He waved his dagger, making sure the King noticed it.

Montagu silently cursed Cumberland and his precious dagger. More than ever his distaste for Cumberland and his sycophants grew. He turned his attention away from the royal box as a loud roar erupted from the audience. Two petite, golden-haired wenches entered the ring, waving Union Jack flags, thus announcing the bout was to begin.

Figg had entered the ring. Jack stood outside the ropes as did the Beast. Once the audience saw Figg, they joyfully chanted his name: *Figg! Figg! Figg!* Then, *Champ! Champ! Champ!* A footman handed him a speaking trumpet. He held it to his mouth and cried out to the audience, "Greetings to all in attendance tonight. I would especially like to acknowledge His Majesty, King George, who graces us with his august presence!"

The King rose as the entire theatre erupted in cheers: *Long live the King! Long live the King!* He waved to the crowd then gestured for Figg to continue.

"Thank you, Your Majesty. I would also like to thank my benefactor, His Majesty's son, Lord Cumberland, for attending our fight tonight. This is our final match this evening. I would like to bring forth into the ring a giant of a man who has journeyed from the Holy Land. I invite the Beast of Tiberias!"

Cheers rang out from parts of the theatre. They were overwhelmed by loud boos as the Beast climbed into the ring. Lights hung from the rafters surrounding the ring and illuminated his mass of reddish-brown hair, making his head and back look like they were on fire. He stood tall, cracking his massive knuckles.

Figg turned his back to the Beast and facing Jack, spoke loudly into the speaking trumpet. "I now invite our waterman from Bristol, who has yet to be defeated . . . Jack Broughton!"

Jack climbed into the ring, the audience stamping their feet and shouting, *"Broughton! Broughton! Broughton!"*

Both men carefully moved towards each other with Figg between them.

"Tonight, these two gladiators will fight until one of them either submits to defeat or cannot pick himself up off the floor," Figg said. "Each round will last ten-minutes, after which we will take a short break for water and mopping up the blood. I will then announce the next round. After one hour we will take a longer respite for drink and food, if so desired, and we will start up again until we have a victor. At no time may a fighter leave the ring. And, please, gentlemen, do not throw anything into the ring to distract the boxers."

He placed his speaking trumpet on the floor. One of his footmen leaped into the ring and took it away. Figg held up both boxers' arms. He could almost feel their hearts beating as he looked at them. The nostrils of the Beast's enormous nose flared like a bull, while sweat already flowed down Jack's neck. Figg dropped their arms and yelled, "FIGHT!" and quickly climbed out of the ring.

Neither boxer moved. The crowd's initial roar died down as anticipation grew. The Beast could not stand the silence. He bellowed out a guttural sound moving forward, wildly swinging his right fist at Jack's head. Jack instantly swung his head to one side and felt a breeze whoosh past. He reared back and pounded his right hand deep into the belly of the Beast. His expectations of quickly ending the fight vanished as his opponent absorbed the blow as if it had never touched him and remained on his feet.

The Beast again lunged forward. This time he did not swing but reached around Jack with both arms and held him in a vise-like grasp. He twisted Jack around, pushing him back to the ropes. Jack hit the ropes so forcefully, he bounced off, right into the Beast's left fist, striking him in the jaw. The Beast's knuckles, hard as carpenter's spikes, tore into his face. Blood began to flow. Jack instinctively retreated.

The Beast stalked closer in pursuit. Using the lessons Figg had taught him, Jack moved quickly to his left, avoiding several attempts to strike him. The more he moved, the more he sensed the frustration growing in his opponent. The Beast lowered his fist and growled. Jack took that moment to strike a hard blow directly to the Beast's chest, this one knocking him backwards. He stumbled and fell to the floor.

Jack looked out to the cheering and cursing crowd. *Could that blow have ended the match?* When he glanced back, the Beast had risen. His head lowered like a crazed animal, he rushed Jack, crashing him into the ropes again. His arms again became a vise, but his sweat caused him to lose his grip. Jack took advantage of the loosened grip and quickly rotated his hip. The leverage threw the Beast down, rolling him into the ropes. As Jack approached, the blood flowed from his cheek and left a trail on the floor. He heard the clanging of the bell and saw the Beast had risen.

Holding up his speaking trumpet, Figg announced a break before the next round. Both fighters retreated to their corners as footmen jumped into the ring and began to mop up the blood and sweat pooled on the floor.

WILLIAM HAD NOT been able to find a seat, so he stood in the aisle halfway back from the ring. He clenched his betting chit. Seeing the blood on Broughton's face gave him hope that tonight he would score a winning chit. From the corner of his eye, he saw William Plunkett, the chemist, better known to those who needed a quiet loan as the best shyster in London.

"Good evening, Mister Haymarket!" Plunkett shouted above the din of the crowd. "I hope your chits pay off for you tonight." He tipped his black felt hat to Haymarket as he walked past.

William pretended he could not hear Plunkett above the chaos in the arena.

Plunkett stopped, turned back to William and in a stern voice that could be heard over the ruckus said, "If you win tonight, I trust you will visit my apothecary in the morning and settle your overdue loan."

Haymarket sighed and held tighter onto his chit as Plunkett walked away.

MONTAGU TURNED HIS attention from the ring and watched the silver-spoons of London seated around the King, all in their silks and velvet attire. He knew most of them had never known the force of a hard blow, or the fear of death. Yet, they chatted away, laughed, and drank the fine wine supplied by Cumberland. He tasted the bile he felt towards them all.

The mate next to Montagu poked him on the shoulder and held out a wineskin. "I say guv'nor, grand fight indeed. Care for some elderberry wine?"

FIGG STOOD NEXT to Jack, as one of his footmen wiped the blood off the boxer's jaw. "Keep as you've been taught; move to his left. He's strong but you can beat him," he said.

Jack said nothing as the young lassies announced the start of another round, and he rose to continue the battle.

For the next hour, they traded blows. Figg stood to announce the end of each round, and as customary, a quarter-hour break. Both men refused as they stood toe-to-toe, flailing at each other, raising purple bruises where the punches landed. Jack was able to avoid many of the hits as he darted left and struck back with his right. Yet the Beast would not fall. Both men were feeling the heat and stale smoke from the crowd, and the exhaustion of their battle. The Beast had lost some of his vigor, his nostrils flaring faster as he attempted to refill his lungs. Jack dodged to the right and landed a quick blow to his opponent's eye. Blood squirted like a geyser and covered Jack's arm. The Beast became confused; he could not see out of his right eye and swung wildly at Jack, but Jack had moved away and circled behind him. He pushed hard and the Beast fell into the ropes again and started to tumble out of the ring. If he landed outside, the fight would be over.

Several of his distraught partisans who had gathered near the ring, rushed forward. Three men acted as one and pushed the Beast back away from the ropes and into the ring. The Beast attempted to wipe the blood from his eye, creating an opening for Jack to land a terrifying strike at his other eye, creating two geysers. The Beast was trying to hold the blood back with one hand and swing with the other. To no avail.

The King rose from his seat, as did Cumberland, cheering Broughton on to victory. William feared his chit would vaporize.

Jack took a moment to size up the damage he had inflicted on his opponent. His own face was bruised from the relentless blows of the Beast. He tasted victory. With all his strength he propelled his fist deep into his opponent's stomach. Jack could feel the hiss of the Beast's breath. He forced his left hand upward, landing squarely under the Beast's chin. Teeth spewed out. The amber fire in his eyes turned black and they rolled upward as the Beast crashed to the floor, his body crumpled and motionless. Blood continued to flow, a dark red pool around his head.

The crowd erupted. Losing bettors tossed their worthless chits into the air, creating a small snowstorm that blanketed the arena. An exhausted Jack stood over his silent foe ready to strike again if he were to rise.

Figg jumped into the ring along with three footmen. He leaned down and put his hand on the Beast's face and pulled his bloodied eyelids open. He felt a slight breath coming from the vanquished boxer. Figg stood and shouted for those who could hear above the cheering, "The Beast of Tiberias is alive, but cannot rise. I pronounce Jack Broughton as the winner!"

The footmen attempted to revive the Beast. They threw several buckets of cold water on him while one of the men kept slapping his bloody face. He stirred but could not rise.

Jack stood in the center of the ring. Salty sweat mixed with his own blood tasted bitter in his mouth. He looked towards the Beast and silently prayed that he had not killed his foe.

William, distraught, ripped his chit into tiny pieces and flung them to the floor as he bulled his way through the crowd to the exit.

Montagu sunk down and ripped his chit. He glanced over to the royal box and saw Lord Cumberland standing and shouting with joy that his man had won again and sent a servant to collect on his winning chits. Once again, Cumberland had bested him.

Figg found his speaking trumpet and stood next to Jack. The King rose and waved to the victor. The crowd, seeing His Majesty standing, quieted as the King began to speak. "You have fought a brave battle and have made us all proud! Mr. Figg, you have a champion amongst your stable! Great fun tonight, indeed!"

The crowd cheered. *Long live the King!* resounded throughout the arena. Figg and Jack both bowed to their King.

"Thank you, Your Majesty," Figg said. "Yes, you are correct, I have a champion in my stable. As I have fought for our king and country over these past fifteen years, tonight I wish to relinquish my title and with Lord Cumberland's approval, pronounce Jack Broughton England's new Boxing Champion!"

The King smiled as did Lord Cumberland who raised his dagger high into the air and shouted, "Tonight, England has a new champion!"

More chits flew into the air and covered Jack as he closed his eyes and took a deep breath, filling his lungs with their cheers. The word *champion* resounded in his ears.

Chapter Eleven

BEFORE DAYBREAK ILLUMINATED the streets of London, William Plunkett's day began, in many ways an extension of the night before. He arrived at his apothecary on Jermyn Street riding a sturdy brown horse laden with several large canvas bags bulging at the seams. He wore a long leather coat and across his back the leather straps holding his blunderbuss pulled taut as the horse pounded the cobblestone street.

His partner, James Macleane, waited outside the shop holding a small lantern. He grabbed the reins from Plunkett and tied the horse to a hitching post while the chemist dismounted. Plunkett fished for his copper key and unlocked the front door. They hastily entered, like conjoined twins, with Macleane leading the way to the back of the store. The lantern illuminated the storage room filled with several shelves holding bottles of lotions, pills, powders, a few stone mortars, and pestles. A small cabinet with bottles of rum nestled in the corner.

With a thud, Macleane dropped his bag on Plunkett's oak desk. Plunkett followed suit. A large chest stood at the rear of the storage area. It looked heavy, but Macleane easily pushed it aside, revealing a door cut into the floorboards. Plunkett grabbed the circular iron latch and pulled the door open. Macleane pointed his lantern toward the opening. His bag in hand, he led the way down into the secret room. Plunkett followed, carefully descending the wooden staircase with his bag.

The concealed room, supported by large timbers, was a dank basement carved into the earth. The flickering candle made the cobwebs shrouding the timbers glow like threads of silver. Shelving was carved into the dirt walls and four large chests stood on the floor. One of the shelves held several Venetian masks, along with saddle bags and a cape. A tall cabinet stood open, revealing several muskets, a blunderbuss, whips, clubs, crowbars, gunpowder, and swords.

A brick archway opened at the rear. A large tapestry depicting a hunting scene hung from the arch, making it difficult for anyone to see into the tunnel concealed behind it. The tunnel led several hundred feet under the streets of London to an opening behind a hedgerow on Burry Street. It had taken Plunkett more than a year to quietly construct this escape route. The hedgerow concealed the door, which was always locked from the inside.

The men proceeded to empty their bags. Plunkett pulled out a lovely silver necklace adorned with large rubies. He chuckled to himself, *honest chemist by day, highwayman by night.*

Last night had been fruitful, indeed. They had known that after the much-heralded prize fight a large crowd would be leaving London and the highwaymen could hide along Hounslow Heath, a dark road outside the city. The road led to lavish estates in Bath and Exeter and the woods, heavy with brush, made it an ideal place to wait and pick out the most promising carriages to rob.

The night had been clear with a half-moon shining above. Several carriages had driven past their lair, each carrying extra coachmen for protection. Finally, a vulnerable coach came into view. It rode low to the ground as it was carrying several passengers. Two horses struggled to pull the coach. Being late at night, the coachman was secretly stealing a sip from a bottle stashed under his seat.

Macleane mounted his horse, slipped on his Venetian mask, and motioned to Plunkett that he would fall behind the carriage. Plunkett had already mounted and was wearing his mask as he quickly led his horse through the brush to block the oncoming coach. He raised his blunderbuss to the sky, a fearsome silhouette against the moon.

"Halt!"

The startled coachman dropped his bottle, and momentarily lost his grip on the reins. They slipped from his hands. The horses charged forward. The coachman fumbled to regain control but could not stop the coach. Several of the passengers had fallen asleep from their long night of food and drink but were rudely awakened and tossed about the cabin. Plunkett chased after the runaway coach. Macleane followed, his long hair flying in the breeze when the wind blew his hat off.

The coachman finally took control, glanced back, saw the two highwaymen, and decided he could outrun them. He snapped his whip, commanding the horses to run faster, but it didn't work. They could not pull any harder or faster. The passengers screamed as the coachman pleaded and cursed his horses to outrace the bandits.

Since Macleane's horse was a younger and more powerful animal, he reached the coach first, racing along the left side, waving his long cane for the coachman to pull to a stop. The coachman saw the highwayman riding tall, cane raised, the moonlight reflecting on his white Venetian mask, giving him the appearance of a phantom. The coachman turned to his right and saw a blunderbuss pointed at him, the rider closing in faster than the coach could go. Wisely, he pulled hard on the reins. The exhausted horses gladly slowed to a walk.

The six passengers were in panic. A portly gentleman reached into his long waistcoat, pulled out a Queen Anne flintlock, and leaned his head and arms out the cabin window. As he was cocking the pistol, a cane with a silver wolf's head came crashing down on his arm, knocking the pistol to the ground. The two female passengers screamed.

The coach rolled to a stop. The coachman, seeing the bandits wearing Venetian masks, knew he was in trouble. Word had spread among the coachmen of London to be wary of the Gentlemen Highwaymen; courteous to women, but brutal to any man who dared to hinder their path.

Plunkett held his blunderbuss cocked and ready to fire. He trotted his horse towards the coachman and pointed the gun at him. "Stand and deliver!"

The coachman stood shaking with his arms held high. He wished he could reach down and have another swig from his bottle, now hopelessly tipped on its side, the rum puddling around his feet.

Macleane moved his horse so he could peer into the coach. He saw four men of wealth and to his delight, two women attired in fine gowns and hats, and visible even in the half-light, glittering jewelry. Macleane pointed to the man who had attempted to use the pistol. "Step out of the cab!"

The man hesitated at first, but from the tone of Macleane's voice, he knew he should obey. He emerged from the coach. Suddenly, Macleane struck the man across the face with his wolf's head cane, knocking him back against the coach.

"My dear sir, that's a warning. If you try any more violence against me," he said, withdrawing the sword concealed inside the cane and pressing the point against the man's chest, "you will regret it. Do you understand?"

The man nodded *yes*, painfully holding his jaw.

Plunkett laughed, then returned his gaze to the coachman. "I assume we have an understanding as well?"

The coachman quickly nodded several times, his legs still wobbling. "Anything you say guv'nor."

"Good."

Macleane asked the other three men to step out of the coach. The youngest of the females began to exit but Macleane said, "Please, my lady, remain seated. You will be much more comfortable where you are."

She saw his handsome smile in the moonlight, blushed, and returned his smile as she sat back into her seat. The older woman gave her a look of disgust and secretly removed her large diamond ring, tucking it in her bodice.

Macleane dismounted, patted his horse for a good chase, and reached into his saddle bag. He pulled out a canvas sack. He walked toward the four men, wielding his sword, and politely said, "My dear friends, and I do call you that as I never hurt my *friends*, only those who oppose me, since you are my friends this evening, I suggest you slowly reach into your pockets and purses and place your money into this sack."

He handed the sack to the first man and kept his sword at the ready. The men all complied. Macleane noticed a large, jeweled ring on one of the men. "Is that an emerald?"

"Yes, it is. It was a gift from my mum, bless her departed soul."

Macleane smiled. "Well, I think if she's looking down on you, it will please her to know that you surrendered it to me." The man's hand shook as he removed the ring. "And what about this other ring, it looks to be silver?"

"Yes, it's my wedding band."

Macleane paused for a moment. "Is the older woman inside your wife?"

"Yes, please don't harm her." He started to remove the silver wedding band.

"Harm her? As I said, I don't harm friends. I respect a man who loves his wife. But really, you have the look of a man of means, and you wear only a silver band?" Macleane pocketed the ring. "All of you please walk toward the front of the coach. If you try anything, my partner's blunderbuss can inflict considerable pain."

They did as ordered while Macleane entered the coach. The young woman and the wife sat nervously, not knowing what to expect.

"Good evening, my dear ladies. I trust you heard my conversation with the men of your party. I intend no harm to either of you and I do apologize for creating any discomfort or fear. I know it's past the witching hour, so if you would kindly remove your jewelry, you will soon be on your way home, with a little less wealth, but a grand story to tell your friends."

The young woman attempted to remove her pearl necklace, but her nervous fingers could not manage the clasp. Macleane smiled and gently whispered, "Allow me."

He reached behind her neck, inhaled her sweet perfume, found the clasp and the necklace fell. The young woman, looking deeply into Macleane's eyes, caught the pearl necklace and held it in her hand. He softly took her hand as if they were lovers and slid the necklace into his pocket, never losing eye contact with her.

He turned his attentions to the wife. "Shall I help remove your ruby necklace?"

The wife ripped off the necklace and tossed it, hitting him squarely in the face. He paid no heed to her action.

"I would also like for you to hand me your tippet. It looks like ermine?" She refused to remove her fur cape. Macleane stroked it. "Are you familiar with the Latin quote, '*potius mori quam foedari?*" No response from the wife. "It means, *rather die than be dishonored.*" Surely, there is no dishonor in giving me your cape . . . and I do not believe you would really rather die."

She scowled and handed him the tippet. He nodded and stepped out of the cabin where the four men stood nervously by the front of the coach. Plunkett had ridden to the other side of the coach to keep an eye on them and the driver. He had ordered the men to toss their hats, silk vests and silver buckles into his canvas sack. He allowed them to keep their leather coats. He glanced over to Macleane. "I think we're done here," he said, tying the bulging sack to his saddle.

"Just a moment if you please." Macleane walked back to the cabin and stuck his head in, looking at the wife. "Earlier, I had spied a wonderous ring on your finger. I assume you now have it hidden somewhere on your person?" He held out his hand. "If you please."

The wife clenched her jaw, reached into her bodice, and pulled out the diamond ring. She handed it to him, followed by a hard slap across his face.

Macleane felt the sting but did not retaliate. He only smiled, then turned to the young woman, gently clasped her hand, and gave it a soft kiss. "Be well my lady, remember this night."

He mounted his horse and trotted to the four men. "Tell your friends the tale of the night you encountered the gentlemen bandits!" He leaned down to the married man, reached into his pocket, and handed back the silver wedding band. "I think you need this more than me."

Macleane spurred his horse and he and Plunkett rode away into the night.

In the secret room, Plunkett and Macleane finished stowing their plunder. As agreed, they divided the take as each had their own storage chest. The more valuable items Plunkett would sell to acquaintances and would split the sale with Macleane.

Once upstairs, they pushed the large chest over the trapdoor.

Macleane quietly departed. The sun was now up, and life was stirring on Jermyn Street.

Chapter Twelve

AT ANY TIME of day or night, the streets of London buzzed with activity. That summer's eve was no exception. Shops were open, the taverns full. Music flowed into the street. Londoners of all kinds were about, some dressed in their finest garb, others in nothing more than rags. A violinist wandered amongst the citizenry, his music blending with the sounds of carriage wheels and hawkers' cries. There were hawkers of fish and oysters, apples, oranges, and nuts; there were knife sharpeners, pot-menders, and candle-makers; sellers of pamphlets and broadsides; ballad sellers; musicians; beggars and pickpockets; cardsharps, jugglers, and magicians; milkwomen and town criers; servants running errands for their masters; and, of course, the lovely ladies selling nosegays, or other "favors" for discerning gentlemen, all of them jostling for space in the rutted streets with sedan chairmen ferrying wealthy passengers, carters delivering goods, and hackney coaches with footmen clinging to their sides.

Street vendors' pushcarts, fired by glowing coals, spewed smoke, forming a thin fog that hung in the air. The merchants served warmed eels, hot sheep's feet, and lamb pies along with other hot and cold items. The various savory scents were a welcome antidote to the stink of horse manure and human piss rising in the streets.

Stefan was right at home as he stood before the Haymarket Theatre, trying to make his voice heard above the cries of the others, intent on earning a few shillings, calling out to the people in the street. He had arrived with the anticipation that his life could change that night. He had thought long and hard about his talk with the Duke of Montagu. He knew Cassandra did not approve, but Stefan was determined; his time had come. Beyond performing street illusions, he was willing to taste the dark magic she had warned him to avoid. He was destined to show the world his true abilities.

The delicious aroma from a nearby pushcart diverted his attention. The vendor shouted, "Hey there, mate, got me some fresh pickled whelks just shipped in from Normandy."

The scent of butter and garlic mixed with the tasty sea snails was intoxicating, but he knew that such a dainty would be too expensive for him. "I thank you kindly, sir, but . . ." He reached into his threadbare coat and drew out two copper half-pence. "What can this purchase from your cart?"

The vendor chuckled and pulled out a small hot pea-pie and exchanged it for the two rusted coins.

Famished, Stefan quickly consumed the small pie, nodded appreciation to the "chef" and hobbled with his walking stick to a spot a few yards from the Haymarket entrance. Not only would this be a spot to attract an audience, hopefully he would also be in a good position to spot the duke.

"Ladies and gentlemen! Step closer, please and prepare to be amazed!"

Some who had seen Stefan perform before moved closer, drawing with them a few new onlookers. Someone said, "Look! It's the trickster who did the card tricks."

Stefan bowed to the audience. He swept his hat from his head and placed it on the ground saying, "*Conjuror*, if you please. Tonight, no card or sleight of hand tricks. Instead, stand back and watch."

Leaning back on his walking stick, he withdrew three apples from the pocket of his coat, tossed them in the air and began to juggle them. The crowd rewarded him with a smattering of polite applause.

A man in the crowd nudged his neighbor and said, "Glad I didn't waste a shilling on this foolish show."

Stefan shot the man a disparaging look then suddenly kicked out the walking stick with his lame leg, sending it skyward. It spun once in the air above him then descended, almost floating, and he moved under it, catching, and balancing it on his nose, the apples still blurring in orbit around him. The grimace on his face revealed the pain he felt standing without the aid of his walking stick but the audience, caught up in his marvelous performance and heartily applauding, did not notice. Stefan, however, noticed the copper flying into his hat.

He returned the apples to his pocket and took hold of his walking stick. "Now, to *completely* mystify you," he said, pressing one end of the stick to his lips. He blew on the stick and the sweet notes of a flute sounded in the air.

"Would you look at that," someone said, "the trickster's cane is also a flute!"

"Why I believe that's a Handel piece!" a woman said. "How does he do that?"

Caught up now in the moment, the crowd cheering, Stefan turned the stick as though it were a trumpet and, sure enough, trumpet blasts echoed in the street, startling the other vendors, bringing them to stunned silence, at least for the moment.

More coins clinked in his hat. He was about to begin another trick when William Haymarket pushed his way through the crowd, his face red with anger, an unlit mashed-up cigar clenched between his teeth. Attendance at his theatre had been sparse enough lately; he didn't need any interlopers cutting into his business.

"What's going on here?" he demanded, the cigar flying into the street. "Pay no attention to this ragged trickster!"

"I'm not a trickster, but a *conjuror!*"

Nearly nose to nose, William bawled, "You smell of a gypsy, look like a beggar, and act like a damned trickster!" He shoved Stefan into the street, where he stumbled a few paces then fell hard on the stone pavers, his apples rolling away. "Get away from my theatre or I'll call the constable!"

Gypsies and constables were like oil and water; they didn't mix, so Stefan crept away on his hands and knees to the rear of the crowd.

William called out to the crowd that was beginning to drift away. "Listen, my friends! Tonight, at the Haymarket, I promise you a show that will thrill and delight you all. The amazing Soho Swami has a beautiful new assistant who will please your discerning eyes. I guarantee it!"

Only a few headed toward the theatre while the others who had gathered to see Stefan walked off, seeking other diversions. William picked up Stefan's walking stick and hurled it into the street. He turned back to the few people left and desperately called, "You won't want to miss the great Swami!" He shook his head and stomped back inside the theatre.

Stefan slowly pushed himself up on all fours then stood, wobbling. He hobbled to his hat which, amazingly, remained on the ground, the coins untouched. He picked it up. He looked at his walking stick and was terrified by what he saw. The stick was no longer a stick but, somehow, had been transformed into a black snake slithering toward him. Fighting his fear, he grabbed the snake, looking around to see if anyone else had seen it. The instant he took hold of the hissing creature, it once again became a walking stick. He stared at it for a few moments.

He put the strange event out of his mind as he reached inside his hat to count the night's earnings. A tap on his back made him jump and he nearly dropped the hat. He turned to find the Duke of Montagu smiling at him.

"Well, I thought I might find you out here," the duke said. "You're looking like the mouse the cat dragged in. A difficult evening?"

"I . . . uh . . . yes, I've had better."

Montagu laughed. He draped his arm over Stefan's shoulder. "Here, come walk with me." Dodging a carriage coming down the street, he led Stefan over to the Haymarket Theatre, pausing outside.

"Would you not rather be inside this magnificent edifice," Montagu said, spreading his arms wide as if he would hold the theatre in their embrace, "performing for the best of London, than panning for a few shekels in the cold night air? I believe in you, so the first step toward fashioning your dreams is for us to go in and watch the Swami perform, and I will get us a meeting with the theatre owner."

Stefan shook his head. "No." He felt a tremor in the walking stick gripped tightly in his hand.

"No?"

"He wouldn't want to talk to me, I'm sure."

"Nonsense. Just leave it to me," Montagu said. "Show me your hat."

Stefan held it out and Montagu plucked out two coins. "This should do it. Follow me." He bought tickets from the girl at the door and the two entered the Haymarket Theatre.

Chapter Thirteen

J⊕NAH AND ABEL had stood at the rear of the crowd watching the lame gypsy perform, their eyes darting from side to side as they sized up possible marks.

"Keep your eyes on that bloke over there," the taller one said, nudging his partner with his elbow. "He looks like he might have some coin about him."

"Which one? The one what's got his hand on that lady's arse?"

"I thought you'd take notice of that, Abel, but no, not him. The tall one in the tan coat with gold braid. And that fancy cane topped with a silver wolf head. That's our man."

Abel raised up on his toes to get a better look over the heads of the people before him. "I see him," he said, "Aye, Jonah, he's dressed like a dandy. Most likely carrying a nice fat purse and easy to snatch, no doubt."

"Shhhh!" Jonah said, pulling Abel back by his coattails. "Do you want the whole blasted city to hear you?"

"Sorry."

"Just keep him in sight, is all."

Up front, the gypsy was entertaining the crowd with some magic tricks but Jonah, his attention focused on the crowd and its lucrative possibilities, paid him no mind until he heard the magician speak.

"Listen," he said to Abel, cocking his head to hear better.

"What?"

"The lad's no Englishman, mate."

"No?"

Jonah shook his head. "He's got a Romani accent. Can't you hear it?"

Abel squinted his eyes as though they were the organs through which he heard. "Hmm, maybe."

"But that's not so much of a surprise, especially if he's from across the channel. I wonder if he is," he mused. He listened intently to the magician's patter. He nodded, as if confirming something to himself. "That's a Romani accent for sure, Abel. But it's not like ours. I detect a different dialect."

"How do you know?"

"Blast it, Abel, I'm a Hunter! You're a Hunter. We're trained to know these things."

Abel shrugged. "Alright then, no need to get huffy."

The gypsy was no longer speaking as he focused on the three apples he had juggling in orbit around him.

"I wonder who his people are," Jonah said. "Could there be Romani around here that we don't know about, or is this bloke a lone wolf? No matter, we should tell Melchior. I'm sure he'll be interested."

"Are you thinking of the book?"

"I'm always thinking of the book, aren't you?"

"Aye, but right now I'm still thinking about that mate with his hand on the lady's rump," Abel said.

Jonah slapped him across the back of his head.

"Hey!" said Abel, rubbing his head.

"Pay attention, you arse."

A bald, cigar-chomping man had come out of the Haymarket Theatre and was berating the gypsy, putting an end to his show. The crowd started melting away. Jonah saw the man in the tan coat about to cross the street. Torn between lifting his quarry's bulging purse or further investigating the young gypsy, Jonah opted for the bird in hand. Besides, how difficult would it be for him to again find the street magician if he needed to, especially after Melchior was made aware of his existence?

Jonah saw that the man in the tan coat had already reached the footpath on the opposite side of the street.

"Let's go, Abel, after him."

The two hurried across the street, following the man in the tan coat and black tricorn at a discrete distance. Carriages and carts rumbled by in the street as Jonah and Abel dodged through pedestrians on the footpath, trying to keep their target in sight. At one point, their passage blocked by two carriages that had collided, they lost sight of the man, but finally threading their way around the wreckage and the opposing footmen and drivers now engaged in violent fisticuffs, they once again spotted the black tricorn bobbing above the heads of the pedestrians.

"There he is!" Jonah said, "And look, he's turning down that alley, a perfect place to waylay him."

The two quickened their pace, turned down the dimly lit alley and spotted the man mere yards away. He had paused, reaching into his pocket, perhaps to check his pocket-watch.

"Now!" Jonah said.

Abel rushed up behind the man and tried to grab his arms from behind while Jonah circled around in front of him. The man slipped from Abel's grasp and spun to one side with the grace of a dancer so that, for an instant the two thieves found themselves grappling with each other.

Jonah pushed away from Abel and turned to charge the man who stood calmly in the street, both hands gripping his cane. Too late, Jonah realized the man had given the head of the cane a quick twist and now withdrew a slender, wicked sword. It flashed through the air so quickly as to render it invisible as it sliced through the sleeve of Jonah's coat so effortlessly that the thief wasn't certain he had been struck. The bright red bloom spreading across his sleeve woke him up.

"Abel, I'm bleeding!" he cried, staggering back from the man who held his ground, watching him.

Abel's eyes were wide with fright. He took one look at his bloodied partner, turned and ran.

"Coward! Son of a whore!" Jonah called after him, but he, too, wasted no time in scurrying away, holding one hand pressed over the wound in his arm.

Their intended victim returned his sword to the cane, calling after them, "Take that as a lesson from James Macleane!" then coolly resumed his walk, none the worse for the bungled robbery.

A few streets away, the two bunglers stumbled into an empty stable. Wincing in pain, Jonah grabbed Abel by the neck and slammed him against the wall, rattling the few teeth left in the man's head. "You pig shit! You miserable dunghill! Why didn't you help me?" He banged Abel's head against the wall. Once. Twice. And would have done it once more if the pain in his arm hadn't halted him.

He tore off his coat and threw it on the ground, swearing under his breath as he examined the wound through the shreds of his sleeve.

Abel stood meekly by. "He had a sword, Abel."

"I bloody well know that don't I? Here, help me with this. Tear off a strip of my sleeve that I could use as a bandage."

His fingers trembling, Abel pulled off a strip, uncovering the wound just below the serpent and book tattoo on Jonah's arm.

Jonah examined the wound. Long but not deep. "I'll say this for him; he left me with a tidy wound, almost like a surgeon. Alright now, Abel, tie the bandage."

Abel wrapped the strip of shirt around the wound and tied it tightly.

"I'm sorry, Jonah, I shouldn't have run off."

"No, you shouldn't have, you pox-ridden cur." He picked up his coat and put it on, Abel carefully assisting him like a valet. "Well, no matter now. What's done is done. Let's go find Melchior."

"He won't be happy if we turn up empty-handed," Abel said, running a hand nervously through his greasy hair. "You know how he can be."

Jonah did know. Melchior was not one to be trifled with, but he needed to hear about the gypsy. As for the botched robbery, there was no help for it. They would have to take what was coming to them.

"Just you don't open your trap," Jonah said. "Things is bad as they be, I don't want you mucking them up more. Let me do the talking and maybe we won't get us a beating. Just play dumb. That shouldn't be too hard for you." He gave Abel a shove toward the stable door. "Let's go."

Chapter Fourteen

· ·

THE BRIGHT LIGHTS and lavish furnishings of the Haymarket Theatre dazzled Stefan almost as much as the lovely hostesses escorting people to their seats. Just as in the streets, people chatted and joked, and ate pickled eggs, sausages, and other delicacies, washing them down with ale or hard cider, all delivered by the buxom hostesses. The theatre was the place for the silver-spoons to see and be seen and, for all the activity going on in the audience, it didn't matter whether anything was happening on the stage.

But this night, the theatre was less than half-filled. Montagu looked around, appraising the crowd. "You could do much better than this, my boy," he said.

They were just about to sit when William spotted them and came running. "Montagu! What's the meaning of this? What's this trickster doing here?"

"Now, William, rein in your horses," Montagu said. "He's with me. Calm down."

"Calm down? He's a dirty gypsy!"

Stefan reached for his walking stick, but the duke put out his hand and stopped him. "There'll be no trouble, William, I promise that. I can vouch for the lad."

William frowned. "Alright. But he better not cause a ruckus in here or I'll bounce him out on his ear." He stalked away mumbling to himself.

Montagu grinned. "Nice fellow, eh?"

But Stefan had lost interest in the debate, his attention diverted by Lucinda, who had appeared on stage setting a small table before the curtain.

"I know that woman!" he said.

Montagu looked up. "Do you?"

"Well, no, not really. I've seen her at the Pig's Head."

"I see. If you stare any harder, your eyeballs will be rolling on the floor." The duke noticed her long brown hair tied back loosely with a green ribbon, the curves of her bosom in her corset. "Although she is a tasty-looking dish." As Lucinda walked off the stage, he caught her eye, startling her, and causing her to trip and almost fall. "But perhaps a bit clumsy."

William mounted the steps and stood beside the table, waiting for the audience to notice him and quiet down. After a few fruitless minutes he began to speak, pitching his voice over those coming from the seats.

"Good evening, ladies and gentlemen! Welcome to the Haymarket Theatre!" The crowd gradually quieted. "I am your host, William Haymarket."

"Boo!" someone yelled.

"So soon?" William said. "I've hardly started."

Montagu chuckled.

"Tonight, we again welcome a rare talent," William said. "A mentalist and prestidigitarian of mystical ability! Fresh from his exotic world tour of Rangoon, Bombay, Cairo, and East Wickersham, please welcome, the Soho Swami!"

As he walked off the stage, the curtain opened. There, in all his glory, stood the Soho Swami, looking like a character from an Arabian fairy-tale. He had wrapped his gaunt frame in a cobalt-blue silk gown, sprinkled with silver stars. His golden slippers tapered to long points that curled up in spirals. He wore an enormous scarlet turban that teetered as he moved, threatening to fall off at any moment.

Stefan was enthralled. "I've never seen anything like it," he whispered to the duke.

"Lucy," the Swami said, "my wand."

Where Stefan had been enthralled before, he was practically rendered unconscious by the sight of Lucinda reappearing on stage, carrying a wand, a red handkerchief, and a deck of cards. She turned to the audience with a smile and a bow. Shrill whistles and some bawdy remarks greeted her.

The Swami took the handkerchief from her and displayed it to the audience. Slowly, he pushed it into his closed fist. He blew on his hand and opened it. The cloth had disappeared.

The audience was unimpressed. "So what?" the man seated beside Montagu yelled.

The Swami was about to respond when suddenly, he clutched at his throat and began coughing. "Oh . . . my!" he choked out. He thrust his fingers into his mouth and extracted a red handkerchief, but tied to it followed a green handkerchief, and tied to *it*, a yellow one, then a blue one, until the Swami had drawn out from his throat ten handkerchiefs tied together like a string of flags. He smiled broadly and took a bow. The audience applauded but cheered even more enthusiastically when Lucinda bowed and curtseyed, treating them to a lovely view of leg and decolletage.

Montagu leaned toward Stefan. "I'm sure you could do that, couldn't you?"

"Do what?" Stefan said, his eyes still trained on Lucinda.

Montagu jabbed him sharply in the ribs. "The trick!"

"Oh. Yes. Child's play."

On stage, the Swami was preparing for his next trick. "And now, I require the assistance of an audience member. My lovely assistant, Lucy, will fetch a volunteer. Do I have any volunteers?" No one spoke up, so the Swami upped the ante. "All volunteers will be rewarded with a free pint of ale at the Pig's Head."

At that, several gentlemen raised their hands and voices to get Lucinda's attention. She descended the steps and walked down the aisle, passing close to where Montagu and Stefan sat. She glanced at Montagu, a slight smile on her lips, but passed on, lightly touching the shoulders or arms of the eager men pressing their case. She stopped before an elderly white-haired man and held out her hand.

"Sir, would you please?" she said sweetly. He took her hand. She could not help but notice the ruby pinky ring he wore. Holding his hand, she led him to the stage where the Swami stood shuffling a deck of cards.

"Thank you, my good man," he said. "Please pick a card from the deck but do not show it to me." The Swami made an elaborate show of turning away his head as the man drew a card from the deck. "Very good. Now, look at it and commit it to memory. Do you have it?" The man nodded. "Perfect. Please hand the card to Lucy."

Addressing his assistant, he said, "Lucy, hold the card to your forehead so that I cannot see it. I will read your mind and divine the card."

Lucinda held the card to her head while the elderly man looked on. The Swami frowned as he concentrated on the card. After a few moments, during which the audience continued to chatter, the Swami announced, "I do believe you are holding the knave of clubs. Is that correct?"

Lucinda revealed the card to be, in fact, the jack of clubs.

"Was that your card, sir?" said the Swami.

"Indeed, it was."

Mild applause drizzled through the theatre as Lucinda took the man by the hand. She led him to the front of the stage and bowed, once again enchanting the men with her charms. After escorting the man to the steps where one of the hostesses led him out of the theatre to claim his ale at the tavern, she returned to the stage. She exchanged a knowing look with the Swami who had noticed the man was no longer wearing his ruby ring.

Montagu stretched and yawned loudly. "I hope I can stay awake," he said. The Swami's performance seemed to go on forever and the duke wondered what he had done to deserve such torture.

On stage, the Swami said, "Lucy! Another volunteer, please."

Montagu groaned. "By Jupiter, no, not another one!"

Lucinda had already descended the stage and was now in the aisle. Slowly, and ignoring the other men calling out to her, she came to where Montagu and Stefan sat. Noticing the duke's upper-class fashion, she said, "You," beckoning to him.

Stefan was beside himself with excitement as he grabbed the seat before him and stood.

"No, not you," she said. "*You*," pointing a slender finger at the handsome Montagu.

Dejected, Stefan slumped back into his seat. Lucinda took the duke's hand and brought him onto the stage. She stood close beside him while the Swami adjusted the turban that was starting to slide off his head.

The Swami said, "Sir, you look like a man of title. How may I address you?"

"Montagu. The Duke of Montagu if you please."

"I would imagine you would have a penny upon your person?"

"I would hope so," said the duke, provoking some laughter from the audience.

"Please hand it to the lovely Lucy. I assure you; it will be returned to you."

Digging deep in his pocket, it took Montagu a few moments before he discovered the coin there and drew it out, giving it to the girl. As their fingers met, he held them briefly, pleased to see a blush rise upon her cheeks.

"Hold out your hands so the audience may see that they are empty," said the Swami.

The Swami then directed the duke to close his hands into fists and told Lucinda to place her hands over his. As they held hands, the intense gaze of the duke's gray eyes caused Lucinda to look away, embarrassed.

The Swami waved his wand over their hands. "Abracadabra!"

Montagu looked at him. "Really?"

"Abracadabra! Open your hands!"

They opened their hands and several coins fell to the floor.

The audience applauded but Montagu suddenly grabbed Lucinda and bent her backward, giving her a long, passionate kiss. With his back to the audience, they could not see his hand snake inside her warm bodice, nor could they see him retrieve the silver snuff box she had hidden in her cleavage.

The audience went wild, cheering and whistling. Only Lucinda heard the duke whisper, "I must insist on having my snuff box returned to me. You could use a little more practice, my sweet."

He released the disheveled and dazed Lucinda and addressed the audience in a loud voice. "As enjoyable as these little tricks have been, I wonder if you fine people would not like to see some truly wondrous feats. Stefan! Come on up, lad!"

Confused, Stefan looked around as though the duke were calling some other Stefan. Surely, he must have been, but no, Montagu was urging him to the stage.

"Come on, Stefan!"

Reluctantly, he limped toward the stage, leaning on his walking stick. William tried to intercept him, but Montagu called out, "Let him come, William!"

He finally made it onto the stage and stood there nervously, wondering what the duke had in mind, and smitten by the presence of the lovely Lucinda so near to him.

"Show them what you can do, Stefan," Montagu said.

"What? I'm not ready," Stefan murmured. "I can't do this."

"Sure you can, you're a conjuror."

Stefan froze.

"He's a fake," the Swami said, "get him off the stage!"

A man in the audience shouted, "Do something mate!"

Something stirred within Stefan and roused him into action. "Hold this for a moment," he said to Montagu, handing him the walking stick. Stefan tried to remove his coat but got his arm caught in the sleeve. Turning in a clumsy circle as he struggled to free himself, he heard the cloth tear, eliciting more laughter from the audience. Finally, he freed his arm and removed the coat. He retrieved the walking stick from Montagu, leaned it against the table and draped the coat over it. With a fierce look of concentration, he slowly waved his hands in the air around the coat, as if he were a mystical potter shaping some invisible vessel with his hands.

"Abracadabra?" the Swami said.

Stefan briskly whisked the coat away. The audience gasped. The walking stick now sprouted several large branches covered with shiny green leaves.

"Now *that's* a trick!" a man shouted from the audience.

Stefan beamed, especially as he noticed how his magic had impressed Lucinda. Suddenly, the magic tree began to lean. Before he could get to it, Lucinda rushed over and caught it.

"Thank you," he said. "Uh, would you be so kind . . . I mean, could you . . . would you hold it up for me?" She nodded. He picked up the Swami's wand, walked over to him, and lightly touched the immense turban. Instantly, three little chirping birds flew out of the turban and over the audience, circling and twittering in the air.

The audience went wild, clapping and cheering.

"How in the blazes did he do that?" the Swami mumbled.

Stefan raised one arm and, as if summoned by a falconer, the birds veered away from the audience, flew back to the stage, and settled on the branches of the tree.

Lucinda's eyes sparkled at such wonderment. She flashed Stefan a big smile. She took his hand and walked him to the front of the stage. Together, they gave the audience a deep bow, ovations thundering in their ears. As they rose, he stumbled and would have fallen into the orchestra pit had she not quickly grabbed him by the arm.

The curtain closed as the cheers continued.

Chapter Fifteen

AS THE VELVET curtain swished closed behind him, Stefan turned, glowing from his triumphant performance. But backstage was pandemonium. Montagu wrestled with an enraged William, whose face was red and eyes wild as they bored into Stefan's. William's arms flailed in the duke's grasp. Had he broken free William would have pitched Stefan off the stage.

"Let me at him!" he screamed. "I'll tan his hide!"

"William! Calm down!" said Montagu. "You're mussing my coat!"

The Swami stood by silently, hoping to remain unentangled in the dispute. He reached up into his gigantic turban and carefully dug out a small bottle, which he opened and immediately brought to his lips.

"Damn you, stop!" Montagu said, pushing William away.

Stefan refused the bottle the Swami silently offered him. He backed away from the two combatants. William panted like a winded racehorse, still shooting eye-daggers at Stefan. Montagu tugged at his coat sleeves and straightened his collar.

"There, much better," he said. "Now William, this was not what I had planned for tonight. I had just hoped to talk with you about a business venture that might interest you concerning Stefan, the most impressive magician I have ever seen." He looked at the Swami. "No disrespect intended."

"None taken," the Swami replied, taking another slug of whisky.

"But when this beautiful lass called me up to the stage, I thought the best way to show you Stefan's talents was, as they say in picklewag, to just jump in."

"This is my theatre. You ruined the night. I should have you arrested. No! In fact, I should have you both arrested." William noticed one of the stagehands sweeping the floor. "Hey, you! Run outside and fetch me a constable at once!"

The man dropped his broom and ran out.

"Come now, William," the duke said. "Have you not known me for years? Have I ever steered you wrong?"

Stefan nervously shuffled a few steps closer. "Sir, I meant no disrespect. Truly, I had no idea . . ."

"Get this ragged gypsy away from me before I strangle him!" William said.

Montagu beckoned to Lucinda. "Come here, lass. Lucy, is it?"

She smiled at him. "Lucinda."

"Would you please escort my young comrade here to the back alley so I can have a private chat with my old friend, William?" She nodded and took Stefan's arm, leading him out. "That's a good girl," Montagu said.

As the door closed behind them, the Swami said, "I see that I'm not needed here." He took a swig from the bottle but only a drop drizzled out. "Drat! So, it's off to me dressing room to find a fresh companion."

"You don't have to leave," William said. "Duke or no duke, this *friend* ruined the night."

"*Au contraire*," replied the Swami. "I'm not sure what that kid did tonight or how he did it, but I might find the answer in another pint of barleycorn." He dropped the empty bottle on the stage and started to walk off but then stopped and turned. "And don't forget, William, you still owe me for my sterling performance."

"Sterling, my arse," he mumbled at the Swami's retreating back.

"Are you willing to listen now?" Montagu asked him once they were alone.

"Go on."

"I'm assuming that tonight's attendance is typical?" William's dour expression told the duke all he needed to know. "If I could promise you a performance that will ensure a full house, no, a house packed to the rafters, would you be interested?"

"What? With that gypsy? Have you lost your wits?"

"William, you saw what he could do. I happen to know that gypsy is actually a conjuror and can bring about mystical events that not only defy logic, but everything known to science. Even the transgression of physical boundaries."

"Bollocks."

"Have you ever heard of the Bottle Conjuration?"

"The what?"

"The Bottle Conjuration," Montagu said. "A magician uses a common wine bottle, which any of the spectators may first examine. He places it on a table in the middle of the stage. He inserts a funnel in the bottle and then, amazingly, our magician enters the bottle."

"The hell he does!" William said.

Montagu ignored the manager's outburst and continued unperturbed. "Once inside, he sings. Any person may handle the bottle and see plainly that it is only a common tavern bottle. Yet, our young lad is very much encased inside."

William stared at him. "Preposterous! You're daft! Looney!"

"You can ask the Swami about this feat as it has been tried in Asia, Africa, and in the Orient, all to no avail. That is . . . until now."

"Even so, what's that got to do with me, and your ruining the show tonight?"

"I repeat," said Montagu. "What if I could guarantee an audience of the highest quality? Not the common riffs who scurry up a pence for your shows, but a theatre full of London's elite. Dukes and duchesses. Countesses and lords!"

"Lords?"

"I can promise you that Lord Cumberland . . ."

"King George's son?" William said in a hushed voice, his eyes wide.

"Actually, the third son, but yes, none other. With Lord Cumberland and his friends in attendance and with the proper promoting, the London snobs will come. Why you could charge five pounds a ticket and even sell standing-room at a premium." He looked around to make sure they were alone, then leaned closer to William. "Think of the extra riches your hostesses would be able to pluck that night," he whispered.

Before William could answer there was a commotion at the door as the stagehand and a constable burst in. The constable looked around suspiciously. "What seems to be the trouble?"

"*Merde*," Montagu said under his breath.

"Trouble? There's no trouble here, Constable," said William. "There's nothing amiss. Isn't that right, Montagu?" He shot the duke a warning look.

Montagu shrugged his shoulders. "None that I know of."

"But this here bloke said there was some kind of ruckus going on," the constable said, holding the squirming stagehand by the scruff of his neck.

William laughed. "No, no, nothing of the sort. He must have misunderstood. Perhaps he's a bit in his cups, I don't know. Everything is fine, Constable," William said, patting the constable on his shoulder. "Sorry to have troubled you."

The constable squinted as if trying to see inside William's thick skull. He sighed. "Alright, then, I'll be on me way. But don't make me come back."

The constable walked out, followed by the stagehand.

"So," Montagu said, "do we have a deal?"

Chapter Sixteen

· ·

LUCINDA AND STEFAN found themselves standing in the
alley, bordered by the theatre on one side and Unicorn Court on the
other. A tall stone wall ran along the court, creating dark shadows. The
alley was used by the theatre to bring in supplies, to haul in set pieces and
served as the employees' entrance. The old cobblestones were in disrepair, weeds sprouting through the cracks.

They stood on the loading dock, the door firmly closed behind them.
Neither knew what to say. Lucinda broke the silence. "What do you suppose they're talking about?"

Stefan hobbled toward two large barrels. "Me." He sat on one, all the
while avoiding looking at her.

"You?"

He scratched his head. "That doesn't sound right, does it? He's trying
to get me a performance here." He finally looked at her and saw confusion on her face. "The duke that is."

Her face glowed and she almost swooned. "Ah, the Duke of Montagu.
Is he per chance, married?"

It was now Stefan's turn to be confused. "Married? I don't believe so,
but I really don't know."

She sat on the other barrel, primping her hair as she spoke. "Such a
handsome man deserves a beautiful wife, don't you think?"

Her proximity made him nervous, and he forgot his words. He simply
stared at her.

Like a teapot ready to whistle, she jumped up and started pacing.
"What's taking him so long?" She stopped mid-stride and turned back to
Stefan. "Tell me, how do you know the Duke of Montagu?"

"Only recently met him. He's seen me do my street conjuring and . . ."

"Like the tricks you did in front of the Pig's Head?"

Embarrassment grew on his face. "Oh, that. I . . . I'm so deeply sorry
about nearly drowning you."

She gave out a sweet laugh. "I'm just teasing. That blunderbuss had no right to treat you or anyone like that." She sat down beside him.

He smiled. "The duke said that he believes in me and would have a talk with the theatre owner, who I don't think likes me. Or any Romani."

"Well, he may not have admitted it, but I'm sure your tricks impressed him. Tell me, how did you do that trick with the fruit tree? I've never seen anything like it."

He shrugged. "Magic is all."

"Just like that? Magic? You're being modest. There must be more."

"Cassandra has been a wonderful teacher."

"Who's she? Your mum?"

"No. My mother died giving me birth."

"Oh! Mine too. Well, not giving me birth, but when I was three, she died of scarlet fever." She unconsciously began twisting the delicate chain that held a simple locket. She looked at the heart-shaped locket and read the inscription: *Let love and faithfulness never leave you.*

She whispered, "Hardly any memories of her, this locket is all that I have."

Stefan watched her silently gazing at the locket. "It's beautiful. You're blessed that you have something to remember her by. I wish I had something that was my mother's."

Lucinda sighed. "But after she died, it was just me and the old man. A sorry bastard he was, the sod!" She turned and spat on the cobblestones.

"My father," he said, and the words took on a hushed tone, "ran off when I was born. Because of this." He pushed out his twisted leg. "I've never even met him. I don't know if he's alive or dead. I suppose I don't really care."

"I ran away from *my* father as soon as I could. I couldn't take being slapped around anymore. He was a mean drunkard."

Their common bond rendered them silent. They simply looked at each other. This time Stefan broke the silence. "And so, here we are, two orphans in a dark alley. Talking."

Lucinda smiled. "Yes, it's nice. I don't have many people I can talk to. I never did."

"I find that hard to believe, Lucinda. I mean . . . you're beautiful."

She blushed. "Thank you, but what about you?"

"Me?"

"Who do you talk to?"

He thought for a moment. "No one, I guess. Just my aunt, Cassandra."

"She taught you magic?"

"That's right," he said, carefully choosing his words, "and how and when not to use it."

She sighed. "I wish I knew some magic. I'd turn myself into a bird and fly away from here."

That remark surprised Stefan and with a laugh, he said, "Really? And where would you go?"

"Don't rightly know." She paused, deep in thought. "Somewhere exotic, maybe. Somewhere with golden sands and coconut trees and monkeys."

"Monkeys?"

She laughed. "Yes, monkeys! And I would be their queen and they would bring me diamonds and rubies from secret mines."

"And bananas?"

"Well, of course, bananas! Monkeys have to eat, don't they?"

"If I could learn that trick, I would make you a queen."

"Would you?"

"Yes."

With a quizzical expression, Lucinda, perhaps seeing something in Stefan she had not noticed before, stood up and minced a few steps. "And I would make you the royal conjuror. You would be famous the world over."

"That would be a dream come true."

She stopped her waltz. "Is that your dream? To be famous?"

"What more do I have?"

Quiet seeped in for a moment.

She sat back down. "You were fantastic, you know. That trick."

"Oh. Thank you."

Suddenly, the large theatre door opened, interrupting their conversation. Out stepped

Montagu looking incredibly pleased. "Let's go my conjuror, we have work to do!"

Confused, Stefan rose from his seat and balanced himself against the barrel. "What?"

"Come on lad, up and at 'em!" shouted the duke.

Lucinda stood as well and primped her hair, smiling with her eyes at the Duke of Montagu. But his eyes darted away to Stefan as he handed him the walking stick he had left behind in the theatre.

"What's happening?" Stefan asked, as he grabbed the stick.

"Great news, Stefan! William is willing to allow you to perform on his stage with the Soho Swami."

"With the Swami!" Lucinda and Stefan said, simultaneously.

"Don't give it a thought, my boy," Montagu said. "We all know you're the star of the show, eh? But that's the only way William would have it."

"Alright. So be it. When?"

With a Jack-O'-lantern's grin, the duke said, "In a fortnight, so there's no time to waste. I need to make sure all of London knows about you. If you can separate yourself from this beauty, you need to rehearse. Let's go!"

Montagu took his arm and led him down the alley, whistling a bright tune as they walked. Stefan glanced over his shoulder at Lucinda. She returned his look with a deep warm smile.

Chapter Seventeen

· ·

THE HAYMARKET THEATRE had several dressing rooms. The largest room was used for operas, plays and larger stage productions. These rooms were sparsely furnished with clothes racks, several mirrors and a variety of tables and chairs. During a performance, the rooms were crowded with actors and actresses humming about. The Swami's dressing room was far down the hall in what was once a storage space. It contained a small armoire for his costumes and a long wooden table whose paint had become a faded memory years ago.

Makeup jars containing bismuth, ceruse, talc, and rouge sat on the table. Small oil lamps were attached to the sides and top of a large tin-framed mirror beside the jars. The glass had a burnt-yellow tinge from the warm light of the lamps.

The Swami sat on a rickety wooden chair. He stared into the mirror. "Truly t'is the winter of our discontent," he mumbled. He took off his turban, placed it gently on the table, and began to remove his makeup. He noticed that he had applied too much pearl powder, making his face white as a ghost now peering back at him from the mirror. "Really? Have you something to say to me?"

But the mirror was silent.

He took a small cloth and started to wipe off the India ink used to darken his eyebrows. Some ink slid into his eye, causing him to wince. He reached over to take a warm sip of whisky but remembered that the empty bottle rolling around the stage floor was his last. He looked into the mirror as if speaking to the last row of the theatre.

"I would give all my fame for a pot of ale and safety," he recited, quoting the Bard. Unlike when he had played in *Henry the Fifth*, no applause rang out.

He started to rub out the rouge on his cheeks and mused to his reflection, "What a journey we've had, from studying theatre at Cambridge, to performing great works of Shakespeare before the royal family, and now, reduced to the role of a swami performing simple feats of amazement to earn enough shillings for a soft bed and a warm meal." He sighed.

The ghost mimicked him in silence. The Swami patted his face with a soft sponge and said to his reflection, "If you remember, there was a time that Fortune found me, as did a paramour or two. Yes, even a duchess and later an earl, but those were mere dalliances. The life of a performer is a life best travelled alone." He erased the last of the rouge from his cheeks. "But things could always be worse," and then, remembering he was out of his barleycorn, said, "Correction; things are worse."

He sat back, free of the stage paint and saw himself in the mirror as the ghost had vanished. He wondered about what had happened tonight and who was this young gypsy?

A rapping on the door interrupted his thoughts and before he could respond, William walked in. Annoyed by the intrusion, the Swami's demeanor softened when he saw William reflected in the mirror holding a flask. The Swami smiled.

William held out the bottle. "A peace offering. For this evening's fiasco."

The Swami, with a touch of indignation in his voice, said, "It was certainly that. A performer of my caliber should never be treated so shabbily. It's disgraceful."

"I'm terribly sorry, Swami. I had nothing to do with it. Had I known what was going to happen, why I would have thrown that upstart . . ."

"Upstart indeed!"

". . . into the street. Please accept my apologies." William handed him the precious vessel. "And this flask of Jamaican rum."

He accepted the flask haughtily and took a dainty sip. "You're forgiven. I will say, though, the upstart has rather pretty ogles."

"Forget it, pretty eyes or not, I don't think he's your type."

Another sip. "They're all my type, dear boy."

William pulled up a stool next to the Swami. "Please, Swami, get serious. I have something important to discuss with you. I've made a deal with Montagu."

The flask froze halfway to the Swami's lips. "A deal?"

"Yes, I'm putting the gypsy, what's his name? Oh, Stefan, on the stage."

"Over my dead body!" the Swami said, slamming the flask on the table.

"I don't think it will have to come to that."

The Swami leaned forward, inches from William's face. "You're replacing me! The great Soho Swami, known worldwide as . . ."

William backed away. "No, no! Not at all. Calm yourself. Listen. The duke assured me his protege . . ."

The Swami's cheeks were red, even without rouge. "Protege, my arse! And who in the blazes is this duke?"

William reached out his hand asking for a sip. Without thinking, the Swami passed the flask to him. After a long pull on it, William said, "Fine. He's just a bugger of a gypsy. By the way, it's the Duke of Montagu from the noble house of Montagu. I've known him for several years. Bit of a gambler and practical joker, but highly regarded by many a society lady. Anyway, Montagu assured me the boy is a good magician. You've seen that for yourself, but the duke said that no one is as good as the Soho Swami."

"He said that?"

Holding his hand to his heart William replied, "I swear on my mum's grave."

"Well, flattered, I am." The Swami took back the flask. "Amazing! Proceed."

"As I said, the gypsy is good, but he needs the teachings of a great master to reach his potential. That's where you come in."

"No."

"Yes! Think of it, Swami." William stood. "You will be billed as not only the great and powerful Soho Swami, but as the world's master of the arcane arts. You will be the gypsy's mentor, and everyone will know that his success is all your doing. Without your tutelage, the lad would be just one more gypsy doing cheap tricks on the street. And a crippled one at that."

The Swami's brow wrinkled in contemplation. "Hmmm . . ."

"I want him on the stage in a fortnight."

"I haven't agreed yet, William."

William placed his arm around the Swami's shoulder, "There will be quite a handbag."

Turning to William, he asked, "How much?"

William pulled away from the Swami and became animated, his arms flying about excitedly. "Montagu said he can entice the rich and powerful to come to the performance, even Lord Cumberland himself. I could charge double, maybe triple. . . No, quadruple my usual admittance!"

"His Grace himself? And you will cut me in?"

"Absolutely. How does five percent sound to your ears?"

"Not as musical as ten percent."

William thrust out his hand, almost poking the Swami in the face. "You drive a hard bargain."

"So, I've been told," he said, with a lascivious wink.

William's hand still hung in the air. "You'll do it?"

The Swami brought the flask to his lips and clasped William's hand. "Alright."

"Good! In a fortnight. Oh. And that bugger, Stefan, will be performing something called the Bottle Conjuration."

The Swami spewed out the rum. "What! That's impossible! Not even in the Far East has it ever been known to succeed."

"Is it impossible, Swami? With you as his mentor?" William's tone grew serious. "Make it so." He headed towards the door, turned back to the Swami, and said, "Two weeks." He closed the door behind him.

The Swami, his head swimming, glanced back at his mirror and was not at all surprised to see that the pale ghost had returned.

Chapter Eighteen

AS HE TRIED the lobby doors of the theater, Stefan had to step around the glue-spattered stagehand who was pasting up a poster advertising the Soho Swami's upcoming performance. The doors were locked. Stefan stepped back to admire the poster and almost kicked over the glue pot.

"Hey, careful there, mate!" said the stagehand.

"Oh, sorry," Stefan mumbled.

The stagehand wiped his hands on his pants. "If ye has business here, use the back door. Bang twice."

Stefan nodded as he read the poster. "I'm going to be working with the great Swami," he said, proudly.

The stagehand picked up his gluepot. "You don't say. Well, I'm leaving for me card game with King George. His carriage should be fetching me any time now." Stefan frowned. "By the way, I'd be watching me backside with that Swami. First chance he has, you'll be buying him some barley-corn."

Just as the stagehand was about to walk off, a corner of the newly glued poster came away from the wall and before he could catch it, the whole thing peeled off. "Damnation!" he said.

Stefan thought it was a good time to make himself scarce, so he headed to the rear of the theatre where he found the door unlocked.

William was in the aisle, giving instructions to a gaggle of hostesses gathered around him, including Lucinda.

"So, if we sell out the house as expected," William said, "not only will there be more quarry for you, but the prey will be of London's finest, making our work even more lucrative."

William saw Stefan standing there. "Speaking of the devil," he said.

Lucinda looked up and gave Stefan a smile.

"Get yourself backstage," said William, "the Swami isn't a patient man like me."

Backstage, the Swami stood by his prop table, practicing card tricks. He wasn't wearing his costume and from the wings, Stefan noticed how gaunt he was, like a field scarecrow. Without his huge turban, his nearly bald pate gleamed in the light.

When he noticed Stefan in the wings, the Swami said, "Come on, lad, I won't bite. If I'm to be your mentor, we best get at it. Your big night is none too soon if you ask me."

As Stefan hobbled toward him, the Swami said, "Are you sure you can perform on stage with that bum leg? I guess you need your walking stick. That's fine, I like it as a prop. It adds a certain, I don't know, let's say panache, to your tricks." He stroked his chin in thought. "Hmm, but we really have to do something about those ragged clothes of yours."

He called down to Lucinda who was just walking up the aisle. "Lucy, fetch me a robe for this ragamuffin. I'm thinking the red . . . wait, no, the gold one, the one I used for the disappearing doves trick. Yes, that'll do nicely."

She appeared backstage with the robe and draped it over a chair. Stefan felt heat rise in his face as she helped him shuck off his coat. She shook out the golden robe. Dust and a few moths flew out, flittering off to the lights. She sneezed. "Sorry," she said.

The robe fit Stefan like a circus tent. It fell to the floor in cascades of silk that threatened to trip him up. His hands were lost in the long sleeves.

"Now, that's better, if I do say so myself," the Swami said. "Do you agree, Lucy?"

Her lips quivered and Stefan was not sure if she was stifling a laugh or another sneeze. "Why I do," she said. "I'd say he's a right handsome sorcerer at that."

"Alright then," the Swami said. "Listen, my sonny-boy, I don't like wasting my precious time on a gypsy, but my task is to teach you a few tricks. Help you with your stage proficiency."

"I understand," Stefan said, "and with your help, I can become a good conjuror."

"I'd be happy if you could master a simple card trick or two. What you do on your big night is of no consequence to me. The way I look at it, I'm being paid if you do your trick or not. But you better understand, if you muddle up my show, you will regret it the rest of your life."

"I won't muddle up. I'll be of assistance to you and more. I will perform the Bottle Conjuration. I promise."

The Swami waved his hand as if brushing off Stefan's comment. "Bottle trick or no bottle trick, some free advice. What's important is to bring in a large crowd. And, if your trick flops, you should stand before the audience, explaining that you attempted the impossible, then exit the stage with your head held high. But I'd be ready for a cabbage or two flung at your head. So, I'd advise you to get off stage as fast as your bum leg will let you. Now that I've imparted my wisdom to you, I'm retiring to my dressing room for an afternoon tea." He fished a small bottle of gin out of his pocket. "Lucy will work with you on props. *Adieu.*"

He walked off, bottle in hand, unexpectedly leaving Stefan alone with Lucinda. He fidgeted with his walking stick, trying not to look at her but incapable of looking away.

"I suppose we should get started," she said, breaking the silence that had settled over them. "The Swami performs mostly card tricks, so all you have to do is bring out a new deck when he asks for it."

He took a deck of cards from the prop table and wordlessly began to shuffle them faster and faster until all she saw was a blur.

"Perhaps we can skip the card tricks for now," she said, amused, taking the deck from him. She picked up a large bowl of artificial fruit from the table. "Now, as you can see, this is not an ordinary bowl of fruit. The fruits are made from sponges brought back from the Americas, dyed, shaped, and colored to look like real fruit. The Swami . . ."

"Lucinda, please," said Stefan. "I'm willing to learn the Swami's tricks if I must, but I want to do more wizardry than cards and fake fruit. I want to astonish the audience."

"Like you did with the tree."

"Yes."

She sighed. "You need to take a breath and bide your time. Learn what you can from the Swami. Remember, a bird must learn to fly before it can leave the nest."

He smiled. "I like your advice."

"About learning from the Swami?"

"No, about learning to fly." Shyly, he took her hand and leaning on his stick, hobbled with her to center stage. "Watch." Cupping his hands, he raised them high over her head. He made a little jump up, then opened his hands. A tiny finch flew from them onto the balcony.

"Very nice," she said.

"Wait," Stefan said. He stood behind her and placed his hands gently over her eyes. He felt that contact like a lightning jolt through his body. He leaned forward, inhaling her scent like lilacs, and whispered in her ear. "Close your eyes and think what it would be like to fly away to a desert island."

She laughed. "One with monkeys?"

"Yes. Monkeys gathering jewels from secret mines." He brought his hands down to rest against the back of her shoulders. "Keep your eyes closed and remember those dreams." He reached out and took up a mirror from the prop table, his walking stick tangling in the oversized robe. He came around her and held the mirror before her.

"Slowly, now, open your eyes."

Her eyes grew wide in astonishment as they found the mirror and the image it held. Two magnificent, snowy-white wings, so beautiful they would make an angel weep in envy, rose behind her, their fine pinions pointed skyward as if ready for flight.

"Oh, Stefan! They're beautiful!" Tears shimmered in her blue eyes. "Just like in my dreams!"

He blushed and was about to speak but before he could find the words, she stopped him by pressing her finger against his lips. "No one has ever done anything as nice for me," she said.

She looked at him for what seemed like an eternity and his heart raced as he imagined what thoughts were going through her mind. She embraced him and slowly, gently, kissed him.

Completely untethered by her kiss, he stumbled, the voluminous robe snagging around him but enveloping her as well as she held him. He lost his grip on the walking stick and now, like a mighty tree felled by the woodsman's axe, he swayed, then toppled over, taking Lucinda down with him. They crashed to the floor in a geyser of white feathers. She landed on top of him. Stunned, they lay there, looking into each other's eyes, feathers still floating down around them.

Thwap! A dirty wet mop barely missed Stefan's head.

"Can I help ye up," said the stagehand mopping the floor, "or do ye want me to mop around ye?"

Chapter Nineteen

AMONG HIS MANY titles, Prince William Augustus, Duke of Cumberland, was also known as Ranger of the Great Park, as he resided in the enormous edifice outside Westminster called the Great Lodge. Surrounded by an immense lawn, and circumscribed by woods, meadows, and a large pond, the lodge had been built by Colonel James Byfield in the middle of the seventeenth century with improvements and additions made by subsequent residents. Now, almost a century later, the three-story red-brick lodge with its crenelated towers and central keep rose like a medieval castle on a modest elevation overlooking the Windsor Great Park. Despite its grandeur, Cumberland was busy adding terraces and gardens to make it even more imposing. He also added a green for lawn bowls, a favorite game of his, prohibited to the low-born by Henry VIII two centuries earlier.

Although a bachelor, Cumberland was more than capable of hosting elaborate dinner parties at the Great Lodge, aided by a talented staff of cooks and servants. His invitations were always eagerly awaited by those who wished to rub elbows with the rich and powerful. There was no dearth of such elbow-rubbers.

Dressed in an emerald-green coat embroidered in gold, buff-colored knee breeches and waistcoat, Cumberland looked every corpulent inch the lord of the manor. He smiled to himself as he surveyed the crowd chattering in Tapestry Hall. The men in their periwigs and ornate coats and the women in their silk and satin dresses, many with outlandish panniers that made it almost impossible for them to pass through doorways. Yes, sycophants for sure, but they were *his* sycophants, born of the same noble class as him, so different from the burgeoning aristocracy~a term he used loosely~rising among some of the guildsmen in central London with their pretensions of sophistication and wealth. Men like the printer Jeppson, a hale enough fellow, but certainly a man who could never rise to the level of a peerage. But Cumberland knew that titles were now easier to obtain; a military hero may find himself knighted or more for some act of bravery on the battlefield. He did not believe such titles were worth the script they were written on.

He sipped a glass of claret as his guests circulated about. In a corner of the hall a chamber orchestra played Bach. Golden light from the westering sun slanted through the immense window at one end of the hall, illuminating the gigantic tapestries on the walls and gilding the crystal and tableware set out on the long table in the center of the room.

A giant of a man stood by the window, towering over three other gentlemen. The man looked ill at ease, despite his size, but Cumberland was not surprised. Jack Broughton may have been a champion bare-knuckles boxer, but conversing with men of privilege, in the Duke of Cumberland's salon, no less, terrified him.

"An exceptional evening, my lord," a man said, at his elbow.

Cumberland turned to find the Earl of Peterborough and his wife standing there. "Ah, Peterborough, I had not seen you arrive; welcome."

The earl bowed and his lady curtseyed, giving Cumberland an eyeful of her delightful décolletage. It was much more pleasant to gaze upon that than to look at the earl, as the man's right eye had a tic that caused it to twitch incessantly.

"We were wondering what delicacies your cooks might be preparing this evening. Each dinner seems more marvelous than the last," Peterborough said.

"Thank you. Wait and see, I'm certain you will be amazed," said Cumberland. "I was just observing my champion over there," he said, nodding toward the window.

"I assume you are well-pleased with him."

"Indeed, I am."

"He's a great ox of a man," Peterborough said, with a laugh.

"More like a prize stallion and, no doubt, as prodigiously endowed as well."

Lady Peterborough's ears perked up. "Your Grace, if I may excuse myself? I spy Lady Abercrombie across the hall and have some news I must impart to her."

"By all means," Cumberland said, with a smile and a nod. "You are a lucky man, Peterborough," he said, watching her cross the room, drifting close to the circle where Broughton stood.

From Peterborough's position, he could not see the expression of awesome wonderment on his wife's face as she stole a furtive glance at the enormous boxer. "Indeed," he said.

Turning back to the earl, Cumberland said, "But still, there are the tavern wenches, eh?"

Peterborough laughed. "How to explain that. I don't know. But there is something . . . exciting about frolicking with the lower classes, don't you think?"

"Yes, good for a tumble or two, I concede. But then, one must lose the stink of such people," Cumberland said.

"Indubitably."

Cumberland set his wine glass on the table. "But seriously, Peterborough, don't you believe the common folk are causing problems for our class with their guilds and associations, pretending to rise to our standards?"

"They are far beneath our standards."

"Precisely, but their arrogance, the airs they put on, as though they *were* of our class, are insufferable."

"True. And yet, while they pretend to wealth, we are the ones being taxed ever higher to support so many wars and God knows what else," Peterborough said.

Servants were now moving about the long table, setting out plates and bowls. The revelers continued chatting and flirting as the airy notes of a Bach sonata floated above the crowd like little cupids.

Cumberland picked up his glass and drained the last of the claret. Immediately, a servant appeared seemingly out of thin air and refilled his glass. "I fear our society is eroding," he sighed. "There are already undesirables pretending to our ranks. Montagu, for example."

"I know how Your Grace disdains the man," Peterborough said.

"Disdains? You put it mildly, Peterborough. The man is an impostor."

"He *is* a duke."

"Balderdash! In name only. His family inherited farmland that happened to have a large vein of coal beneath it. From farmers to colliers in a generation or two. And wealthy colliers at that," said Cumberland, incensed. "But Montagu is a wastrel, a dissolute scoundrel, so much so that even his family wants nothing to do with him. He is the Duke of Penury."

The house steward entered the room and declared in a loud voice, "My lords and ladies, dinner is served."

While the orchestra continued to play, the guests found their places at the table, each seat designated with a name card. It turned out that Peterborough was to be seated at Cumberland's right, while Lady Peterborough would be on his left.

Even as they took their seats, Cumberland, still vexed by thoughts of

Montagu, said to Peterborough, "He is such a pompous ass. I would love to take him down a notch or two. Put him in his proper place."

Peterborough smiled. "Yes, and what a ridiculous notion he had about that ragged gypsy trickster. A man inside a bottle! Insanity!"

"Hmm, I had forgotten about that, Peterborough," Cumberland said, tucking a linen handkerchief beneath both chins, "but that gives me an idea." He leaned closer to the earl and whispered, "Perhaps a sizeable wager with Montagu about whether that trick could be performed or not would cut him down to size."

"He is a man who would bet on whether the sun will rise in the morning," Peterborough said.

"Yes, he is that. Perhaps, I shall do it; offer him a wager to see if his purse will back up his mouth."

Noticing that the room had gone quiet as his guests waited for him to give the word, Cumberland smiled and inhaled deeply. "Ah, the roast lamb smells delicious. Once again, my cooks have outdone themselves. Please, everyone, begin. Let it not grow cold!"

Instantly, the clinking of glasses and rattle of silverware once again mingled with animated conversation as the diners were served delightful heaping portions of the cooks' sumptuous delicacies.

Yes, Cumberland thought, bayoneting a chunk of lamb with his fork, it would be quite pleasurable to humiliate the Duke of Montagu.

Chapter Twenty

· ·

HIS TARNISHED GOLD‑PLATED pocket-watch glowed in the morning sunlight. Even after all these years, it kept precise time. It was one of the few items he had from his father, a parting gift, as Montagu left home to find his way in life. He shook the watch, but the time didn't change, and as usual he was late for a scheduled meeting, this one with Jeppson.

Jeppson was not just a printer; he had risen to become a Master in the Worshipful Company of Stationers guild and with Lord Cumberland as a client, his status had increased.

Montagu quickened his pace and soon turned the corner onto Chancery Lane. From there, it was only a few blocks to Fleet Street where the best printers were located. He arrived at the Jeppson Bookbinder & Print Shop, housed in a two-story brick and stone building with small white columns enhancing the large, frosted glass door. Printed copies of the news of the day, pamphlets, and examples of various leather-bound books filled a bay window. Midday crowds would form to read the latest news posted in the window. A few gawkers were reading about the latest bold robbery, the mysterious thieves hiding their faces behind Venetian masks. This most recent affair deprived Sir Thomas Robinson, one of the wealthiest men in London, of several valuable personal items.

Inside the shop, Jeppson vociferously reprimanded one of his apprentices, spittle flying from his mouth, while the apprentice kept his head down. Another journeyman grinned, remembering days past when he had drawn Jeppson's wrath. The printer held up a misaligned page and before more profanity could fly from his lips, the bell at the front door jingled as Montagu walked in.

"I may be a bit late, Jeppson, but don't stop what you're doing. I heard you half a block away," the duke said.

Jeppson took a deep breath and looked at the cowering apprentice. "Go on now, fix the type and heat up the glue pots for when we start on the binding." The shocked apprentice didn't move, as if his feet were glued to the floor. "Now!" Like a rat being chased by a broom, he scurried to the back room.

"Well, Monty, glad you're here. I've worked up the poster that we spoke about. Let's see, where did I put it?"

He turned to look around as the journeyman came forward with several posters. "Yes, that's it, thank you Willard. Best go back and check up on our apprentice before he burns down our establishment."

Montagu took a poster and held it at arms' length. He read aloud, "*The Most Extraordinary Performance Ever to Be Seen in London!*" He set the poster down. "Not bad Jeppson, not bad. We can have these posted all around town."

"I'm glad you approve. I would be more pleased if I knew you could pay for the work in advance."

Montagu flashed his well-rehearsed smile. "Of course. I have a few darlings who will financially support my plan. It is their way to pinch their gullywag husbands."

Jeppson moved over to the letterpress and removed a newly printed broadside. "I took the copy you sent me for the advertisement and did a quick press. Take a listen. '*On Monday, next, a gypsy. . .*'"

Montagu shook his head. "We should say, *conjuror.* That sounds more exotic, don't you agree?"

The printer thought for a moment. "Yes, I do agree." He walked the broadside over to a large wooden table, pushing aside a bundle of hemp cords, rollers, and a brass binder stamp to make room for the document. "I'll make that change." He grabbed a quill and bottle of ink to make notes.

Montagu, standing over the broadside, read the ad to himself. "I think we need to be more dramatic. This needs to grab the imagination of all London."

Jeppson sat on a stool, not sure what to change. "Any ideas, Monty?"

"Not really. Why not read it aloud to me? I'll close my eyes and see if I can imagine this mystical performance."

Jeppson adjusted his spectacles and read, "*On Monday, next, a conjuror will perform several most surprising things. To wit, he will take a walking stick. . .*"

"Let's make it a common walking stick."

"*To wit, he will take a common walking stick and thereupon play the music of every instrument known in use.*" Jeppson looked up. "How in the blazes does he do that?"

Montagu sat with his eyes closed. "Hush, I can see it. First, he would take the common stick to his lips and when he blows into it, sweet flute music will flow. Turning it another way, it will sound like a French horn."

"If you say so." Jeppson made a few scratches and continued to read. "*To his lips the common stick will play music of every known instrument like flutes, French Horns and likewise he will sing to surprising perfection.*"

"Jeppson, that's good." Montagu opened his eyes. "We should also describe the wine bottle."

The printer again took quill to ink and said, "Perhaps we should say *a common wine bottle which is presented to any of the spectators who may first examine . . .*"

Montagu closed his eyes again. "Wait. I see a bottle being placed on a small table alone on the stage with a chair next to the table and, yes, a funnel placed in the neck of the bottle."

Scratching as fast as his fingers would allow, Jeppson said, "Slow down, Monty." He finished writing and read, "*This bottle . . . wine bottle, is placed on a table in the middle of the stage, and without any equivocation, the conjuror goes into it, in sight of all the spectators, and while encased, he begins to sing.*"

"Yes! That's the spirit!" Montagu said.

Jeppson set the broadside down and removed his spectacles. He sighed. "Will anyone believe this nonsense, Monty? It is more than bombastic. Can people really be so gullible?"

"I believe so."

"Even Lord Cumberland and his gang of sycophants?"

Montagu turned and looked out the bay window. "Especially them. Oh, they will claim the trick is impossible. They will say anyone who believes it can be done is a fool. Yet, they will come to the theatre to see the act, mark my words. Why? They will come precisely to see it fail, to prove they were smarter than everyone else and right all along."

"There's that," replied Jeppson.

Montagu turned back to him. "But do they need to come to see the act if they know it is impossible? After all, the gypsy's spectacular failure will be bruited all around London in minutes. No, but they will come because deep down inside they doubt their convictions. They want to make sure the trick *can't* be done. They must see it, or not see it, with their own eyes."

"Gullible."

"As gullible as the people who burned witches at the stake."

Jeppson took a cloth and rubbed the thick lenses of his spectacles. "It will be great fun to fool them."

"Fool, yes. Making them the laughingstock of all Britain is even better."

Jeppson placed his spectacles back on, adjusting the nose guards. "Monty, this all sounds good, but there is another side to this coin. Cumberland and many of his associates, snobs or not, do support my establishment. I have to protect myself."

"I fully understand," Montagu said, "and I will allude to using another printer if Cumberland inquires. Better yet, who is your chief competitor?"

Jeppson paused but decided against antagonizing a brother guildsman. "This gypsy, what's his name again?"

"Stefan."

"Stefan thinks he can do the trick?"

"Most certainly. The lad may be misguided, but he is sincere. He's a dreamer, that one, naive to the ways of the world. In other words, the perfect foil for our plot."

"He has no suspicions?"

"Not a one."

Jeppson grabbed a tray to reset the type. "It should be a most interesting night. If for no other reason than to see the gypsy's lovely assistant again."

Montagu's smile beamed like glowing coals in a pot-belly stove. "You're right, and she can be our accomplice."

Jeppson seemed confused. "How would she do that? How do you propose to win her over?"

"Leave that all to me," replied Montagu. "If you loan me a few farthings, I'll get it done."

Chapter Twenty-One

EXCEPT FOR THE oil lamps casting their dim light upon the stage, the theatre was dark, no performances having been scheduled for the evening. Instead, Stefan, Lucinda, and the Swami were gathered on stage rehearsing. The Swami's props table sat center stage loaded with assorted cups, balls, cards, and the Swami's enormous turban. In the background, almost lost in the shadows stood another table, barren except for a magnum wine bottle and a funnel.

William appeared on stage, pulling on his coat. "I'm through for the day, Swami. I'm going home, but remember next Monday is our special performance. Do your best with that gypsy trickster, will you?" He tossed a set of keys to the Swami. "Make sure you lock up when you're done."

"Worry not," replied the Swami, catching the keys in mid-air. He blew on his fist, then opened his hand to show the keys had disappeared. He smiled, but the smile died a sudden death when the keys fell out of the sleeve of his robe and dropped to the floor with a loud *clang!*

William sighed and shook his head. "I should have gone into medicine," he mumbled as he walked off stage and exited the theatre.

The Swami turned to Stefan and Lucinda and withdrew a bouquet of flowers from his sleeve, which did not impress his assistants. He handed her the flowers. "Remember, Lucy, to show the audience the flowers and hold them high as you take a deep, long bow," the Swami said. "Try it."

Lucinda bowed.

"No. Lower," the Swami said, his eyes focused on her low-cut bodice. "A bit more." Lucinda bowed so low she nearly toppled over. "Raise your chin a little. Ah, yes, lovely. That'll do."

"Now, lad," he said to Stefan, "when she takes her bow, you walk over and pick up a deck of cards from the table."

"Cards? Should I not prepare for my bottle feat?" Stefan said.

"You really don't understand the ways of the stage, do you? We need to build anticipation for your, uh, *piece de resistance*." Stefan seemed confused. "Your bottle trick!"

"It's no trick," Stefan said. "It's real and only a conjuror can evoke the powers to do it."

"Oh, of course, yes," said the Swami. "In my travels through India and beyond I've heard tales about it. I've also heard that no one has ever been able to do it." He sighed. "But we're wasting time. William has persuaded me to help make the performance an unforgettable event. First, we will open the evening with some rowdy songs from our hostesses as they circulate among the audience. Then I will perform a few of my most mystifying illusions." The Swami took the flowers from Lucinda and placed them on the table. "Lucy, you will be escorting our audience volunteers to the stage. Choose carefully, only the *creme de la creme* will do."

"I understand," she said. "The rich blokes."

"After I do a few tricks, I will introduce you as my protégé," the Swami said to Stefan, "whom I am mentoring in the grand mystic arts. We should probably start with one or two card tricks." He gave Stefan a deck of cards. "I'll show you how to guess what card a volunteer has selected. It's actually the easiest trick to do."

Stefan was not paying attention but was riffling through the deck, shuffling the cards faster and faster, using the Hindu shuffle. Amazed by his dexterity, the Swami stood speechless.

"I grew up with cards," Stefan said, hobbling over to Lucinda. "Not so much for card games, but to tell one's future."

"Like Tarot cards?" she said.

"Something like that, but even an ordinary deck like this will do." He fanned the cards out face-down. Slowly, one card rose from the deck. "Take it," he said.

She took the card. "The ace of diamonds."

"That means great wealth," Stefan said.

Another card rose from the deck. She picked it out.

"Ah, the lovely queen of hearts," he said. "That means love may be near."

"Rubbish," the Swami said.

Stefan ignored him. He took back the cards and reshuffled the deck. "Now, let's see which card is your true fortune."

He held the deck before her. "Think carefully and select only one card from the deck. That will be the true future awaiting you."

Lucinda hesitated for a moment; her brows knit in concentration. Then, she removed the top card of the deck. "It's the queen of hearts," she said.

He looked into her eyes and said softly, "True love waits for you." He noticed the sad expression on her face. "Are you disappointed?"

Still looking at the card, she said, "Well, I was hoping for the ace of diamonds again."

"Here, give me those cards," said the Swami, indignantly. "I assume *this* is the ace," he said, drawing the next card from the deck. With a flourish he turned the card over to reveal . . . the jack of clubs. He frowned. "Alright, what does this card mean?"

Stefan shrugged. "Nothing, really."

"Nothing?"

"It's just the rogue," Stefan answered. "One who cannot be trusted."

At that moment, the door at the rear of the theatre opened and the Duke of Montagu walked in. "Excellent!" he said, as he bounded for the stage. "Seeing the three of you hard at it! Bloody good!"

Lucinda held out her hand to help him onto the stage. Still holding her hand, he smiled and brought it to his lips, kissing it. "Thank you, my lovely," the duke said. "Listen, all of you, I have great news. I've been working on printing up posters and broadsides to promote next week's spectacular." He reached into a pocket of his coat and withdrew a sheet of paper from which he read, "*On Monday the sixteenth, at the Haymarket Theatre, a feat of pure mystical power will be presented. The night will include performances by the acclaimed Soho Swami.* The text goes on, but the point is this should bring in the curious, the men of learning, and of course, the finest of London."

The Swami snatched the paper from the duke and stared at it. "I'll be the talk of the town!"

"Stefan, can you really do your trick?" asked Lucinda, worried.

"Of course, the lad can," Montagu said, "but time is of the essence, so I suggest that Stefan and the Swami get back to practicing."

The Swami nodded in agreement. "This will truly be the night of all nights and the Soho Swami will be at his best."

Montagu once again took hold of Lucinda's hand. "It would be best if they practiced alone, Lucinda. I have ideas I would like to discuss with you about a special guest at the show. Come with me, we'll have dinner and talk."

"If it's alright with the Swami," she said.

The Swami shooed her away with his hand.

"Then, let us go." Montagu led her toward the steps.

"I will return soon after dinner," Lucinda said.

Stefan, gripping his walking stick, watched her go to the front of the stage, as if she were a ship sailing to unknown horizons. "Promise?"

She turned back and said, "Rest assured."

But as the smiling duke led her away by the hand, Stefan felt anything but assured.

Chapter Twenty-Two

· ·

THE FARMS AND meadows surrounding the village of Hackney
supplied the horses used by the coachmen in London. William Haymarket spotted a weather-beaten hackney outside the theatre. He noted the
medium-sized pale horse hitched to it. That size of horse and cab was gen-
erally desired by lady passengers, as it provided a slower, smoother journey. As expected, a woman wearing a large pink bonnet emerged from the
cab, paid the driver, and received a tip of his tall hat as a thank you from
the coachman. William considered waiting for another larger, faster cab,
but decided a slower ride home would help him shed the chains of the
day. He waved to the coachman and was signaled to hop aboard.

Once inside, he noticed a placard stating that his coachman, Alberton,
was a member in good standing of the Worshipful Company of Hackney
Drivers and had successfully passed the Knowledge Test. William was
pleased to know that his driver was highly qualified with an intimate
knowledge of London streets and important buildings. It should be a
peaceful ride. He gave the driver the address of his townhouse on Winchester Walk.

"Yes, sir, I do know the area. Bit of a ride, but nice, I might say," the
coachman replied.

The drive, William thought, should take about forty-five minutes, but
with the age of the horse, it might take longer. They would travel along
the Thames, over the London Bridge and then a few minutes later onto
Winchester Walk. At night, indeed a peaceful ride.

The sounds of the barters on Haymarket were left behind and he began to relax. *How did he get to this place in his life?* Born into a working-class
family in the east end of London, he knew he did not want to work like
his father, pushing a coal-cart throughout the city. As a child, he would
sneak into local theatres, and watch plays, song and dance shows, even
an opera. He dreamt of being on stage, but as he grew up, his immediate
need to earn a living and the sad realization that he did not have any tal-

ent in the theatrical arts locked those dreams in a closet. His only talent was gambling.

His best bet had been when he met Rosalind. She was standing in line to enter the Mayfair Theatre. She stood about twenty feet behind him. He heard her voice before he saw her. If a voice could taste sweet, hers would be like honey. He turned and noticed her long auburn hair gently waving as she shook her head. She glowed as she animatedly talked to the woman beside her. It was obvious they were friends. He felt himself staring at her and quickly turned away. At thirty, he was almost bald, and felt embarrassed about his looks. Yet, he had the notion of taking a chance. He approached the ticket booth and looked back at the two girls. Did the girl with the auburn hair just smile at him?

The ticket attendant broke his spell. "It's a quid for the show." She started to tear out a ticket for him.

William whispered into the booth, "Do you see the woman behind me with the auburn hair and the pearl broach?" The attendant nodded. "Also, the short woman next to her, with the blue scarf? I will pay for their tickets, but you must ensure that they will sit next to me." Nonchalantly, she took the money and tore out tickets for them. "It's a surprise. Just hand them the tickets when they come to your window. Tell them it's their lucky day—free tickets!" He handed her another quid for helping him.

She smiled and gave him a wink.

When the girls arrived at the ticket window, the attendant played the game like an actress. The girls were surprised but delighted to have received free tickets, graciously took them, and entered the theatre.

William's plan worked. He found himself seated next to the auburn beauty. That had been twenty-five years ago, and he was as happy today as the day he purchased the tickets. During their early years, he was able to use his winnings from the various card games, horse races and boxing matches to provide a nice life for Rosalind. Fate also dealt him a good hand as, unbeknownst to him, he discovered that her parents were part of the growing aristocracy and gave her a healthy dowry. With that, they purchased the townhouse on Winchester Walk. But, over time, the gods of gambling turned on him. His losses started to mount. Then he went to Hell. Lower Hell.

There were two types of gambling halls in London. Hell was for the elites and for the commoners, there was Lower Hell, usually found in coffee houses, taverns, or abandoned buildings. One had to walk through two sets of heavy red curtains to enter. They were designed to keep the gambling hall as dark as possible and separated from the public areas.

William had played a high-priced game of backgammon. His opponent was losing. It was only a matter of time before William would be able to collect the cash. His opponent, sweat forming on his brow, raised the stakes. He took the doubling cube and moved it to sixty-four. William felt moisture on his brow. If he took the bet and lost, he would be broken. He would never be able to explain that to Rosalind. Earlier, he had promised her he would stop gambling and find honest work. Yet here he was. He took a deep breath and accepted the wager. He pulled out the money he had in his purse and placed it on the table. He still had twenty pounds sterling left, tucked in the heel of his boot. His opponent parleyed up his wager, his hands shaking as he reached for the dice-cup.

"Wait!" exclaimed William, taking a long drag on his cigar. "Let's say I not only match your wager but increase it by twenty pounds." He took off his boot, removed the notes and added them to the pile. The onlookers crowded the gaming table. Tension filled the hall.

His opponent placed the cup down. "My friend, a bet is a bet. The cube stands at sixty-four, and I'm afraid that is all the money I have."

William sat stoically in his chair and puffed smoke that caused him to momentarily disappear. "Well, sorry old chap, but the rules of this fine establishment are that a bet can be added as long as the dice remain in the cup. If you can't match it, then the spoils are mine."

Several of the bystanders shouted, "Here, here! The bloke's correct."

William felt some guilt, but not enough to let the old chap out of the bet. He pulled the cash toward him.

"Wait!" shouted his opponent. "I have something that I think is worth more than your twenty pounds." He reached into his vest pocket and pulled out a folded parchment. As he unfolded it, William saw "DEED" printed on it. "This," his opponent said, his voice cracking, "is the deed to the Duchess, a property that I own. If you accept, I will add this to my wager. . ."

William took the paper and examined it. His first inclination was to reject the offer, but as he looked at the deed, he saw that the Duchess was an opera house. He sat for a moment gathering his thoughts.

The owner of the Lower Hell shouted out, "That's a fair wager and under house rules, you must accept. Or you can cancel all the bets and each one takes back their wagers."

William always wanted to be in the theatre; if he won, he would not only have money to bring back to Rosalind, but he could now leave gambling behind and run a theatre. "Where, perchance, is this theatre located?"

"It's a fine place, needs some renovation, but has been around for fifty years or so. Worth more than your twenty. . ."

William interrupted him. "Again, fine sir, where is it located?"

His opponent sat back in his chair. "On Haymarket street near Suffolk."

William smiled. He knew Fate had kissed him. Not only a theatre, but incredibly, one located on a street that bore his surname. Fate could not be denied.

"Roll the dice!"

That was fifteen years ago, and William had been the proud proprietor of the Duchess, now renamed the Haymarket Theatre, ever since.

The coachman pulled on the reins and guided the horse to make a right turn onto London Bridge. The horse fought the change and challenged the driver, but with a quick crack of the coachman's whip, the animal relented, and the carriage made the turn. The coach jostled him from his thoughts. He looked at his pocket watch, seeing that he should be home in twenty minutes. He snapped the watch cover shut, placed the watch back in his pocket, and resumed his reverie.

He enjoyed the excitement of an opening night, watching the shows, the music, and of course, the girls. Especially those who would reward him with a personal performance. He loved owning the Haymarket. Love was fleeting, though, especially when the bills came due. The cost to run the theatre was far more than he was bringing in. With the condition of the property, most of the audiences comprised the lower classes of London, while those of means and titles enjoyed the larger, more elegant theatres in town.

Like the crossroads the cab had arrived at, he too had arrived at a decision. To create wealth, he needed to borrow funds to upgrade the Haymarket, add special boxes for those of title and turn the place into a palace. He also needed to find talent that would draw in crowds. The banks denied him the funds he needed, and he refused to borrow money from Rosalind's parents. His only choice was to find a shylock.

Instinctively, he knew this was a bad idea, but the gambler in him won out. He found a well-known chemist in town who also dabbled in the art of moneylending. The terms were tough, as was the rumor about how the chemist and his partner dealt with those who crossed them. But, if his plans fell into place, he would be able to repay the loan with interest. Rosalind would be none the wiser.

The coach had arrived at Winchester Walk, moments from his door.

The trip had gone faster than he thought, but maybe it just seemed that way. The time flew, as did the time for his loan to be repaid. He was now two weeks past due, and he would have to stall as much as he could. If Montagu's plan worked, he would be able to cover the loan and more.

He stuck his head out the window and shouted to the coachman, "Three houses more, the two-story brick with the white trim and the black wrought-iron gate."

The cab came to a slow crawl and finally stopped. "That'd be one-quid and half-pence, if you please," said the coachman.

William took out his coin-purse, and by the light of the oil streetlamp counted out the fare and a nice tip, or as he called it, *to insure promptitude*, the next time he used the service of this coachman. The coachman smiled and tipped his hat.

William walked toward his house and opened the gate, which gave out a rusted groan as it opened. *Must take care of this gate in the morning.* As he closed it, he noticed a dark figure standing under the streetlamp. The flickering of the yellow flames made the silhouette seem gigantic, drawing out long shadows into the street. William walked up the steps, quietly opened the front door, and glanced back at the streetlamp. The silhouette was gone. He entered the hallway. All was quiet; his wife was probably asleep. As he started up the stairs to his bedroom, he felt tired. The long, heavy chains had returned.

The coachman had paused to adjust the harness on the mare and was about to jump back onto his seat, when a man, dressed in a long black coat approached. He wore a white Venetian mask and pointed to the open cab door. The coachman nodded for the man to enter.

Chapter Twenty-Three

THERE WAS A chill in the air, unusual for this time of year. Lucinda was glad that Molly had loaned her a black knitted shawl that morning. She warmly embraced it as she walked with Montagu to the Pig's Head Tavern.

The duke noticed Lucinda clutching her shawl, and gently tucked her arm under his, pulling her closer. He gave her a smile. When they arrived at the tavern entrance, he grasped the wrought-iron handle fashioned as a pig's head, opened the door, and allowed her to enter first.

She thought this was probably the first time a man had ever opened a door for her.

The noise and smoke of the tavern greeted them.

"This is a boisterous place," Montagu said. "I've reserved the snug for us, so we can talk privately."

Having worked at the Pig's Head, Lucinda was familiar with the snug. Most popular taverns had a private room—a snug—located away from the bar crowd. She had often served a fine Bordeaux to a vicar or two who would reserve a table in the snug so as not to be seen by the public while they imbibed, or perhaps, held a *tête a tête* with a woman of dubious repute. Chestnut tables set with red cloths and oil lamps crowded the snug. A stone fireplace nestled in the corner. Opaque glass block windows filtered light in but kept anyone outside from seeing who might be inside.

They were comfortably seated in a corner with enough distance from the other patrons to allow them privacy. Lucinda glanced around the room. "I feel like a fish out of water. I've never eaten a supper here, only served them."

He smiled. "You are worthy of a fine dinner, Lucinda. A woman like you deserves fine things." He waved over a barmaid.

"Can I get you some ale or wine?" she asked.

Montagu thought for a moment. "No. Would you bring over a bottle of your finest gin?"

She gave him a mischievous wink as she turned away with his order.

He turned to Lucinda. "There are probably a hundred ale houses in London that serve 'mother's ruin,' but what they bottle here, I think is the best in town. Do you agree?"

"I've never tried a drop of it."

"You are in for a real treat, then" he replied, as the barmaid returned with two glasses and a small bottle. She was about to pour, but Montagu took the bottle from her hand. "I'll do the honors," he said, as he poured the clear liquid into Lucinda's glass. "And we would like to order. We will have the leg of mutton and Lenten pie." He glanced at Lucinda. "Sorry, do you approve?"

She blushed. "Whatever you wish, my lord."

The barmaid promptly left, and Montagu lifted his glass. "To finer things!"

"Yes!" she replied, toasting with her glass, and taking her first sip, the gin causing her to cough. She put her glass down and leaned closer to him. "Ah, but you already have all the finer things you might want."

He took a moment to respond and looked at her meaningfully. "Not yet, but soon perhaps."

She took another swallow of gin. "But a duke has so much already. A fine estate with many servants. Paintings on the walls. A beautiful garden. Orchards, perhaps."

Montagu had looked away for a moment as though he was deep in thought. "Orchards? Why not?"

The barmaid appeared with their supper. Lucinda's eyes, a bit glassy from her first experience with gin, grew large on seeing the meal. She immediately took to the mutton as if she hadn't eaten in a week. Montagu, amused, poured more gin into her glass. "Slow down, my lady. Take time to savor this dish."

She paused. "You must have a fine coach with coachmen in red coats and silk hats."

He raised his knife in the air. "How about two coaches!"

"A box at the royal opera. Invitations to fancy balls . . ."

Waving his hand, he said, "Mere trifles."

Her eyes were as wide as his smile. "Trifles, m 'lord? I think not! They're wonderful!"

Montagu shrugged nonchalantly while he poured more gin into her glass. "Have you tried your Lenten Pie yet? And, please Lucinda, call me John."

"John?"

"Yes. I think we are friends, are we not?"

"Oh, yes!"

Montagu leaned closer to her. "Then call me by my birthname."

Softly she replied, "John."

He touched her lips with his finger. "It sounds like music on your lovely lips."

Loud and rowdy shouts and cheers from the tavern bar shattered their quiet moment. Montagu looked toward the door. "Guess those bloody gypsies have arrived. Another reason why I secured this table away from the riffraff."

As if in a trance, Lucinda did not notice the noise. Her eyes were locked on him. She hoped that he would kiss her and had moved her head to accept a kiss when the doors burst open.

Several of the gypsy women, including Sophia, entered playing their tambourines and singing. Before Henry Roberts could shoo them away, Sophia noticed Montagu sitting with a woman at the far table. Tambourine in hand, she swayed and danced toward them. She struck the zils with her fingertips in several short taps. She stood beside their table and dragged her thumb in a circular motion on the zils, creating a loud sustained jangling near Montagu's ear.

Montagu, annoyed, covered his ear.

Sophia shook the instrument one last time. "I thought that was you I spied. Good evening, Monty!"

Looking up at her, he coldly replied, "Good evening. . . Madam."

"Madam?" Sophia glanced at Lucinda. "Oh, *madam*. I understand." She bestowed a wink on him and gave her single hoop earring a little tug. "I don't wish to disturb you, so I'll be on my way before master Henry comes after me with his cricket bat." She swirled her flowing skirt like a mini-whirlwind, and again started to shake the tambourine.

Montagu watched her walk away. He turned to Lucinda with a peeved look. "A clear case of mistaken identity."

"She called you Monty."

He quickly grabbed the bottle. "Did she now? Yes, well . . . More of this wonderful gin?" He poured the last of the small bottle's contents into her glass. "Tell me, how long have you been the Swami's assistant?"

She watched the glass being filled, looked back to him, and responded as if the encounter with Sophia had never transpired. "Only for a few weeks."

"I must say, you are yourself excelled at the sleight of hand." He took her hand and softly held it. "Quite intelligent fingers you have. You almost made off with my silver snuff box. It has sentimental value to me, as it was a gift from my departed mum." He wiped an invisible tear from his eye.

She nearly swooned as he held her hand and gently massaged her fingers. "I'm so sorry m'lord. I mean, *John*."

"You are forgiven, Lucinda. I quite enjoyed retrieving the box from your bodice." His eyes went there once more and noticed a locket peeping above her blouse.

Embarrassed, she turned away, then came to her senses and withdrew her hand from his. "And you reminded me that I am supposed to be helping Stefan and the Swami with their rehearsal. I really should be getting back."

"Nonsense, my dear. There's plenty of time. What say we finish off this lovely supper with a nice glass of cognac? Then, I will escort you back to the theatre."

She hesitated before responding, "But Stefan. . ."

Montagu signaled to the barmaid as she approached the table and said, "Bring us two glasses of your finest cognac."

The barmaid stopped and gave him a disbelieving look. "Really?"

He reached into his waistcoat, pulled out a coin purse and opened it, revealing a treasure of coins. Impressed, she headed to the bar.

"Now, what were you saying, my dear?"

Lucinda noticed that her hands were entangled with his. The warmth of the gin had enveloped her, and she found it not only hard to think, but also difficult to answer him.

The barmaid arrived carrying a tray with two amber glasses filled with cognac and placed them on the table. "Will that be all, my lord?" She held out her tray for payment and a much-deserved tip.

Montagu ignored the barmaid and handed a cognac to Lucinda.

She took the glass. "I guess one last drink couldn't hurt," she said.

The barmaid repeated her question, this time putting her tray directly in his face. "If that be all, you owe two pounds, three shillings."

"Two pounds!" Montagu held his tongue and reached into his vest with a sigh. "Yes, indeed the meal was divine as was the drink." He handed the coins to her.

She carefully counted them as he dropped them on her tray. She stood firm and took a breath. "Did we forget something, guv'nor?"

With a sigh, he reached back into his coin purse and tossed in a half penny. The barmaid knew the battle was over. She took the half-penny from the tray and hid it in her blouse. With a smirk, she curtseyed, then faded away.

He turned back to Lucinda. "What again were we discussing?"

She said, "I don't mean to pry . . . John, but will the duchess be attending the performance?"

"The duchess?"

"Your wife."

Montagu quietly laughed. "Oh, that duchess. No. There is no Duchess of Montagu."

"No?"

"No."

It was Lucinda's turn to laugh. "A pity."

Montagu looked forlorn. "Perhaps someday I will meet my true love, someone I can lavish my gifts upon."

Longingly, she looked into his eyes. "Gifts. Maybe there will be someone soon."

"One never knows," he replied. "So, tell me, Lucinda. Where did you learn to be such an accomplished pocket thief?"

"Here and there. A girl raised on the street learns how to survive. I'm not proud of it."

"Is that how you got this?" he asked, reaching over, and lifting her locket by the chain. He flipped it open before she could stop him and saw the woman's portrait. "And this old dowager, is she the hag you robbed?"

Lucinda sat as though struck dumb. At last, she whispered, "That's my mother."

The duke's hand froze, the locket dangling from his fingers. "Your mother. Ah, yes, well" was all he could muster. She took the locket from him and tucked it securely in her bodice. After what seemed like an eternity, he finally said, "My apologies, my dear."

Lucinda nodded, willing to forgive him but still shaken by his callous comment.

Montagu raised his cognac, signaling for her to also take a drink. "To our mothers," he said, trying on a smile.

They drank and Lucinda pushed all thoughts of her past into the dustbin of her mind, preferring to concentrate instead on the handsome duke.

"But you should be proud of your prowess as a pocket thief!" he persisted. "It's a rare talent and quite useful skill." They placed their glasses down and the duke took her hand again. "In fact, your skills might be of service to me."

She looked into his eyes as the drink had invited cherubs to dance above her. "I would love to be of slurpluss. . . service to you!"

Softly squeezing her hand, he said, "Would you?"

"Oh, yes, m'lord!"

Smiling, he tapped her hands. "Such a good girl! But we mustn't speak here. Too many ears. Let's speak in private."

The cherubs started to dance faster around her head. "What?"

Montagu stood up and reached out his hand to her. "I think you have had enough to drink my dear. Come with me."

She tried to stand but her legs felt like those of a fawn attempting to walk, as she started to slip. He quickly moved around the table and placed his arm around her waist, pulling her close, ostensibly to help her walk.

"Oh! That's nice!" She leaned against him as he led her towards the door.

He began to weave her through the tavern and into the street. Outside, he turned them left, away from the theatre.

She noticed the theatre drifting away from them and with a slur asked, "Where are we going?"

"I have an apartment near here. We can talk there."

"Will you give me a gift?"

Montagu smiled. "I intend to."

With Lucinda gone, the theatre suddenly became darker. Stefan could not put his finger on the anxiety inside him, but somehow, he knew that she was its source. She was supposed to be helping him and the Swami with their routine. Why had she left with the duke? She said she would return soon but "soon" had already come and gone.

Stefan tried to lose himself in practicing his tricks even though his mind was somewhere in the streets of London looking for Lucinda. *Concentrate, damn it!* The second time he dropped several cards from the deck, he knew it was useless to go on, yet he pushed even harder, much to the consternation of the Swami, who looked like he was in dire need of sleep or drink or both.

"I must say, you are persistent," said the Swami, bending down to retrieve the fallen cards, "but, lad, it's going on the witching hour and my weary bones need to stop."

Stefan looked crestfallen. "Just one more time," he said, "maybe something with the vanishing fruit."

"Really?" the Swami said, sadly shaking his head. He placed his hands on Stefan's shoulders. "You know she' s not coming back."

"Of course, she is," Stefan said. The Swami gently squeezed his shoulders, looking intently into his eyes. Stefan looked away, scanning the dark theatre as if searching for her. Turning back to the Swami, he said softly, "She said she would be back. Where is she?"

"I don't think you are that naive."

No, he wasn't, and his heart would not accept the lie he wanted it to believe. Lucinda wasn't coming back.

"Stefan," the Swami said, kindly, "I've come to learn that a woman's heart, like the magic arts, should never be trusted." Stefan was mute. "Let's call it a night, son. There's always tomorrow."

The stage grew darker as the Swami turned down the oil lamps.

Stefan stood there in the last pool of light, wondering if he really wanted to know what tomorrow would bring.

Chapter Twenty-Four

THE LAVENDER COACH raced through the countryside at breakneck speed. It was adorned with enormous peacock feathers streaming in the wind like military flags. Two white steeds galloped forward, nostrils flaring, hooves pounding like thunderclaps. From the coach window she saw a wagon that a common day-laborer would use. It was approaching faster than she was traveling and soon overtook her. The driver of the wagon, his face turned away, was snapping the reins as it raced by. She could not identify him.

"Faster!" she shouted to the driver. "Faster, now!"

She heard the cracking of a whip. Suddenly, her coach began to lift upward, leaving the ground below them. Up and up the horses pulled her into the clouds. She leaned out the window and saw a castle, high atop a mountain, a drawbridge open, waiting for her to enter. She ducked her head back inside the coach. She saw the duke sleeping, his head nestled against the back of the seat. *How could he possibly be sleeping?* She gently shook him. *Wake up, wake up.*

"I'm awake, my sweet one," Montagu replied.

The rays of sunlight, streaming through a break in the apartment curtains, softly lit her body. She murmured yet was fast asleep. Smiling, he leaned over and gave her a soft kiss.

She stirred languidly, draping an arm across his chest. In a hushed voice, she said, "Good morning, m'lord."

Montagu kissed her passionately and whispered into her ear, "John."

She opened her eyes. "Yes. . . John." She stretched as he kissed her neck. He turned and started to get out of bed. Lucinda held him back. "No. Stay with me."

He sat on the edge of the bed and caressed her cheek. "If it were possible, I would. Unfortunately, I have work to do."

She kissed his hand. "I think you've already done it."

Montagu grinned. "Work of a different nature. Not as pleasant, I'll admit." He began to dress. "That must have been some dream you were having."

"Dream?" She lowered her head on the feather pillows. "Oh, yes, a dream. I was in a lavender coach racing through the countryside. Then it just rose upwards into the clouds towards a castle. It was glorious!"

He kissed her forehead. "Flying coaches. Castles. Sounds divine. But I must get ready for a long day ahead."

She pouted. "You would leave me so easily?"

"Leave you? Not at all, love." He tucked his shirt into his pants and turned to her. "In fact, I need you."

Excited, she sat up, holding the sheet over her breasts. "You need me?"

"Yes, I do. But . . . No. No, I cannot ask that of you." He turned from her as he adjusted his shirt.

"What is it, John? What do you mean?" He walked to the window, opened the drape, turned back to her, and started to say something, but thought better of it. "Please, John, talk to me."

"Forget I said anything, Lucinda, please. It's too dangerous."

She clutched the sheets. "Dangerous!" She leaned forward. "But you said you needed me. Tell me what you mean. Please!"

He shook his head. He looked out the window of his second-story apartment. The apartment was on Jermyn Lane, a busy street lined with a variety of apartments, townhouses, small shops, and a chemist. As he was carefully choosing his next words, he spotted Sophia loitering in the street. She happened to look up and saw him. She tugged on her hoop earring and blew him a kiss. Quickly, he drew the curtains over the window so hard that dust flew, and the curtain rod shook.

"John, please don't be angry, I just want to help," she said, nervously.

He turned away from the window and walked over to the bed, his expression serious. "I'm not angry. Very well." He cleared his throat. "I am planning a thievery."

"What?"

"On the night of that bloody gypsy's performance, I plan to steal Lord Cumberland's jeweled dagger."

"But why would you do that? You're rich . . . aren't you?"

He waved his hand dismissively. "Yes, yes, of course. Coaches. Paintings. Orchards."

"Then, I don't understand."

Montagu fell to one knee by the bed and took her hand. "I don't need the jewels, mind you. You know that. I have a personal score to settle with that gundiguts, Cumberland. I have a list of grievances against him that

I can tell you about someday, but not now. Stealing his precious dagger would be sweet, sweet revenge."

"Steal his dagger for revenge? But, why?"

He glanced at the closed window curtains and back to Lucinda. "For now, all I can say is that Cumberland and I have had many grievances beginning when we were both in the service of our King during the bloody Netherlands Campaign."

"You were in the war? Is that where the scars on your back came from?"

"Scars?"

"Scratches," she said. "Like from a cat. Or maybe a tiger!"

"Oh, those scars. Uh, I really don't want to talk about them. Or the campaign, except to say the dagger does not rightfully belong to Cumberland. No matter how many times he declares it is his."

"Who does it belong to, then?"

"To my best friend. I mean my late best friend, Lieutenant Lawrence." He paused, gathering his thoughts. "During a violent skirmish, my friend fought a French Grenadier to the death. In the soldier's possession was a jeweled dagger." Montagu lingered as if he was holding in a long ago hurt. "Lawrence made me vow that, if he died in battle, I was to sell the dagger as the bounty would provide for his widow and their six children."

Lucinda's heart stirred. "How did the Duke of Cumberland get possession of the dagger?"

Montagu thought. *Hmm, how indeed?*

"Another long story to be sure, but when he found out about the dagger, Cumberland demanded Lawrence forfeit it to him. My friend refused. Cumberland had him shot for disobeying an order. Leaving his widow with nothing. Not even a pension."

A tear formed in Lucinda's eye. "What a horrible and cruel man!"

Montagu held back a wry smile, proud of his storytelling abilities.

"Yes, and my plan is to steal the dagger, quickly sell it to those who deal with that sort of thing and give the funds to Lawrence's widow. But the best revenge will be the joy of seeing Cumberland squirm over losing something he prizes so highly."

Lucinda saw that he was distraught. She leaned over and kissed his hand. "John, you still have not told me how you need me." She placed his hand on her breast. "What is it you want from me? You know I'll give you anything."

"Oh, yes, I do know." He took his hand back.

She looked into his eyes. "What do you want?"

"I want you to steal Cumberland's dagger."

"Me? Steal the dagger?"

"Yes."

"From the King's son. Really?"

"Yes."

"How? When?" He remained silent, knowing that she knew the answers to her questions. She lowered her head and whispered, "During Stefan's performance."

"Yes."

"Are you mad?"

"No."

"John, that's impossible! I would do it for you if it could be done. You know I would."

He smiled. "It can be done, and you can do it, Lucinda. With your charms and nimble fingers, it would be child's play for you to lift his dagger."

"You said it was dangerous."

"Only if you're caught," he replied. "And you won't be, Lucinda, trust me."

He leaned over and gave her a long passionate kiss.

When the kiss ended, she took a moment to catch her breath. "I do trust you. But . . ."

He surprised her with another kiss, distracting her thought. "But what?"

She opened her eyes and saw him looking at her with anticipation. "Nothing," she replied. "And you will be there?"

"Of course. I will be with you every step of the way."

She searched his face, her heart racing. She knew she could not say no to him. "Alright my love, I'll do it. . . .. I will do it for you." Her eyes closed as she leaned in to kiss him.

Montagu sprang up. "Excellent!"

Startled, she opened her eyes to see him heading to the door. "Where are you going?"

He reached for the doorknob. "Out. To put my plan into action."

She stood up. "What about me?"

Montagu, seemingly puzzled, noticed her dress hung over a chair. He took two quicksteps and tossed it to her. "You? I don't know. Get dressed, I suppose. You're probably needed at the theatre. Now, I really must go." He opened the door and, like a racehorse, bolted out of the room.

The door slammed. Forlornly, she mouthed, *No kiss goodbye?* She grabbed her linen dress and slipped it on. She tossed her hair and walked over to the window, pulling the curtains aside. The light streamed in, blinding her for a moment. As her eyes adjusted to the bright sunlight, she looked out the window and saw the morning bustle of London below her. She spied Montagu talking to a woman. The woman was tall and had a large hoop earring. The duke and this woman appeared to be having an intimate conversation. Something about the woman seemed familiar but her mind was still cloudy from the night before and she couldn't quite place her. She watched as the couple, arm in arm, walked down the street, turned left, and faded from view. A tear formed like a raindrop and left a moist trail down her cheek.

Chapter Twenty-Five

SOPHIA STOOD ACROSS from Montagu's apartment, upset that the scoundrel had not shown up last night as promised. His behavior had been more vexing over the past several weeks. The late morning sun was in her face making it difficult to see into his second story window. The curtains were drawn, not a good sign, as he only closed them when he was entertaining someone. *But who could it be?*

When he did not show last night, it was too late for her to return to her camp, so she wandered to the Vicar Wesleyan's church. It had a separate entrance for men and women, and she knew gypsies were welcomed there. She was not surprised to find the room spotless and the straw beds more than comfortable. The women who volunteered to work there called themselves "Sisters" and were members of the vicar's church. Sarah Peters led them and held the title, *Visitor*. She also had spiritual duties at Newgate prison and called on the sick.

Sophia tired of waiting for Montagu. She decided she would burst into his apartment and confront him with his doxie. She took a deep breath as she was about to cross the street. Suddenly, the curtains opened. She saw Montagu clad in his finest white linen shirt. His back was turned to the window, and he seemed to be talking to someone. Again, she thought, *who?*

He turned and looked out the window. She knew that he had seen her. She pulled on her hoop earring and blew him a kiss, a signal that he had better come to her. Abruptly, the drapes snapped shut.

She stepped back onto the sidewalk and paced like a teapot ready to boil as she waited for him. She stopped in front of the apothecary and, seeing her reflection in the glass, admired her hair. *Who would have taken her place with him last night? It must be a wench with wealth, maybe even a duchess.* She felt a jealous heat tighten around her like a green-eyed beast, its sharp talons squeezing the breath out of her. The words Sister Sarah had read to her from Proverbs in the good book came to mind, *"A tranquil heart gives life to the flesh, but envy makes the bones rot.*"

She calmed herself with those thoughts, knowing that Montagu had no love for the wealthy dollies, only for their money and influence. This was not the first time he had changed their plans to dine with a lady of means. She thought, if he was a man of means, what did he need them for? He had confided in her that, after the war, circumstances arose which depleted his holdings and wealth but never told her anything more. Maybe he was not as he advertised, perhaps not even a duke at all.

Now the beast came back, and she whispered, "I will take care of whoever this latest roundheels is and find a way to rot his bones." As she adjusted her skirt, Montagu's reflection appeared in the apothecary window.

"My dear Sophia." He placed his arm around her waist and turned her toward him. "Before you say anything, I must sincerely apologize for not meeting you last night."

Sophia kept the beast at bay but pushed back his advances and let the fire in her eyes shine in his.

"Please, my dear let me explain." Again, he reached his arm around her waist. "What I did last night was a means to an end, one that will bring us great happiness."

She grabbed his arm, tightened her grip on it and seethed, "I don't trust you for a moment. You're nothing but a liar, a cheat, and I don't believe you're even a duke."

Her anger surprised him, but he mustered his well-rehearsed smile. "But I am a duke," he said.

She quickly shot back, "Then why were you with some duchess or some aristocrat's wife last night?"

He looked deep into her eyes. "I wasn't with a duchess or anyone's wife. Indeed, I was with the great Swami's nubile assistant, Lucy. She has a talent that you and I will need for us to carry out my plan. Why, she means naught to me. She's nothing more than a hedge whore."

"Plan? What plan and what does it have to do with me?"

He looked around, noting the street had come alive with people. He gently took her arm. "What I have to tell you cannot be spoken in public. Around this corner there is a small park with benches where we can have more privacy."

She hesitated, but finally nodded her assent. He led her to the street corner where they turned toward the small park. No words were spoken during their short walk. She sensed that he was deep in thought.

The park formed a small rectangle alive with cherry trees, a small fountain bordered by a hedgerow and several oak benches. He pointed to a seat and as they settled, he asked her, "Tell me, at your camp, how well do you know this Stefan who claims he is a conjuror of sorts?"

"There's not much to tell. I've watched him practice his tricks and more than once fall on his face without his walking stick. Conjuror? I'm not so sure about that." She hesitated then said, "I can tell you that I'm not very fond of him or his aunt."

Montagu sat back. "Tell me more."

"Many in the tribe consider her our elder, which I do respect, but I fear there is an uneasiness about her. She made an enemy of another Romani clan, the Shaitaans, a tribe that follows the ways of darkness. We fear her feud with them could endanger everyone."

"Sounds interesting, maybe they could be of use as my plan develops," he said. He took her hand and lightly kissed it. "I know this will seem confusing to you and yes, as you suspect, I have not been true to you. Not for lust or for riches, but for revenge." She sat mute, waiting for more. "I have been simmering a pot of stew for many years over the harassments, lies, and the belittlement that Cumberland has thrown at me since our time together in the military. I have wanted to find a way to embarrass that oaf, along with his toadies. I wanted to show how gullible they were as they followed Cumberland's every lead in so many ways."

"So, what does that have to do with me? With us? And, if you are truly a duke as you claim, why not just live your life of title and wealth?"

He ignored her questions and continued, "I have met that young conjuror and seen his sleight of hand tricks, which are quite good. He claims he can do an impossible feat and if I am correct, I can have our conjuror perform at the Haymarket to a full house with that blunderbuss Cumberland in attendance."

"So, how does that embarrass the king's son?"

"For starters, to even attend such a sham, will be the joke of London. Secondly, I plan to steal his jeweled dagger, his most favored possession. And that, my dear, is where both you and our little Lucy come in."

Sophia bristled at the thought of the other woman and leaned away from him.

"At first all I saw was revenge, but as my idea developed, I saw a chance to steal from the rich, and take their ill-gotten gains for us. You will help me to pilfer the box office during the performance. Our young dewy-eyed wench has a wonderous talent for picking pockets and will lift the dagger."

"What happens to her?"

"Who cares? You will secure us two fast horses, saddles, and bags. After I obtain the dagger from her, we will leave her in the dust. With the money and the jeweled dagger, we will have enough wealth to leave London. We can escape to the sunny coast of Spain for a life of leisure . . . together." He took her hand and kissed it. "How does that sound to your pretty little ears?'

Her mind was telling her not to believe him, but what did she have to lose? Could she stand another night at the Vicar's or living at the camp? "I understand," she said, "but I have no money to acquire horses, bags . . ."

He leaned closer, keeping his voice low. "I happen to know the owner of the apothecary you were standing in front of. William Plunkett. He is known in some circles as a shyster. He can also help us sneak out of England."

The plan was making sense to her, and the green-eyed beast ran off as Montagu embraced her.

"There is another small favor I will need from you," he said.

"What?"

"To secure the loan from Plunkett, I will need something of value to use as collateral. I noticed that lovely silver chatelaine you carry hooked to your belt."

He lifted the chatelaine in his hand, admiring the star-shaped medallion that held the chains. Attached to the chains were a pearl handle pocket-knife, a silver perfume vial, and a brass key.

"This will do very nicely," he said, as he unhooked the chatelaine from her belt. "If I may and, oh, a lovely jasper healing stone, too." Before she could object, he placed the chatelaine in his jacket pocket. "Don't fret, my sweet, you will get this back once we complete our plan and I pay back Plunkett with interest. Time is of the essence. We need to be discreet and stay away from each other as much as possible until the time is ripe for our plan to unfold. I will leave you now and go meet with Plunkett. Once I have the funds, I will look for you so you can take care of the horses. Where can I find you?"

"Don't worry," she replied, "I have ways to find you."

Montagu stood, gave her a kiss on the cheek, and headed back to the apothecary.

Sophia remained on the bench watching him saunter away. She understood she needed to be wary of this plan and this *Lucy. How do I know she isn't more involved with the duke than he is saying?*

The beast was back. *Be wary of a double-cross,* it whispered.

Chapter Twenty-Six

MONTAGU NONCHALANTLY WHISTLED a bawdy tune as he walked down Jermyn Street. The morning had started with sunshine bathing his bedroom in golden rays revealing Lucinda's smooth, pastel-white skin, and curvaceous body. This image stuck in his mind. Maybe she could be even more useful, and perchance there would be more evenings like last night in his future. His thoughts changed to Sophia's smoldering eyes and the imaginary fire erupting from them destroyed his quiet morning reverie.

His plan was beginning to take shape. He must tread lightly, like walking on a frozen lake, careful and steady. The plan must come first. A shame he thought; Lucy would make a splendid mistress, but Sophia's fury had no mercy and he needed them both.

He arrived at seventy-one Jermyn Street, the apothecary of Plunkett the chemist. Several sea-crabs walked out of the shop. They were dressed in white britches, blue waistcoats with shoulders and cuffs trimmed in gold, all dressed to announce that they were on shore leave. Each of them carried a tiny vial of mercury and sulphur pills to be used later that night if the need arose. If they were lucky.

Montagu waited for them to pass before he entered the apothecary. The clerk was a tall, young man, a jack-of-legs who stood more than six feet tall. He possessed a thin elongated neck and his rusty hair indicated to Montagu that he was a Scott. A stubble of hair, a sorry excuse for a beard, sprouted from his chin. He looked up from where he stood behind the counter and greeted Montagu. "May I be of service?"

"Good day to you my fine young friend," the duke said.

"If you be needing the cure for the flapdragon, like those sailors, I think we are out of the mercury."

Montagu smiled. "Actually, I had hoped to have a chat with the owner."

The young man placed the jar of sulphur pills on the counter. "That'd be Mister Plunkett. He's in the back. He gets upset if I yell for him, so let me go into the backroom. Who shall I say wishes to see him?"

Montagu reached into his vest pocket and pulled out his calling card, recently printed by his friend, Jeppson. The card read, *John Montagu, the Duke of Montagu.* The young man stared at the card, moved it closer to his eyes and stood and swayed without saying a word.

Montagu quietly said, "It says that I'm John Montagu, the Duke of Montagu."

"Right sir, I mean, My Lord. I'll go fetch Mister Plunkett." The young man turned and stepped like a giraffe into the back room.

Montagu looked around the store. Several oak barrels stood beside the counter. Tea filled one to the top. Another held an assortment of roots and herbs. Set to the side were two large, ornate cherry-wood cabinets, carved twisted pillars framing each of them. Doors made of interlaced brass webbing kept the contents secured but visible. There were colorful bottles, porcelain jars, and tin boxes. One tin was labeled *Turds of Goose and Pigeons.* Another tin with a skull and crossbones image was labeled, *Nightshade.* He shuddered when he saw a swarm of slithering black leeches in one of the bottles.

Plunkett not only mixed healing potions and made powders and pills, but also performed basic medical procedures and examinations for his customers. The sign posted above the counter said it all: *Bleeding & Cupping & Tooth Drawing.*

The duke walked back to the counter where he saw a leather-bound book titled, *Pharmacopoeia Londinensis.* Bored, he was about to peruse the volume when Plunkett, dressed in a soiled apron and looking like a man who did not have a good night's slumber, emerged from the back room.

When his assistant had brought the duke's card to him, the chemist recognized the name. Plunkett made it his business to service those of title living in London and Montagu had been an occasional customer. He cleared his throat to gain Montagu's attention. "My Lord, what can I do for you? Does something ail you this morn'?"

"Good morning to you," replied Montagu. "No, actually I'm feeling rather spritely."

"Then, if I recall, do you need to purchase a soothing medicine for your lady, or ladies?"

Montagu smiled. "Not this time. I'm here to ask you for two favors."

"Favors?"

"Yes," replied the duke, as he reached into his coat pocket. He retrieved a broadside, unrolled it, and placed it on the counter. "As you can see, this broadside announces a most amazing occurrence that will take place at the Haymarket Theatre.”

Plunkett read the broadside. “A conjuror will enter into a wine bottle?” He looked up at Montagu with a quizzical expression. “Balderdash!”

“Quite so, but what if? You’re a man of science. I would think such a thing would intrigue you. I happen to have seen this conjuror perform and without a doubt his magic goes beyond mere trickery to something, dare I say, mystical? I have helped him secure a special performance at the Haymarket. We hope to have the theatre filled with those of title and the elites of London to witness the impossible.”

Plunkett, tired from his night’s work, tapped his fingers on the leather book. “So, what has this to do with me?”

“As I have been a loyal customer of your shop, could I indulge your cooperation and have copies of this broadside sent over to hand out to your customers, and perchance posted in your shop’s window?”

Plunkett thought for a few moments, his fingers lightly tapping. “Those of title attending?”

“Why, yes, even His Grace, the Duke of Cumberland and his friends will be in attendance.”

Plunkett’s fingers ceased tapping. “I’ve never met the man but would love to have him as a customer.”

“Indeed,” replied Montagu. “I’m sure many of his associates utilize your services. A handbill inserted into their packages might be useful to your business as well.”

“Maybe,” he replied. “You said two favors. What’s the other?”

It was now Montagu who cleared his throat. “I have been told by a few in confidence that you are not only the best chemist in London, but you have a special, let’s say, quiet enterprise of loaning funds to those who would not want to deal with bloody bankers.”

Plunkett’s assistant entered from the backroom. Plunkett picked up his pharmacopeia and handed the heavy book to him. “Take this to my desk and sweep out the back. I’ll finish up with our customer.” Once he had left the room, Plunkett turned to Montagu and said, “I only service those who I know and trust.”

The duke reached into his other pocket. “Well, my friend, I have been a customer for some time, so we do know each other. As for trust . . .” He pulled out Sophia’s silver chatelaine. The tiny items attached to the chains danced like a miniature wind chime as he handed the chatelaine to Plunkett. “I would temporarily give away this keepsake. It’s worth more than money to me, as it is a precious memory of my departed grandmum, the Duchess of Montagu. She handed this to me on her deathbed. But, to stitch up our trust, you may hold on to this and kindly return it to me when I pay back the loan. With interest, of course."

"Loan?"

"Not much, a trivial sum, really. With the unexpected expense of promoting the performance, and with my pension not arriving for another few weeks, I have a need for this temporary loan. Seventy-five pounds is what I was hoping to acquire."

"Trivial? Maybe to a duke, but not to a working man." Plunkett inspected the chatelaine. He held it up to the light that was pouring from the bay window, took his fingernail, scratched the surface, and chuckled. "If this be from your dear grandmum, I suggest you never part with it. To me it's worthless, especially not worth seventy-five pounds." He handed the trinket back to Montagu.

"I can probably get by with fifty pounds," Montagu said, the forsaken chatelaine lying in his palm.

Plunkett stood still. The long night had caught up with him and his patience. "You have been a loyal customer and for that I am grateful."

Montagu smiled and pushed the chatelaine back towards Plunkett.

"Here is what I can do for you," replied the chemist. "Have your broadsides sent over and I will post them in my shop's window. I'll hand out copies to my clients. So, if there is no other business? I have much to do."

Montagu stood like a rat caught stealing from the waste bin, eyes now red, not knowing how to proceed. Before he could come up with another tactic, Plunkett emerged from behind the counter and led him to the door.

"I hope your conjuror is successful and please come again." He opened the door. A cool breeze greeted him, followed by the hollow rumble of thunder echoing down Jermyn Street.

THE CLOUDS WEIGHING down on Montagu were a dismal accompaniment to the dark clouds in his mind. The weight of Sophia's chatelaine in his pocket dragged him down further. Worthless. And, of course, turning his face up to the sky, the first cold drops of a London rain found him. He pulled his tricorn down firmly on his head, hunched his shoulders against the rain, and was about to set off to the Pig's Head to think when a coach pulled up alongside, splashing his legs with cold water, and a voice called out, "My Lord!"

He squinted up through the rain and saw it was a woman, peering beneath the half-rolled blind over the window.

"Montagu!" she called, waving a gloved hand at him. Even through the rain he recognized the chestnut hair and amber eyes of the lovely Baroness Smithfield. "Where are you going? Come inside, I'll give you a ride."

The footman opened the door and Montagu wasted no time scurrying inside, settling himself on the seat opposite the baroness.

"My goodness, you are soaked through!" she said, with a laugh. "You look like a drowned man."

"It's a pleasure to see you, too, my lady," said Montagu. "Lovely as ever."

His eyes traveled over the light blue silk dress that accentuated the swell of her breasts, the lovely ringlets of hair cascading down to her shoulders, and those amber eyes so deep he felt he could fall into them. "Thank you for your assistance," he finally said.

"It is my pleasure," she said, her lips opening like a glorious rose. "Now, tell me, where can I take you?"

"I was on my way to the Pig's Head."

She frowned and wrinkled her nose. "Ugh, such a ghastly place. Why would you want to go there?"

"A bit of liquid refreshment always helps me to think better."

"And you have something to think about?"

"Indeed," he said, with a theatrical sigh, already thinking of a scheme that might get him the money he needed. He shook his head forlornly. "I have much to think about."

She leaned forward on the seat. "Would you care to share your thoughts, Monty?"

He was encouraged when she called him by his nickname. He felt like a fisherman who discerns that first faint nibble on the line. Careful, now. Careful. He waited her out and, sure enough, she was the first to break the silence.

"You seem so sad," she said. "Perhaps I can be of some help if you tell me what is on your mind. Why don't you come back to my home where we can talk?"

"Oh, Josephine," he said, deliberately using the familiar with her, "I certainly cannot impose upon your hospitality."

"It would be no imposition, I assure you. We could have some tea and you could dry out beside the hearth as you tell me what is troubling you."

"But surely, Baron Smithfield is busy with work. I would be an interruption."

Josephine smiled. "Not at all. My husband has business in Scotland that has called him away for a fortnight. I insist."

And there it was, that little fish making a sudden, unexpected move that only embedded the hook deeper. "Well," he said, "if you insist."

She tapped the roof of the coach with her parasol and called out to the driver, "Stuart, home!"

The coach lurched and started to roll down the cobblestones.

The Smithfield townhouse sat in a neighborhood in transition, although it was difficult to tell if the transition was trending upward to more affluence, or downward to the ranks of cobblers and cabinetmakers. Not unlike the Smithfield's themselves, Montagu thought, at the bottom ranks of the peerage, yet hoping for future elevation. He knew from experience that trying to keep up with the more affluent was a dangerous gamble, one that could easily reduce Baron Smithfield to repairing some other lord's boots instead of investigating new business opportunities in Scotland as he was apparently doing at that moment. Still, the coach from which they descended was the baron's property and the house was furnished comfortably enough, one might say almost fashionably.

"Here, come sit by the fire," Josephine said. "You need to get dry."

Montagu took a seat beside the hearth.

Josephine tugged on the bellpull for the maid. "Take this," the baroness said to the young maid, handing her the parasol, "and bring us some tea and scones. Now then," she said, turning to the duke and seating herself on a small couch, "what is it that has you so troubled?"

Troubled? Ah, yes, he had almost forgotten. He sighed deeply and tried on his best hang-dog expression. "There is so much trouble in this world, isn't there, Josephine? So much poverty. Why, just the other day I came across a most interesting magician performing outside the Pig's Head."

"Magician?"

"Yes, a gypsy by the looks of him. He was just a lad and the most beggarly, destitute person I have ever seen."

His speech was interrupted when the maid entered again, carrying a tray with tea bowls, a silver teapot, and a plate of scones. She set the tray down on a low table between them and as she bent over, she noticed where his eyes wandered and gave him a secret smile before standing upright and heading for the door.

"Elizabeth, please close the door behind you as you leave and see that we are not disturbed," Josephine said.

"Yes, ma'am," the girl said, shooting a last glance at Montagu before leaving the room.

Josephine poured tea into the two small bowls. She was about to rise to hand the duke a bowl, but he said, "Please, don't exert yourself," and moved to sit beside her on the couch.

It was a bold move, one that brought a blush to her cheek, but he had always believed in fortune favoring the bold. She did not shy away from his proximity and handed him a tea bowl. They sipped their tea, their eyes held on each other. He noticed the rise and fall of her bosom and realized how small was the gap between their lips. As if suddenly awakened from sleep, she set down her bowl a little too brusquely, spilling a few drops of tea on the tray.

"You were saying? About the gypsy?"

"Yes," he said, placing his bowl on the tray, "a raggedy lad and, as though the heavens had opened and the sun shone forth, I suddenly became aware of so many poor, homeless waifs wandering the streets of London. Of course, I had seen them before, many times, but it was now a revelation. I felt as though I was Paul on the road to Damascus. I tell you, Josephine, the scales fell from my eyes."

He looked down and she thought perhaps she spotted a tear in his eye. She took his hand and turned to him. "Oh, John, that must have been quite an epiphany for you."

He nodded. "Indeed." She gently squeezed his hand. He covered it with his free hand. "I asked myself how I could help these poor unfortunates."

"And?" she said, almost breathlessly, leaning closer to him.

"I decided to create a home for these cast-off boys, a place where they would be sheltered and fed, where they would be taught a trade so that they would become useful members of our great society and not be reduced to thievery and all sorts of criminal activities to survive."

"You are a saint, John!" she said, moving even closer so that now their lips were mere inches away.

He shook his head sadly. "No."

"Yes, you are!" Her eyes gleamed. "I think that's wonderful."

What he found wonderful was that when he moved in to kiss her, she did not resist, was in fact, ready for him, and what was even more wonderful was how easily her bodice opened, revealing her milky-white breasts and how her petticoats offered no resistance to his vigorous probing. And when they were finished, she lay back on the couch pillow, spent, while he refastened his breeches.

"We've spilled the tea," he said, with a smile, noticing the brown puddle spreading across the table.

She gestured languidly with her hand. "I don't care."

After a few minutes, she rearranged her disheveled attire and sat up. Montagu was retrieving his tea-spattered coat which had fallen to the floor. As he picked it up, Sophia's chatelaine fell out of his pocket.

"What's that?" Josephine said.

"This?" he said, quickly picking it up. "This?" *Think, Monty, think!* "Why, this is my sainted mother's chatelaine. I carry it with me everywhere I go."

"You do?"

"Yes. It's all I have left from her, and it reminds me of all her travails."

"Travails."

"Yes, my dear mum was born poor, not a farthing to her name. Had she not met my father who felt sorry for her, she might very well have died in the poorhouse." He looked up at her. "Perhaps that's why I feel so drawn to help those unfortunate street urchins."

She didn't know if there were tears in his eyes but there were in hers. "That's so beautiful, Monty," she whispered.

He gently held her. "But, alas, I fear my idea is doomed from the start. It would take more money than I currently have available to start my charity."

"Oh?"

"With luck, I hope to elicit donations from the gentry. Such good people are willing to share their largesse with the more unfortunate. I am hoping the Duke of Cumberland himself will be my first patron."

"The Duke of Cumberland?" she breathed.

He nodded. She suddenly pushed away from him.

"John," she said, "*I* want to be your first patron!"

"Oh, my dear, that is so thoughtful of you but, no, I couldn't ask you for that."

"Please," she said, "let me. If the Duke of Cumberland is willing to set the example, why shouldn't the rest of us nobles follow it?" She stood. "How much do you need?"

"Josephine, I'm speechless. I don't know what to say."

"How much?" she repeated, a haughty smile on her face.

"Well, if you insist, might I trouble you for twenty-five pounds? I hope that's not too much to ask?"

Her smile froze and it took her a few seconds to respond. "Too much? No, of course not. My husband can well afford it."

"He is away, is he not?" Montagu said.

"No matter. I will get you the twenty-five pounds."

Before he could say another word, the baroness left the room. He stood and slipped his coat on. This had been easier than he had expected, and it had been entertaining as well.

Josephine came back with a small leather pouch. He heard the coins clinking inside. She placed the bag in his hand and closed hers over it. "Let this be a start for your wonderful venture. You are doing a great thing, John, a truly great thing."

He kissed her hand then dropped the pouch in his pocket. From his other pocket he withdrew the chatelaine. "And I would like you to have this," he said, placing it in her hand.

"Oh, I couldn't," she said.

"Yes, please. I know my sainted mother would want you to have it."

Again, she felt tears in her eyes. She kissed him. "I will treasure it always."

When he once again stood on the front steps of the Smithfield house, the rain had stopped. Keeping one hand in the pocket containing the twenty-five pounds, he jauntily set off down the street.

Now, to find Sophia.

Chapter Twenty-Seven

JEPPSON HAD DONE his job well. The ragged street urchins he had hired for a few pence a day, some of them barefoot, had blanketed London with handbills and broadsides advertising the upcoming spectacular feat of the Bottle Conjuror. Everyone was talking about it.

A well-dressed gent sitting on a bench in Hyde Park squinted through his monocle as he read the notice in *The Penny London Post*. He could not believe what he had read~a man in a bottle? *Poppycock!*

Four powdered and bewigged men standing before Westminster Abbey were engaged in a heated and wildly gesticulated debate.

"I tell you, Cavendish, only a fool would believe such tripe! It cannot be done!"

"So, you say, but I aver there are stranger things in our cosmology. What about the Hindu fakirs who disappear in thin air by climbing up a rope?"

The other man, a fat squire by the name of Simpson, ripped the broadside with its picture of a harlequin disappearing into a wine bottle off the wall and tore it to shreds, scattering the pieces to the winds. "If you're so all-fired sure, then let's lay a bet on it. Ten pounds says it can't be done."

"I'll take that bet," Cavendish said.

Six ladies, fashionably corseted and with finger-curl coiffures, sipped from China tea bowls at Mrs. Worthington's social. They could speak of nothing other than the unbelievable, but somehow titillating notion of a man squeezing himself into a wine bottle.

"Would that not be extremely . . . painful?" one asked.

"Mercies!" said Mrs. Worthington, waving a fan furiously before her face. "The mister himself has said I shall not be suffered to see such a thing. But, of course, he will attend."

And at St. George's Church in Hanover Square, that very minister held up a broadside from the pulpit and admonished his congregation to avoid the event, as seductive as it may sound, by saying, "Remember, my children, believe only in the Lord, not magic. As the good book says, *suffer not a sorcerer to live.*"

Had the Duke of Montagu heard those words uttered by the minister he might have entertained doubts about whether his enterprise was worth risking eternal perdition, but Montagu was not often troubled by doubt, nor did he lose sleep over worrying about his soul if, indeed, he had one. He stood a few doors down from the theatre, watching as one of Jeppson's hirelings, a tall gangly boy of thirteen or thereabouts, finished pasting up yet another broadside on a lamp post. The duke stood back to admire the picture of the disappearing harlequin.

"Good work, my lad," he said to the boy.

"It's a funny picture, sir," the boy said, scratching his mop of hair, "a bloke in a bottle. Can't say I've ever seen the likes of it afore."

"Nor I, lad," he said, more to himself than the boy, who was now walking off, the glue pot in one hand, a stack of broadsides tucked under his arm.

The duke heard the galloping horses in just enough time to scurry out of the way of the speeding coach. He turned and was about to hurl some choice words at the driver, words that would make a sailor blush, when he stopped short, recognizing the royal crest emblazoned on the coach.

Cumberland.

The coach came to a stop and the Duke of Cumberland poked his head out through the window. "Well, well, my old friend, you are certainly making quite a fuss around town."

Montagu drew near to the coach. "I hope you can attend, Your Grace. Trust me, your eyes will be amazed."

Cumberland laughed. "Trust you? Never have, never will." The coachman clinging to the rear of the coach snickered. "But I'm growing weary of all this trumpeting of your gypsy conjuror," Cumberland continued, "so I'm prepared right now to bet you fifty pounds sterling that it can't be done. The so-called conjuror will fail miserably."

"That's a hefty wager, Your Grace, but I will accept it, with one proviso and that is, that you will agree to settle the bet immediately after the performance."

"Of course. As, will you?"

"Done!" Montagu said thrusting his hand through the window to seal the deal with Cumberland.

Montagu smiled as the coach pulled away. *Fifty pounds sterling! Indeed!*

Chapter Twenty-Eight

MELCHIOR TRUDGED UP from the docks along the Thames where he had labored all that hot day unloading boats of their cargoes. Hard work, indeed, even for someone as tall and strong as he was and he felt that labor in every bone in his body, smelled the stink of his sweat upon him. He needed a bit of respite--food and drink--before finding his bed. He thought of the Pig's Head tavern as he bulled his way through the crowded streets rising from the waterfront. People scurried out of his way, at least partly cowed by the eye-patch over his left eye and his mahogany-colored complexion. Coming at them, his body looming as a dark shadow against the sun setting at his back, they must have thought of him as the Devil incarnate. He smiled at the thought. It's almost as if they knew the name of his clan, the Shaitaan, meant "demon" in Hindi.

As he passed a tavern frequented by Royal Marines, a drunken boot-neck backed out the door and staggered into him. The man turned angrily, fist raised, but when he saw Melchior's face, he thought better of it and decided, even through his gin-fueled haze, perhaps that day was not a good one to pick a fight. He stumbled away, mumbling curses.

Melchior watched him go. He had no desire to fight either. All he wanted was food and drink. He knew Henry, the jackass proprietor of the Pig's Head hated gypsies, gypsy men, anyway and banned them from his tavern. But Henry wasn't quite sure where to place Melchior in his pantheon of xenophobia, so he tolerated the big man's visits. And Melchior always paid his debts.

He arrived at the Pig's Head, pushed open the door and entered, causing an immediate cessation of the usual hubbub, not so much from the regulars who had grown accustomed to seeing the strange man there, as from the newcomers who were now reconsidering their decision to drink at the Pig's Head. But once he took a seat in the corner, quietly minding his own business, the chatter resumed. All were safe.

A barmaid placed a tankard of ale before him, giving him a smile and a polite, "Good evening, sir."

His face softened, the closest he could come to a smile at that time. She was pretty and had waited on him several times in the past. Her name, *Mercy*? He wasn't sure about that, but he was sure he could probably have her if he wanted her. Even though a Shaitaan Hunter pledged not to marry, or even have a meaningful relationship with a woman, there was no prohibition against taking one up against the wall. He was mulling the possibilities of such an event when a raggedy youth carrying a sheaf of papers warily approached his table.

"Go away, lad. Don't bother me," Melchior said, and that was enough for the boy to boldly slap a handbill face down on the table and then run off.

He took a swallow of ale and idly turned the paper over. The tankard froze in his hand then slowly found its way to the table as he stared at the paper. *Is it true? How can this be?*

The handbill advertised an upcoming performance by a magician, no, a *conjuror*, at the Haymarket Theatre. The performance would be the Bottle Conjuration, an ancient feat that some had attempted but none succeeded, a feat that Melchior knew required the black arts. As part of his training as a Hunter, the Shaitaan elders had schooled him well on clues that could lead him to *The Book of Shadows*. Anyone who could perform the Bottle Conjuration must surely know of the book. Could this conjuror be the one Jonah and Abel had recently seen performing in the street? Where had he come from, but more importantly, did he have the book?

He tucked the handbill into his shirt, quickly downed the last of the ale and hurried out of the tavern, thoughts humming in his head like a million hornets. He needed to get home. To think. His belly objected, reminding him of his hunger, and he stopped just long enough to buy a minced meat pie from a street vendor.

He turned down a narrow, twisting alley to the two-story decrepit building in which he rented one little room on the second floor. A single window looked out over an old cemetery, the tombstones leaning in the sod like rotten teeth.

He locked the door, set the pie on the table, and lit a candle. The room was stifling, and he stripped off his sweat-soaked shirt, tossing it on the straw mattress. He pulled a chair up to the table and tucked into his dinner, the candlelight making the snake tattoo on his chest appear to writhe around the book held in its coils. As he plowed his way through the pie, he studied the handbill once more as if the letters could speak to him and answer all his questions: *Who was this conjuror? Did he possess The*

Book of Shadows?

It had been several years~the last time, in Normandy~since he, or any other Hunter, had uncovered even a single clue about the book's whereabouts. Melchior believed they were close to finding it, but before they could take another step, the French Catholic clergy expelled the Shaitaan out of the country. He knew the Romani had already been roaming Great Britain for several years before his own people were exiled. The Shaitaan crossed the channel to Britain, with most of them settling in Wales, with a handful of Hunters moving east and finding shelter in the teeming city of London. Of course, he knew about the Romani encampment outside the city. As a Hunter, it was his business to know about them. They were Padura, a Romani clan, and had been there for several months, but his investigation had not discovered any link between them and the book. At least, not so far. But this conjuror—*who was he?* Romani or not, if he could perform the Bottle Conjuration, then he must have possession of the Bloodstone, and if he had the stone, he must also have the *The Book of Shadows*. No one would be foolhardy enough to perform the conjuration without it.

His meal finished, Melchior sat back in the chair, the evening shadows falling around him. Perhaps it was luck, perhaps it was Fate, he didn't know. What he *did* know was all that he had been trained for since he was a youth was again being called into play. After centuries, maybe this time the Shaitaan would be successful.

Time to notify the others.

Chapter Twenty-Nine

· ·

IT WAS ALREADY late morning by the time Lucinda eventually wandered back to the Haymarket Theatre. The spirits that had danced so gaily in her head last night had vanished, murdered by gigantic gin-soaked ogres hammering inside her skull. The rear door to the theatre creaked as she opened it, the sound like a knife-blade cutting into her head.

She heard someone onstage and, fumbling her way through the curtains, saw Stefan practicing, juggling apples. *Had he been there all night?* The fog in her brain cleared long enough to allow her to feel embarrassment, although she wasn't quite lucid enough to understand what it was that embarrassed her.

He saw her and the spinning apples fell to the floor. His expression was stoic as he picked up the apples, ignoring her.

She took a step closer. "I'm not sure what to say, Stefan, but I'm sorry about last night. The time got away from me and . . ."

"Forget it," he said, without looking at her. "Doesn't matter."

She could see he was hurt. Angry. *It did matter, he was her friend.* "Stefan, please understand," she said. "I had every intention of returning after dinner, but . . ."

"But?"

"I had a bit too much wine . . . gin, come to think of it."

He waved her away, turning his back to her, pretending to be busy with the props on the table.

"You're very important to me," she continued, drawing near. "You're the only person who I feel understands me."

He sighed. "What I understand is you promised you would return."

"I know, and I did not mean to break my promise, but the duke . . ."

"Montagu?" he said, turning to face her. She did not know what to say, even though she knew he was expecting some reply, some explanation. He waited until he could wait no longer, then turned away from her once more. "I need to practice."

At that moment, the Swami walked in. One look at the stony expressions on the faces of his two assistants told him something was amiss, but he wasn't one to pry and possibly get himself embroiled in personal situations that would be of no benefit to him. "Lad," the Swami said, "I could use your help in preparing the silk handkerchief trick."

"That's an easy one. Could we do that later?"

"Why? Do you have something more important to do? Cognac with the king, perhaps?"

Stefan shook his head. "No, of course not," he mumbled, "but with my performance coming up shortly, there are some items I need to retrieve from my camp. Especially for the Bottle Conjuration."

Hands on his hips, the Swami said, "You're testing my patience, Stefan, but if you need your props, you need your props."

"Thank you. Do you have a horse and cart I could borrow?"

"And perhaps you'd like me to drive you as well? I don't bloody well have a bloody horse or cart!"

"William does," Lucinda said. Her reply was so soft the men almost didn't hear her. "He owes me a favor," she continued, drawing closer to them. "I can ask him."

"You would do that?" said Stefan.

"On one condition," she replied.

"And what would that be?"

"That I go with you to the camp."

"That's not a good idea," he said, "I'm not sure . . ."

"I won't take no for an answer," she said. "And besides, you can introduce me to the woman you always talk about. Cassandra."

"Well . . ."

"And it will give us time to talk," she said.

Something in her voice, a gentleness he had not heard before, persuaded him to give her a chance. "Alright," he said, "ask William."

Chapter Thirty

HE WAS NO longer a child, of course she knew that, but it was still difficult to let him go, to watch him stumble though life, although Cassandra realized that was the way it was meant to be. The Fates had already decided that when Anna died giving birth to him and his father, Belasco, ran off, abandoning him. Cassandra was to be the mother Stefan never knew. She accepted that role lovingly and patiently and raised him as if she were his mother instead of his aunt.

It had not been easy, as the Romani way of life was never easy. Everywhere her people went they confronted fear, prejudice. Hatred. Often, those feelings boiled over into violence against them. She remembered a memory from childhood; weeping Romani women dressed in black, huddled together, mourning the murder of two young men~she still remembered their names, Valerian and Matthias~hanged by a mob for stealing a horse. The Romani fled the area that night, fearful of more savage reprisals, and were too far away to hear the news of the real horse thieves caught in the act a few weeks after the lynching. No matter, it wouldn't have brought those two innocent boys back. Nor would it have brought justice to the murderers who, after all, had simply killed two gypsies.

A lifetime of such memories caused her to safeguard Stefan from danger. A naive and maimed~some people said with the Devil's mark~young man, Cassandra worried that the cruel world could easily open beneath his feet and swallow him whole.

She watched worriedly as Stefan's magical skills developed and he became bolder. She feared he would attempt the Bottle Conjuration; she made the sign of the cross even as she thought about it. There was so much he did not know about the conjuration. Even though she did not know all its mysteries, she knew enough to understand that malevolent unnatural forces clung to it like a spider's web. Once someone attempted to master the conjuration, he could become forever enmeshed in its evil. Lost. Only a wise and powerful conjuror could successfully conquer its dark forces.

All these thoughts passed through her head as she sat in her vardo, a candle shedding its weak light on the tarot cards laid out before her. She had cast the cards a few times for Stefan over the last few weeks while he was away in London. She had seen nothing in them to alert her fears. Also, she had heard from other Romani going to and from the city that he was safe and working magic at a theatre, which relieved her anxiety.

She smiled when she turned over the next card and set it down. The Magician. *Of course.* The card following that was The Lovers, usually a positive card, but it was reversed upside-down when she drew it, indicating ambivalence. She placed it beside The Magician and picked out the last card from the deck. She held the card in her hand for a few moments, staring at the goat-headed creature on it. Baphomet. Below his imposing horned figure stood a naked man and woman, chains around their necks. Her hand trembling, Cassandra placed the card in the last remaining position of her layout. Even before she had set the card down, she could divine the message the cards were sending. *No! This can't be!*

The night wind picked up, swirling around the vardo, carrying with it the rumble of thunder and the scent of wet earth. The candle guttered in the breeze from the open window, casting weird, flickering shadows across the walls. She drew her shawl closer around her and pulled the shutter closed. The cards were barely visible in the candle's penumbra, but she didn't need to see them. Only once before had she seen cards laid out like that. They were not good then and Cassandra feared they did not bode well now.

Chapter Thirty-One

THE MORNING WAS damp, as a storm had passed through before sunrise. Stefan held the reins to the cart Lucinda had obtained from William. The cart was old but sturdy, like the mule that pulled it. Lucinda sat next to him, neither of them speaking as the mule clopped through the streets of London taking them into the countryside to the Romani camp.

"I think I like London best in the morning," she said, trying to break the tense silence that covered them like a shroud. No reply. "The air smells sweet. The streets are quiet. Even the pigeons seem happy and free."

He pulled on the reins and without looking at her said, "*Cushats* are nothing but rats with wings."

"Cushats?"

"Pigeons," he said.

Sensing that maybe the ice encasing him was about to crack, she warmly replied, "That's probably true." She decided to change the subject. "Where do you stay at night while you are rehearsing?"

He really didn't want to talk, but knowing they had a bit of a journey ahead, he reluctantly kept the conversation going. "Down by Bonhill Street there is an abandoned foundry where they once made cannons. Vicar Wesley is using the space as a church. He allows Romanies to stay overnight. But you have to listen to a sermon or two in return for your lodging."

"Church?" She looked upward as if angels were listening. "I've gone into Saint James a few times to look at the beautiful windows. I also like the quietness when the church is empty. I've never been much of a churchgoer, though being raised by my tosser father. Only time he'd been to a church was for a funeral or two. And one of them was his own." She looked over at him. "Are you a church person?"

He snorted. "Most churches don't allow us in. Cassandra often said to me that we are like millions of stars scattered in the sight of God."

"I don't really know much about your people. What is it like being a gypsy?"

Rough stone and dirt now replaced cobblestone pavement, making the cart bounce.

"*Your people?*" he snapped back. "What is *that* supposed to mean? I thought, maybe you were different from the other *gadjos*. I suppose you think we are all dirty scavengers. Tramps and thieves."

She realized she had upset him. "No, Stefan, I don't think of you that way! Or your gypsies."

He turned to look at her. "Romani."

"What?"

"We are *Romani*. Proud people. Not gypsies. We live by the rules of Romano law, *Zakano*. We believe in *baxt* . . . "He saw confusion on her face. "It means clean. We also believe in *ladz*, or unclean, full of shame. Being *baxt* is how you live your life. Honorably, taking care of your family and your tribe. Our blood is strong."

She did not know how to respond, did not want to upset him any further, as she sat quietly next to him on the wagon.

"Let me tell you a story, Lucinda. There once was a Persian king named Bahram, who loved music more than anything. Because he was rich, he hired the finest musicians to entertain him. One day, he came to learn that the poor in his kingdom could not afford to enjoy music. This saddened the king. He asked the King of India to send him ten thousand lute players. When the *luris* arrived, Bahram provided each player with one ox, one donkey, and a load of wheat. The *luris* could now live off the land and play music to the poor and the music would be free."

He looked back at her and saw she was intently listening. "But it came to pass that the *luris* ate the oxen, and the wheat. A year had gone by and with their cheeks hollow with hunger, they approached the king for help. Angered with the *luris* for wasting what he had given them instead of settling down, he ordered them to pack up their belongings and exiled them to forever wander the world on their donkeys. That was the beginning of my people. Wandering is our fate. We have no country of our own and we don't need to own land. Our territory lies across the souls of men."

"Stefan, that is truly a sad story. I never thought of you, or your heritage, as evil. I don't think of you as dirty or a thief. Look at me, at what I have had to do to survive! You are proud and your conjuring should also make you proud."

The wagon entered the peaceful countryside leaving the streets of London behind. The dirt road took them past orchards, fields, and an estate with a tranquil brook. Planted in the fork in the road was a sign with the emblem of a wheel painted on it.

"What's that sign?" she asked.

"A *patrin*. We place these to lead fellow Romanies to a camp."

The road passed through a field of purple lavender flowers. It stretched as far as the eye could see.

"I've never seen anything so beautiful," she said.

He slowed the grey mule's pace so they could breathe in the scent of the flowers.

"Stefan, I didn't mean to hurt you," she said, softly. He stopped the wagon. "You're a sweet man and I've grown fond of you. I care about you."

"What about the duke?"

She grew tense. "What about him?" She looked across the field of flowers. A breeze crept up and set the flowers swaying. "Maybe, he's a means to an end, I don't know. Aren't riches more important than childhood dreams? Maybe I'm destined to be without love. But think of the life of ease I could have with a duke! Oh, I'm so confused!"

Stefan snapped the reins. The mule took one slow step after another, pulling the wagon forward. He glanced at her and saw a tear about to fall from her eye, and a feeling of compassion overcame him. "Alright. Perhaps there is some way we can clear up your confusion."

"You can do that?"

He laughed. "Me? What do you think I am, some kind of fortune teller? No, I had Cassandra in mind."

They drove around a bend. The lavender fields receded from view.

Chapter Thirty-Two

THE DIRT R⊕AD became more trail than road. The hills and meadows gradually disappeared and were replaced by brush, then pine, oak, and walnut trees. On the left side of the trail, a collection of branches was placed in a large pile about fifteen hands high. Stefan slowed the mule and guided him toward a path next to the pile of branches.

"Another Romani sign?" asked Lucinda.

He smiled and nodded. It pleased him that she was observant and without any mention by him, saw the pile of branches as a marker to lead them to the camp. He was also pleased that she used the word *Romani*. The trees became taller and began to engulf them the farther they drove down the path. Rays of sunlight had to fight their way through the forest canopy. Although it was not yet midday, it felt like twilight.

"Woods have always frightened me," she said. "I'm afraid of getting lost, and of things that may lurk in the shadows."

"Don't be frightened. With me you will not be lost. And the camp is only a few minutes from here. What do you think lurks in the shadows?"

"Well, wild beasts for one, and I've heard stories about hunters entering forests and never returning."

"Wait!" Stefan pulled hard on the reins, forcing the mule to stop in its tracks.

The wagon lurched. Frightened, Lucinda clung to him. He looked down where a large snake with yellow eyes slithered across their path. The mule kicked its front legs into the air, planted them back on the ground and stood at the ready. The snake hissed, then crept past them into the bushes.

When Stefan was sure the serpent was gone, he flicked the reins, and the mule began moving forward. "Sorry about that," he said, glancing at her. "Yes, there are beasts in the forest, but they have a right to live as well. We Romanies have learned to share our home with all creatures." She was still clinging to him, which pleased him. "I want to teach you a

Romani phrase to say when you first meet Cassandra." He looked at her and slowly said, "*Devlesa araklam tume*. Try it."

She cleared her throat. "Day-lisa araklam tomb."

He smiled. "Close. Please, try again, *Devlesa araklam tume*."

"*Devlesa. . . araklam. . . tume*."

"Perfect," he replied.

"What does it mean?"

"*It is with God, that we found you*."

He snapped the reins to hurry the mule. The outline of the camp became visible. He guided the cart to a clearing just outside the circle of wagons. He reached into the cart and pulled out a canvas feed bag and draped it over the neck of the mule. He stood by the wagon and held out his hand for Lucinda to descend. His other hand gripped the walking stick. She felt as light as a sparrow as he guided her down.

"Why thank you, my lord," she said, as her feet touched the ground.

The many wagons encircling the camp amazed her. She also noticed several dwellings made of thatch, branches and canvas scattered about the camp. A large fire was crackling in the middle of the encampment. She saw people wandering about, a few children chasing a cat.

"This looks wonderful," she said.

"Cassandra's *vardo* is over there." He pointed across the circle to a large wagon painted with an unusual design.

Lucinda had seen the symbol before. She knew it as a shield knot, a looped square, that had no beginning or end, formed with a single thread weaving and intertwined upon itself. The outer loop was painted green, the inner loop was yellow. The four loops stood at the corners of a single square. She understood the symbol was for protection against evil spirits.

As they walked toward his aunt's vardo, Stefan spotted her sitting by a small campfire with her back toward the wagon. He took Lucinda's arm and led her to his aunt.

"Cassandra, this is Lucinda, the woman I've told you about."

"Ah, yes, the magician's assistant." She sat in her chair and let out a puff of smoke from her whalebone pipe, apparently unsurprised to see them in camp.

Lucinda curtseyed and said, "*Devlesa araklam tume*."

Cassandra held her thought for a second, smiled and replied, "*Devlesa avilan*."

Stefan whispered in her ear. "It means. *It is God who brought you*."

Cassandra spoke again in Romani, "*Vacare romane?*" She noticed the blank expression on Lucinda's face.

"She's only learned one phrase so far, Cassandra," Stefan said.

Cassandra nodded. "Please, sit with me. I find the fire warms my old bones." She gestured for Lucinda to sit in the empty wicker chair next to her. Stefan sat on a large log beside her.

"You have a warm smile. I see honesty in your heart," Cassandra said. She turned to Stefan. "I thought you would be busy rehearsing with the *gorgers*, or have you given up on your chimera?"

"Yes, I mean, no. I was."

Lucinda stifled a laugh at his clumsy answer while Cassandra quietly sat with her pipe.

"So, which is it? Are you still planning on doing your conjuration?" asked Cassandra.

"Yes, but I needed to retrieve some clothes and a few props for my tricks."

She removed her pipe, turned to the fire, and spat into it, causing the flames to dance and flicker brighter.

When the flames died down, Lucinda noticed a woman walking by. "That woman. I think I know her."

Stefan looked around. "Which woman?"

She pointed to a tall woman with raven hair. "Over there, with the hoop earring. I feel I have seen her before."

Cassandra looked across the circle and recognized the woman. "That would be Sophia. You may very well have seen her before as she takes many trips to London. She is very, shall I say, 'sociable'?"

Stefan smirked. "That's *one* way of putting it."

Cassandra cackled and shook her head. "She's always getting into mischief, that one. Now, I hear she's got her claws in an . . . earl.

Stefan interjected, "Some duke. Not an earl."

"What?" asked Lucinda.

Cassandra took her pipe and banged it against her chair, making a sound like a woodpecker at work. "Never mind, I shouldn't gossip, but I pity the duke, whoever he is." She stood up and inspected the campfire. "Stefan, the fire is starting to die. Would you mind getting us some more firewood?"

He quickly stood. "Yes, of course."

He nodded to Lucinda and headed toward the woods beyond Cassandra's *vardo*. As he neared her wagon, he looked back to see if she was watching him.

Silence crept in and made itself at home. Cassandra stared into the flames, then whisked the intrusive silence away saying, "Have you noticed the flames as they flicker, from a single flame becoming twin flames?"

Lucinda looked into the fire and was surprised at what Cassandra had observed. "Oh, now I see it. I hadn't noticed that before."

"We have a word for twin flames, *pereches*. It means soulmates."

Lucinda looked away to see if Stefan was coming back and turned back to the fire, deep in her own thoughts.

"Are you not feeling well, dear?" asked Cassandra.

"Oh . . . no, I'm fine. Just . . . thinking."

Cassandra looked at her shrewdly. "Give me your hand, girl." She took Lucinda's hand, turned it up, and carefully studied the lines crossing her palm. "I see. Yes, a bright, happy future for you, but. . . "

"But?"

"I also see an obstacle in your path right now. You are in love?"

Lucinda stared at the lines of her palm. "In love? I don't know. Yes, maybe."

"As I thought, you are confused. Sometimes, Lucinda, what seems like love may be as false as the flowers pulled from the magician's sleeve. Don't let your eyes be fooled by outward appearances." Her aged finger traced a small line that went from Lucinda's index finger to the middle of her palm. "I sense you have not yet found your true love."

"How will I know when I do?"

Cassandra closed Lucinda's hand and gave it a warm pat. "You will know it when your heart feels like it is soaring on angels' wings."

Chapter Thirty-Three

A PART OF him said that he really shouldn't do it, that it was a betrayal of Cassandra's trust, but when Stefan passed behind her vardo and saw the door partly ajar, he convinced himself that it was an omen, an invitation from unseen forces.

He looked around. No one was in sight. Quickly, he mounted the steps and ducked inside the wagon, pulling the door closed behind him. With the window shut, there was only dim light inside but enough for him to catch sight of a small, leather-bound book tucked behind a pillow.

So, that's where she had been hiding it!

When he opened the book to the parchment pages, yellowed with age, he read *Librum Umbrarum* in spidery script on the title page. He tucked the book inside his coat pocket. Just as he was about to slip out of the vardo he noticed the distinctive shape of a large wine bottle tucked in a corner beneath an old blanket. He whisked off the blanket and there it was~a magnum wine bottle with an odd label depicting a harlequin disappearing into a funnel inserted into the neck of a wine bottle. The conjuration bottle!

Stefan reached for the bottle, hesitating only for a moment as his dream of fame and glory bludgeoned his integrity. He was aware of the magical power of the bottle, which he had learned about from studying the black arts~a practice Cassandra would have abhorred if she had known about it. He grabbed the bottle, wrapping it in the blanket. He concealed it as best he could beneath his coat.

The cart was not far off, the mule casually munching from its feedbag. Stefan made a beeline for it. As he neared the cart, the mule suddenly reared up, wildly kicking, which caused him to drop the bottle. Before he could retrieve it, the bottle slammed against a rock. Horrified, he scrambled after it. The bottle rolled a few feet away but somehow ended upright. Stefan picked it up and was amazed to find it intact. Not even a crack. He carefully wrapped the blanket around it again and hid it beneath the seat.

Remembering he was supposed to be gathering firewood, he quick-hobbled into the woods and scoured it for firewood, gathering up an armful. He hastened from the woods but slowed to a casual walk, leaning more heavily on his walking stick, as he neared the camp to where Cassandra and Lucinda sat by the fire.

Cassandra looked up. "There you are!" she said. "I thought maybe the devil had gotten hold of you."

No. Not yet anyway. He smiled weakly and set down the load of firewood.

The thought of the bottle in the cart nagged at him. He was impatient to head back to the city. The longer he stayed in camp, the greater the chances of his theft being discovered.

"Lucinda, we should be getting back," he said.

"So soon?" Cassandra said. "We were just getting acquainted."

"Yes, now! I mean . . . we really should be on our way. It's getting late."

"Alright," said Lucinda as she stood, "if you say so."

Cassandra embraced him as they started to leave. She held him tightly, as if trying to hold him there. After a few moments she released him, but not before whispering, "Good luck to you, Stefan. May Fortune smile upon you."

He studied the face he had known and loved for so long. Was it sorrow he saw written there? Or something else? Whatever it was unnerved him. He slowly backed away. "Come, Lucinda," he said, "we're leaving."

He walked to the cart without looking back. Lucinda trailed behind him. She glanced back to see Cassandra standing still as stone watching them go.

Cassandra waited until the cart disappeared out of sight. She felt a heaviness in her heart that seemed a harbinger of something dreadful, although she could not name her fear. With a sigh, she retired to her vardo. She stopped when she noticed the door was open. *Had she left it like that?* She was usually more careful, but perhaps she had, or maybe a sudden breeze had caught the door and pried it open.

But no, that wasn't what had happened.

She saw that the conjuration bottle was gone. Worse, the conjuring book, her personal grimoire was also gone. Her hand flew to her heart, her knees suddenly went weak. She staggered, grabbing at the wagon for support. She looked into the distance, searching for the cart but it was gone, replaced now by a slowly sinking sun painting the landscape crimson.

Oh, Stefan! What have you done?

Chapter Thirty-Four

THE RIDE BACK from the Romani camp was tense but Lucinda could not understand why. They did not stop to enjoy the countryside, winding brooks, or the lavender fields. Stefan kept pushing the mule forward, determined to get back to London before dark, almost as if he were afraid of beasts that might be lurking in the shadows. As if something terrible pursued them.

She tried not to think about that. "I can see why you honor your auntie as you do," she said. "I was nervous when you first introduced me to her, not sure if I pronounced my greeting correctly . . ."

"You said it perfectly. Like a life-long Romani."

"While you were gathering wood, we had a wonderful talk. She even told me my fortune, as it were. I can tell that she loves you with all her heart."

He was distracted and did not bother to ask about her fortune. They had now entered London. "You live on Spring Garden Street?"

She was surprised that he knew. "I do. How did you know?"

He smiled. "Maybe Cassandra told me from her crystal ball, or I heard you talking about it one night at the theatre. If you like, I can take you home. Then I will drop off the props and return the cart."

"I was planning on meeting my friend, Molly, on Market Lane for some fish'n chips about this time. Why don't you join us?"

"No, I'd rather get the props properly stowed before the Swami gets in, so I'll drop you off to meet your friend."

Market Lane ran parallel to Haymarket Street, so it would be a quick journey from there to the theater's loading dock on Unicorn Court. He dropped her off by a tavern, waved goodbye and headed to the theatre. He had to bang on the service door several times before a workman answered.

Once inside, he made sure the prop room was open. It took him only two trips, but he was able to bring the items from the cart into the room.

He carefully set the wine bottle on a lower shelf and to conceal it, draped a blanket over it. The prop room was always a mess; the bottle would not be noticed and would be secure. As he walked toward the door, he thought he saw the bottle move. He stood looking at it for a moment. It remained still.

He grabbed the duffle bag containing his clothes. He reached into his coat pocket and pulled out the stolen grimoire. He felt guilty as he held the book in his hands, riffling through the ancient pages, but not guilty enough to want to return it. Even such a cursory look told him the book held instructions on conjuring tricks and secret verses of dark magic. Cassandra would be furious if she knew he had it. He carefully placed the book in his bag, locking the prop room behind him.

⊕N MARKET LANE, Lucinda viewed the various street peddlers, shoppers, and outdoor cafes, alive with patrons. The lamplighters were putting torches to the streetlamps. They carried small ladders strapped to their backs and kept an eye out for any potential riffraff who could disrupt the streets they served. The local merchants paid them well for this additional protection.

Lucinda saw Molly and waved to her from across the street. Molly's free hand hooked the arm of a bloody-back in full dress uniform. From a distance, Lucinda thought he might be an officer. The way Molly smiled Lucinda knew her friend would not be dining with her after all. She crossed the street. The soldier politely bowed to her as she approached them.

Molly said, "Lucinda, this is Warrant Officer Michael O'Malley."

Lucinda held out her hand.

"Please, just call me Mike," he said, as he kissed her hand.

Molly pulled him closer. "I know we had plans, but Officer Michael is only in London for a few days, so if you don't mind . . ."

"Not at all. I was looking for you to tell you that I had spent the day at the Romani camp and was hoping to make it a short night anyway."

"Romani camp? What's that?" asked Molly.

The warrant officer replied, "It's a gypsy camp. Not to be rude, but it would be a better world if we could remove such vermin. No offense, ma'am."

Before Lucinda could reply, Molly grabbed the officer's arm. "Let's not have such talk. Time is precious. Shall we go? And don't wait up for me, Lucinda." Her smile grew bright as she turned her gentleman around and walked down the street.

Lucinda thought that since the Haymarket was only a short stroll away, she might be able to catch Stefan still at the theatre. She walked down Norris Street and made a right on Haymarket to the theater. She knew the front entrance would be locked, so she went down the alley into Unicorn Court to the stage door entrance. To her surprise the door was open. She noticed that the cart she and Stefan had borrowed was gone.

As she walked up the steps, a workman appeared carrying out trash. "Good evening, my lady. Thought you were not here today."

"I was out, helping Stefan gather his supplies."

"You just missed the lad. He took the wagon back to the stables for me."

She sighed and peered into the theater. "Thank you," she said, disappointed.

"If yer looking for Master William, I think he be in his office. Got some duke with him, he does."

"Yes, I would like to thank him for lending us the mule and cart."

He returned her smile and carried the trash out to the skip bin.

Lucinda entered the back of the theatre. All seemed quiet. Suddenly, a loud angry voice bellowed down the hallway. She quickly walked to William's office. The door was closed. She placed her ear to the door and heard Montagu's muffled voice. *What was he doing there?*

"Are you serious, William?" Montagu said. "How can you be having second thoughts now? The show is Monday night!"

"This could ruin me," said William.

"Ruin you? It can make you a rich man!"

"If that bloody gypsy can't perform that damn bottle trick of his, and I am beginning to doubt more than ever that he can, I will be the laughingstock of all London."

"Nonsense!"

"I'll be out of business, I tell you!"

"No, you won't, William. Listen to me. If things go awry with Stefan . . ."

"What if he doesn't show up?"

"So much the better. If *anything* goes wrong, we put all the blame on that unlicked cub. We claim he was a fraud. He deceived you. No one will blame you. You will say you had no idea he was a charlatan. Stefan will . . ."

Lucinda had heard enough. She turned the knob and stormed into the office. "Stefan will what?" she demanded. The men were taken by surprise and simply stared at her. "I heard your conversation. You can't do that to him!

Montagu took a step toward her and said, "This is none of your concern, Lucinda."

"It is! I'm his friend." Her face red with anger, she turned to go back out the door. "I'm going to tell him!"

The duke grabbed her by the arm. "I think not." He roughly pushed her to a chair next to a small wooden table. "Sit down!"

She fell into the chair, shaking with anger. Montagu turned to William. "I brought a small wooden box in here earlier. It's there, on that shelf. Would you fetch it, please?"

Puzzled, William took the box from the shelf. It had a brass hasp and lock. He handed it to Montagu. The duke placed the box on the table next to Lucinda. He reached into his vest pocket and fished out a black key, handing it to her.

"Open the box." Her hand shook as she tried to unlock the box. She looked up at him. "Open it!"

The brass hinges creaked when she lifted the lid. Inside were broaches, a ruby pinky ring, and various other pieces of jewelry. She sat back in the chair dumbfounded. "Where did you get these?"

Montagu sneered. "Isn't that a question I should be asking you? Or perhaps that's a question the King's constable should be asking you."

William approached the table and gazed into the box. "What is this, Montagu?"

"Your insurance policy, William."

"I don't understand." William plucked out the pinky ring and inspected it. "Lucy, you broke your promise! Our agreement was that *all* items are to be turned in each night. After I pawn them, we divide the spoils. Why you're nothing but a common cheat to boot!"

Montagu clamped his hand on her shoulder. "Lucy, if the Bow Street Runners knew about your ill-gotten goods, you'd find yourself sweeping out the cells in Newgate."

She pushed his arm from her shoulder. "How did you find them?"

"I have ways. I would be only too happy to conceal your thievery in return for your silence. Keep your lips sealed. Remember our discussion the other morning?"

Her mind was racing and could not focus on any one thought. She sat silent and confused. The fear of Newgate grew on her face.

"You haven't forgotten our time together have you, Lucy?" asked Montagu.

"I regret that I can't forget that night and the feelings I thought you had for me."

"In any case, I need you to steal Lord Cumberland's dagger, but tell

Stefan and . . . "

Furious, she looked into his eyes, which she noticed had turned from grey to black. In defeat, she lowered her head. "I understand."

"Do you?"

She nodded. "Yes, you're a monster."

His eyes blazed. He politely replied, "No, not a monster, a Montagu."

Chapter Thirty-Five

· ·

THE DOOR BANGED shut behind her. Lucinda leaned against it, trembling with anger. She gulped the evening air as if she were drowning. *How dare he blackmail her! And how could they do that to Stefan?* Gradually, she calmed herself and tried to clear her mind. She needed to think. There had to be a way out of her dilemma . . . and Stefan's. She closed her eyes. *Think!*

A shuffling sound in the deserted alley roused her. Except for a few patches where moonlight pierced the gaps between the surrounding buildings and weakly pooled along the cobblestones, the alley lay shrouded in deep shadow. She took a cautious step forward and peered into the darkness. Something or someone appeared to be moving there. At first, she could not distinguish a human form but as it grew closer, footsteps echoing on the cobblestones, the figure of a woman gradually revealed itself, only to be swallowed up again as it passed from moonlight to shadow. Emerging once more in a moonbeam, Lucinda recognized the figure.

"Cassandra, is that you?" The woman did not respond but continued to walk slowly and determinedly toward her. "Why are you here?"

Cassandra stood silently before her, the moonlight revealing lines of sadness and worry upon her face. Her eyes held Lucinda's and seemed to bore into her mind. Lucinda shifted uneasily, but finally found her voice. "Why . . .?"

"I've come to put a curse on you, girl," Cassandra said. She spoke the words softly and, rather than anger, Lucinda heard disappointment and regret in her voice.

Lucinda took a step back. "I don't understand."

"You stole the conjuror bottle from my vardo is what I understand. You and Stefan!"

Lucinda was puzzled. "Cassandra, I've never been in your wagon! But . . ."

"Yes?"

"I did see a large bottle that Stefan had in the cart. I thought it was one of his props."

Cassandra sighed. A skilled reader of people's emotions, she could see the girl was speaking the truth. "My dear, you do not know anything."

Lucinda said, "I'm beginning to understand there are people who would like to make a fool of Stefan. They would try to ruin his performance if they could. That may be easy since, no doubt, it's all a clever use of mirrors or perhaps Stefan casting his voice as if he were inside the bottle. It's a trick, after all."

Cassandra shook her head and slowly lowered herself to a crate sitting by the door. Whatever anger had enveloped her before dissipated. She seemed weary. "Would that it were," she said, "but the Bottle Conjuration is no trick, no illusion. There is a dark wizardry behind it. Stefan is becoming a master conjuror. I see him growing more powerful every day, but mark me, if he finds the dark power and enters the bottle, he will be doomed."

Lucinda sat beside her on the crate. "That doesn't seem possible. And, even if Stefan could get inside the bottle, he should be able to come out again or simply break it to escape."

"No. It is said that once entered, forever sealed. Only once before has someone attempted it and . . ." She dropped her head sadly and said softly, "Why would Stefan want to do this?"

"I don't know," replied Lucinda.

"It must be either love of fame or love itself that drives him."

"I care for Stefan," Lucinda said, "I won't let anything happen to him."

"Then you must stop him."

"Somehow, I will. Maybe I should break the bottle."

"It can't be broken, Lucinda. Not with rocks, or clubs, or even gunpowder."

Lucinda shook her head. She felt tears forming in her eyes. "This is a nightmare."

"It is told that only the power of the Bloodstone can break the bottle."

"Bloodstone?"

"Yes, a rare gem that holds within it untold powers—ancient, awesome powers. Sadly, it's been in the possession of the royal family of England for centuries, although they have no inkling of its power. To them, it's just another pretty bauble."

Even as Cassandra had been speaking, Lucinda's mind raced ahead, seeing Stefan on stage. A plan to save him began to take shape. She took Cassandra's hand in her own. She squeezed gently, saying, "Don't worry, I can stop Stefan from performing."

AS EAGER AS Stefan was to study *The Book of Shadows*, he knew he would have to do it in secret. Too many men called the foundry their home, at least for a night or two. Strangers all, Stefan could not trust these men who would be as likely to steal your socks as they would your coin purse.

He kept the book hidden in the inner pocket of his coat and wore the coat as he slept, making sure to secure it tightly around him so that even the slightest mouse-like movement would awaken him. It had worked so far, but he didn't know how long he could continue to keep the book safe with so many others nosing around.

But he had to study the book.

The foundry was a sprawling building, mostly in disrepair, with one large room renovated with beds for the homeless. Stefan slipped away from the others and explored the dark recesses of the foundry, eventually stumbling upon a padlocked door. Padlocks meant nothing to him, especially locks as old and rusted as the one he now snapped open with a little metal pick retrieved from his pocket.

The door opened into a tiny storage space crowded with boxes and crates. Judging by the layers of dust enshrouding them, they had not been touched in years. Rat droppings littered the floor. Cobwebs hung like bed curtains from the ceiling. A thin ray of moonlight filtered into the room through a gap in the boards crudely nailed across a little window. The room was perfect.

Stefan made sure the door was closed, then seated himself on a crate near the window where he could make use of the moonlight. He took off his coat and withdrew the book from the pocket, the cracked leather cover warm to his touch.

He set the book on his lap and carefully opened it, mindful of the parchment-thin pages. A strange symbol was set below the title—*Librum Umbrarum*, The Book of Shadows—a serpent entwined around a book. The book bore no date nor an author's name; it was as though it had simply appeared from the mists of time on its own accord. A preface from the anonymous author explained that the book was a grimoire, a collection of spells, conjurations, and talismans gathered over many years from many arcane sources. The author warned the reader that anything he attempted from the book, he did at his own risk.

The author wrote: *I have let myself be seduced to vanity at times by believing that I have performed these works under my own power. I confess that I have learned from the writings of famous philosophers that have most penetrated these arts with great power, applying everything secret within all of nature.*

Stefan felt a chill course up his spine as he read those words and wondered who those "famous philosophers" were and what was behind the "great power" that revealed to them the secrets of all nature. He was aware of what Cassandra called "black magic," or the "black arts." Was this grimoire the bible for those who practiced such magic?

He marveled at the hodgepodge list of contents: *To Cause a Girl to Dance Naked, To Prosper at Gambling, To Ward Off Wolves, The Ring of Invisibility, The Secret Stick For Travelers, Turning Lead Into Gold,* and so many other wondrous subjects. His eyes focused on an entry titled *Hand of Glory;* a talisman made by thieves to render their victims immobile. The instructions on how to make the talisman were quite detailed and specific:

They take the hand of a man hanged by a road; it is wrapped in a piece of shroud, and it is pressed therein to release enough blood to make the shroud adhere to it. Then, it is put in an earthen vessel with vinegar, saltpeter, salt, and black pepper, all ground up. It is left for fifteen days in the pot, then it is removed and exposed in the sunlight of the midday until it dries completely. If the sun is not sufficient, they put it in an oven that is heated with fern and verbena. A candle is then made with the fat of the hanged man, virgin wax, and sesame oil, and the hand of glory is then used as a candlestick to hold the candle when lit, by placing it between the second and third fingers of the hand. In all the places where one shall go, all onlookers will become immobile.

He paused in his reading, suddenly alert to a sound outside the door. His heart thumped as he sat nervously in the room, expecting to be discovered, but slowed when he finally recognized the sound as that of a rat prowling through the building.

The moonlight was beginning to ebb, so he quickly scanned the pages and then, there it was, the secret of the Bottle Conjuration. A crude sketch of a harlequin half inserted into a wine bottle was on the page. A pentacle rose above the bottle. Stefan knew the symbol was often associated with the black arts, sometimes with devil-worshippers. Seeing it there gave him pause. If he pursued the conjuration, would he be practicing the black arts, or putting himself under their power? But performing the conjuration would make him the greatest conjuror the world had ever seen. Wouldn't such celebrity be worth the risk?

As if in a hypnotic trance, Stefan began to read. He became absorbed in the reading as it promised to demonstrate how one could become a shapeshifter, transforming oneself into something fluid and amorphous, an entity that could enter a wine bottle! He shuddered as he read those words, his heart racing. Here, in his hands, was proof the conjuration could be done, and he could be the one to do it.

Blood was required. Following the instructions in the book, Stefan withdrew the lockpick from his pocket. He winced as he pressed it into the palm of his hand and sliced a small wound from which the blood began to seep. Squeezing his palm to increase the flow, he used his finger to paint the Greek letter *alpha*, on his forehead. Then, he painted the letter *omega* on the floor.

He settled himself on the floor, the symbol before him, the book at his side and he began to read aloud an invocation written in Latin. He had learned a little bit of Latin from other magical books, but he did not understand much of what he now read. The one phrase the book instructed him to repeat, chantlike, while concentrating on the omega symbol was clear to him—*sicut papilio denuo orti*—like a butterfly, born again.

His eyes watered as he stared at the symbol, repeating the mantra.

Sicut papilio denuo orti.

Sicut papilio denuo orti.

Sicut papilio denuo orti.

The wound in his palm began to tingle, the sensation gradually spreading over his hand. It felt like hundreds of tiny needles jabbing him repeatedly, not a pleasant feeling. His hand grew warm, the heat creeping up his forearm. He pushed up his shirt sleeve. His skin was taking on a reddish tinge. The warmth spread through his body. He felt feverish and weak. Sweat oozed from his skin. Still, he persisted.

Sicut papilio denuo orti.

The book lay open at his side, but his eyes focused on his hand and arm. A faint light shimmered around them, and it began to glow, gathering in intensity until his forearm and hand became luminously translucent. Barely able to breathe and growing weaker by the second, Stefan struggled to keep from fainting. The walls, the crates, the floor all seemed to slip away from him as though he were floating in some celestial void. He could no longer feel his body. For a moment he wondered if his soul had left it, if it now floated in that void, looking down on the shell of his body. But even as the room grew ever darker and his consciousness started to fade, he kept his eyes fixed on his arm.

And then it happened.

A lightning bolt of pain suddenly shot from his fingertips to his shoulder, rocking him back against the crate. He wanted to scream but stifled his cries, biting down, feeling his mouth fill with blood when he bit into his tongue.

But my hand! My arm!

The light that enveloped his arm was so bright he was barely able to discern the appendage. All he saw was mere shadow, a vague likeness of an arm, a hand, and fingers, looking more like an anatomist's skeletal model than flesh and blood.

And the shadow was shrinking!

On the cusp of unconsciousness, he didn't know if he was hallucinating, but his entire arm, fingertips to shoulder, was growing smaller, collapsing in on itself like a spyglass. He watched through heavy eyelids, horrified and yet, entranced, as his arm shrank to half its size. It was still moving, rearranging itself, shifting its atoms, when he finally lost consciousness and slumped to the floor.

He had no idea how long he had been insensible, but when he regained consciousness, he found the room to be completely dark, except for a thin ribbon of light from a streetlamp finding its way in through the crack in the boards over the window. In that wan light, he saw that his arm was whole, his hand a normal size. He wiggled his fingers and shook out his arm. Yes, everything was normal once again.

He slowly pushed himself up from the floor, his aching body unwilling to fully cooperate. He tasted blood in his mouth and spat out a glob. He retrieved the grimoire from the floor, put it back in his coat pocket and put the coat on. He remembered the blood he had smeared on his forehead and swiped the sleeve of his coat across it to wipe it clean. He took hold of his walking stick. Leaning heavily on it, he staggered out of the room.

Chapter Thirty-Six

· ·

IT WAS NO use, thought Lucinda, as she tossed in bed, kicking the rumpled sheets onto the floor. She could not calm herself to sleep. Her thoughts constantly revolved, like water flowing into the buckets of a water wheel. Never settling, just turning over and over in her mind. Montagu only wanted to use her and whatever his plan was, it would do harm to her and to Stefan. The image of Cassandra, her shoulders hunched, her voice trembling as she spoke about the dangers Stefan faced, occupied her mind. Wide-eyed, she could not force away the fear that choked her.

She turned to her side, burying her head in her grass-stuffed pillow, as her thoughts turned to how and when would be the best time to talk with Stefan. It had to be soon, as the show date was fast approaching. What words would convince him not to do the performance? Nothing came to mind. Why should she care, anyway? If Stefan was bullheaded enough to attempt his dark magic, what concern was that of hers?

Maybe she should sneak out of London and travel far away so Montagu, or the Bow Street Runners, would not find her. She turned onto her back, the pillow, now flat and damp from her sweat, of no comfort. She closed her eyes. Again, her mind turned to Stefan. Maybe she needed a way to prevent him from entering the theatre that night. She remembered Molly had some powder that when dropped into a gentleman's wine, would cause him to fall into a deep sleep. She called it her emergency 'pinch.' It had kept her safe against the brutes who enjoyed bruising their ladies.

On the oak rafters above her, a spider had been franticly weaving an intricate web. Once completed it would snare the plump flies that entered through the open window. A gust of wind rushed through the opening. The spider clung to its web, but the wind was too strong. The silk tore away from the rafter, pushing the spider and its woven trap down on Lucinda. Tangled in the web, she choked back a scream as she scurried out of bed trying to shake off the spider, with its long black legs dancing on her shoulder.

She ran to the dresser, swatting at the beast, but the monster's legs clung to her nightgown. She grabbed a pitcher of water from the dresser and dowsed the spider, which instinctively wrapped its legs around its body like a ball of wool and rolled off her shoulder onto the floor. It scampered away, hiding under a nearby bed. Lucinda cupped her hands with water and feverishly washed her face, ridding herself of the spider's silk. She stood in the darkened room, heart pulsating, sweat mingled with the water, her nightgown sticking to her damp skin. A roommate, flushed with anger from being woken, sat up in bed.

Lucinda whispered to her, "I'm sorry, a spider..."

The roommate groggily responded, "I really don't care what you are up to, just be quiet. You'll wake the dead or worse, you'll wake Edna."

Lucinda stripped off her soaked gown and quietly dressed. She softly tip-toed down the rickety stairs and went outside. Guided by the dim light of the half-moon, she walked to a small riverside park overlooking the Thames. The wind carried in the morning fog, making the river appear to be meandering through the clouds, a stream flowing in the sky. She had stumbled upon this quiet place months ago and had often found refuge beneath a tall elm tree. It had become her sanctuary, an area where she could be alone with her thoughts and dreams.

STEFAN FOUND HIMSELF outside the foundry, the moon's curved shape providing enough light to reveal his location. He was exhausted. His body ached. He knew he could not go back to his straw bed and sleep. Besides the pain, his mind was buzzing with a thousand thoughts on how to proceed with the magic he now knew he could master. Lost in his thoughts, he ambled down the deserted street heading for the park on the riverbank where he sometimes practiced his magic. In the early mornings the empty park provided the space and stillness he needed to concentrate and perfect his skills. He would fill his pockets with apples and practice his juggling, and once pleased with his progress, would sit and enjoy watching the river as it flowed through the heart of London, and of course, he would feast on the apples as well.

The fog thickened the closer he came to the riverbank. The early morning air, heavy with moisture, sat on his shoulders. Fog nestled low to the ground. It reminded him of the times when he would join Cassandra hunting for mushrooms outside of camp and how the fog would often cling to her feet but would be whisked away by the swipe of her hands. He laughed to himself, stopped, and waved his hands at the fog, but it would not obey his commands.

"Cassandra," he whispered.

He knew she was concerned about his safety, and her wisdom should not be questioned, yet if she could have seen what he had achieved that night! He banished those thoughts; it would not matter to her. The fog became heavier and for a moment, he felt lost and alone. Maybe he should heed her warning.

No! I can do the magic!

He raised his walking stick and waved it several times in the fog. As he did, the fog parted and slowly lifted and melted away. The lifting fog revealed that he was at the riverbank, the cleansing sound of the flowing water comforting him.

The large elm tree that provided welcome shade during the hot afternoons stood in the distance before him. Someone leaned against the trunk. The dawn had arrived, and the image became clearer to him. He stopped and called out, "Lucinda? Is that you?"

The figure turned away from the river, recognized him, and waved.

"This is a surprise! Have you been out here all night? Is Molly here as well?"

A mixture of surprise and happiness crossed her face. "Molly? No, that's a long story. What are *you* doing here?"

"Also, a long story. I couldn't sleep, and I often come to this park to be alone and practice my conjuring skills."

She gestured for him to sit with her and said, "I, too, could not sleep. A night of tossing and turning, then a damned spider dropped on me. I hate those awful beasts."

He laughed. "Truth be told, I also hate them. How did you find this place in the dark?"

"This elm tree has been my guidepost. I like to come here after work and listen to the sounds of the river and let the frustrations of the day wash away. Once I get to the common house, I know I won't be able to find peace until Edna yells, *Lights out!* What about you?"

"I have a nice enough bed at Vicar Wesley's foundry, but between the number of men arriving each night, the prayer times and work details, I needed a quiet place to escape." He turned and looked at the light now washing over the park and the sunlight sparkling on the river. "Amazing that you discovered the same place."

"Amazing, yes, or maybe something more." She leaned over and hugged him tightly.

He returned her hug. For a few moments, neither spoke, but only took comfort in their embrace. Finally, Stefan said, "I'm glad you're here, I have something wondrous to tell you."

"I also wanted to talk with you, and it is very important."

"Alright, ladies first. Tell me your important news."

She paused, trying to organize the words she had been practicing in her mind. She looked at his arms and saw the spots of blood smeared on his shirt sleeve. "Is that blood?"

"Blood?" He glanced down and saw the stains. "No. Oh, maybe. Nothing really to be concerned about."

"Being concerned is why I wanted to talk to you."

Stefan's brow narrowed. "Really it's nothing, but I'm glad you're concerned about me."

"Cassandra is very concerned about you, too, Stefan."

"Cassandra?" He sat up straight. "What does she have to do with anything? What did she tell you at the camp?"

Lucinda attempted to take his hand, but he resisted. "Not at the camp. Last night, in the alley behind the Haymarket."

"What?"

She took a breath. "After we returned, I found that Molly had other plans. She had her claws in some dashing bloody-back. I left them and went back to the theatre to hopefully find you, but you had left. I went into the theatre, and . . . let's say I found out I cannot trust that arsworm, William. Or that bloody Montagu."

"I don't understand."

She searched for the right words and not finding them, said, "I have to ask you, did you take the conjuror bottle from Cassandra's vardo?"

"No. What bottle?" Her eyes told him that she knew. "I did take a wine bottle for my performance along with other props. And that is the news I wanted to share with you. I know now for sure. I can master the mystical bottle conjuration!"

"Stefan, that's why Casandra was so upset! She accused *me* of taking the bottle and was going to put a curse on my soul! She told me how dangerous were the dark powers needed for the conjuration and she's afraid that you will be harmed."

He did not want to hear her. He shook his head. "Cassandra is not aware of what I have already mastered."

"Stefan, she has raised you, taught you, and loved you. For her sake, please do not attempt this magic! You must not show up at the Haymarket."

His face flushed with frustration. "Not show up? All of London is talking about this night. Even His Grace, the Duke of Cumberland will attend. With such an audience I can show them all that I am not a gypsy trickster, but a true Romani conjuror. When I enter the bottle, all will be amazed, and I shall bring pride to all Romanies!"

She grabbed his hand and held it tightly. It felt hot. Feverish. "Please, I beg of you, don't do it!"

He tore his hand from her grasp. The argument they were having felt like when he argued with Cassandra. "Why would you not want me to succeed? I thought you believed in me. I . . . I care for you, and I had hoped you would also care for me, but I don't think you do."

"I *do* believe in you," she said, wiping away her tears.

"I think not! Although I despise how you look at Montagu, he at least believes in my abilities and wants me to succeed."

"No, Stefan! Montagu is not who you think he is. Take that from someone who has found the bitter truth." She attempted to hold him, but he pushed her away. She cried out, "I fear that terrible things will happen! Please, Stefan, Montagu is not a man who can be trusted!"

His vision blurred and his walking stick shook in his grasp. He reached into his coat pocket and yanked out the grimoire. He thrust the book at her. "This is what I trust. The magic in this book will keep me safe and make me the greatest conjuror!"

No more was said, the silence an unbridgeable chasm between them. He felt his walking stick calm now as he took a deep breath. Somewhere above them an unseen willow warbler broke into song. Stefan saw Lucinda's tears flowing and wondered if his book had a spell to stop them. Slowly, he placed the book back into his pocket, then reached out and held her trembling hands.

"Please, I can understand you not caring for me, a crippled gypsy, yet someday, when I do become famous, then I can bring you all that you deserve. I . . ." He gently held her hand in his, but his tongue would not shape the words he wanted to speak. Instead, he quietly said, "Don't worry, please."

She stood, as if caught in a sorcerer's trance, and watched as he turned and started to walk away. She tried to call back to him, but the music of the willow warblers drowned out her softly uttered, "But I do care for you."

Chapter Thirty-Seven

A BOISTEROUS CROWD gathered outside the Haymarket Theatre. This was the night that had been ballyhooed throughout all of London, the night when a man would do the impossible and vanish inside a wine bottle, or fail spectacularly, either of which would be a worthy show for the price.

Carriages and cabs jostled for space in the street as they brought their well-heeled customers to the front doors of the theatre. Jostling of a more unpleasant nature ensued as the bluebloods and social-climbing guildsmen pressed cheek to jowl with the London riffraff, all seeking admission to the theatre. The rank odor of too much perfume--or too little--hung like a cloud in the air.

A barker standing on a crate called out, "Only a few seats left, friends! You can purchase them at a real bargain. First come, first served!" Those unfortunates who had not previously bought a ticket surged around the barker, sharks surrounding an unfortunate sailor.

The Duke of Montagu stood at the fringe of the crowd, paying little attention to it, scanning the street instead. He snapped open his pocket-watch and checked the time. *Where was Cumberland?* He looked around one last time before pushing through the crowd and entering the theatre.

Inside, all was hurry and bustle as candles were lit, dust shaken out of the curtains, floors swept until the varnish gleamed, and chairs arranged just so in the expensive boxes, especially the royal box. All in expectation of the performance that would not only feature a man disappearing into a wine bottle but, even more, would feature the presence of the Duke of Cumberland, son of King George II.

That is, if all went well, thought William, nervously consulting his pocket-watch for perhaps the hundredth time that evening. "You there," he called out to two stagehands hauling a table and props to the stage, "careful with those! I'll have your damned hides if you break that bottle!"

He stomped off backstage. Lucinda and a bevy of hostesses were slathering even more layers of rouge and powder on their painted faces. "Look lively, lassies, look lively! You need to be out and about, ready to greet our guests momentarily."

He turned to Lucinda. "And you, Lucy, hurry it up. The Swami's waiting for you."

She glared at him as he strode out of the room.

Stefan stood onstage, half-hidden in the wings. He saw William heading for his office. The Swami was still in his dressing room and the stagehands were busy with other chores, leaving the prop table with the wine bottle unattended. This was his chance. He crept to the table and removed the funnel from the bottle. One more glance around to make sure he had not been seen and Stefan grabbed the bottle, scurrying off to the prop room.

If time were a genie, then the genie had escaped its lamp, Stefan thought. He hobbled down the theatre's back hallway, balancing himself with one hand on his walking stick, the other hand clutching the wine bottle.

It was hard to believe that tonight was the night of the conjuration. He was ready to perform the usual routines the Swami had taught him. In some ways, those would be fun, and he hoped they would help calm his racing heart and mind before he performed the final act. After tonight, he would be famous. He would bring pride to the Romani people and maybe draw closer to winning Lucinda's heart. If not, it would be Lady Fame to soothe his heart.

At the prop room door, he placed the bottle on the floor. He turned the doorknob. Locked. *Damnation!* Time was running out. He needed to switch the prop bottle with Cassandra's before the Swami arrived. Frustrated, he tried the knob again.

"Hold on mate," a passing stagehand said. "I've got the key here on my ring." He unlocked the door and gave Stefan the key. "I've got more to do out back. Lock up when you're done, and I'll retrieve the key from you later."

Stefan nodded. The stagehand left without paying attention to the bottle sitting on the floor. Stefan picked it up and entered the room, closing the door behind him. Unbeknownst to him the warped door partially reopened, as so often happened in the aged theatre.

The prop room was as he had left it the other night. Cluttered. There was no order to the room as objects were strewn about by anyone who had left them, and they were rarely returned to their original location. Several wooden shelves bordered the room. A large oak table sat in the middle.

One of its legs was cracked and made the table wobble when placing articles on it, but other than its age and blemish, it was a workable table.

He turned to the shelf where he had stowed Cassandra's bottle. It was safe and secure under the blanket. He used his cane like a hook to remove the blanket. He lifted the bottle and placed it on the table. He put the prop bottle on the shelf. How strange, he thought, as he examined the bottle. All these years sitting in her vardo, and he never realized what she had. Combined with the verses from the *Book of Shadows*, the bottle had powers that he still did not fully understand.

The door suddenly opened, startling him. He turned to see Lucinda entering.

"Stefan! I saw the door was ajar and hoped you would be here."

He was at a loss for words and moved between her and the table, trying to hide the bottle. His leg bumped the table, making the bottle wobble, attracting her attention.

"Is that the conjuror bottle?" she asked. "You *did* take it."

"How do you know about that?"

She moved toward the bottle. "Cassandra told me everything. You can't do the trick, it's too dangerous."

"I've been studying . . ."

"Studying?"

"It doesn't matter, I will do it."

Lucinda grabbed his walking stick and shook it. "No!" Her voice trembled. "Turn this stick into a snake or something. Anything. But don't do the bottle trick!" She tossed the stick out the door. It clattered somewhere in the hallway.

His face twisted in anger. "What are you doing?" She reached behind him for the bottle. He made a wild grab for it and a tug -of-war ensued. "Lucinda, you don't understand what you are doing! Give it to me!"

"It's you who does not know what you're doing, the danger you would be in if you attempt the conjuration." She pulled harder. "I made a sacred vow to Cassandra. I won't let you do this!" She summoned up a burst of strength and tugged mightily on the bottle.

Stefan stumbled. "Lucinda! Stop!" He fell backwards to the floor, cracking his head against the edge of the table. Blackness surrounded him.

She stood over him, holding Cassandra's bottle. Alarmed to see him lifeless, she bent down and placed her ear on his chest. She heard his heart beating. She felt his breath against her cheek. "Ah, he breathes! Thank the angels!" She gave him a soft kiss. "I'm so sorry, Stefan," she whispered, "but it has to be this way."

She saw the prop room key on the floor and picked it up, the conjuror bottle in hand. She left the room and firmly closed the door, locking Stefan inside. She tucked the key in her bodice. "Please forgive me, Stefan," she said, through the door, "it's for your own good."

She turned and looked around anxiously for a safe place to hide the bottle. She saw a dusty muslin cloth near a column at the far end of the stage. She placed the bottle behind the column and draped the muslin over it. She made sure the bottle was out of the way and would not be noticed. Glancing once again at the locked prop room, she took a deep breath and hurriedly left for the stage.

Chapter Thirty-Eight

· ·

MONTAGU WALKED INTO the theatre and saw William standing near the stage. The curtains were drawn across the stage as the manager frantically paced the floor. The duke approached, taking him aside.

"Where's Lucinda?" Montagu asked. "There's quite a large crowd gathering outside. I need her out front to escort Cumberland when he arrives."

"You mean *if* he arrives," William said, nodding toward the royal box. Montagu looked up and saw the box was empty. "Are you sure he'll come?"

Montagu sighed and put his hand on the manager's shoulder. "Don't worry, he'll be here."

"He'd better be."

Before the duke could respond, he noticed Lucinda making her way down the aisle, pushing through the crowd. "Ah, there you are!"

As she came closer, he saw that her clothes were in disarray, her cheeks flushed. His eyes narrowed. "What have you been doing? Never mind, I don't want to know." He grabbed her by the arm. "We have work to do." He walked her back to the door. "All you have to do is smile and look pretty when Lord Cumberland shows up."

"That's all?"

"And escort him to the royal box, of course. He won't refuse such an offer. Can you manage that?"

"What if his lady is with him?" said Lucinda.

"What lady would that be? Cumberland remains a bachelor. . ."

"Oh, I didn't know. A bachelor . . ."

"Yes, well there are rumors but, in any case, he is *still* amenable to the charms of a lovely young lady so when you make your curtsey, make it a nice deep bow, eh? Give our lordship something to think about."

"Are all men such pigs?" she said, her voice rising.

"Some more than others, my dear."

"I'm nervous, I don't think I can do this."

He squeezed her arm. She winced in pain. He dragged her out through the door. "You can and you will," he said, his mouth close to her ear. "Remember our little arrangement. Just take Cumberland up to the box and keep your eyes open for the chance to lift that precious dagger of his. Look sharp now, here he is!"

Montagu drew himself up as Cumberland's royal coach, preceded by his men in handsome livery clearing away the crowd, came to a stop. A second, less elegant coach followed behind, with only two footmen.

Cumberland's coachman and postilion held the horses in check as a servant placed a footstool by the door bearing Cumberland's royal crest and opened it. The Duke of Cumberland's large bulk, swathed in an emerald-green coat, appeared in the doorway. The crowd cheered when they saw him, but surreptitious laughter bubbled up here and there as Cumberland attempted to exit the coach only to be seemingly stuck in the doorway. The servant offered his hand to assist his master. Cumberland angrily swatted it away as he tried to squirm through the door.

Montagu stifled a laugh with his hand.

Cumberland's coat hung open while he struggled to get out, revealing a flash of bejeweled gold that caught Montagu's eye. He nudged Lucinda. "Do you see it?" he whispered. "The dagger?" She nodded. "Should be easy pickings for you."

As Cumberland squirmed, the door of the second coach opened and Jack Broughton stepped out to hearty cheers from the crowd, who showed more interest in the massive brawler than they did in the third son of King George II.

Realizing the impossibility of his position and the knowledge that the longer he delayed, the more ridiculous he looked to the people, Cumberland let himself be unceremoniously yanked by the arm out of the coach, like a cork popping from a champagne bottle. Haughtily adjusting his waistcoat in the street as if that was how one always exited the royal coach, he shot the helpful servant a withering look.

"Your Grace!" Montagu said, approaching him with Lucinda in tow. "Welcome!"

Cumberland sneered. "Monty, I must commend you on what you have achieved so far. Very impressive, promoting this farce," he said, looking around at the people gawking at him. "You had better have your fifty pounds sterling or there will be hell to pay," he said, loudly.

"I assure you, all debts will be paid, should I be unfortunate enough to lose our bet so, please, enjoy the performance of a lifetime," said Montagu.

Cumberland snorted. "Ha, and who might this lovely lass be?" he asked, turning to Lucinda.

"My name is Lucinda, Your Grace," she answered, delivering exactly the deep curtsey Montagu had suggested.

Cumberland's eyes widened.

"Lucinda will escort you to the royal box," Montagu said.

Cumberland eagerly snatched up the hand she proffered him. "This evening is looking better," he said, as she walked him into the theatre.

Indeed, thought Montagu.

Chapter Thirty-Nine

· ·

WILLIAM NERVOUSLY PACED behind the crimson velvet curtains. He gave up referring to his pocket-watch; time was moving at a bangtail pace. He strode forward and back, his mind racing between the debt he owed his shysters and the utter insanity of agreeing to Montagu's plan. *What have I gotten myself into?* The audience poured in, but without Lord Cumberland and his party this could be a night of embarrassment and not the embarrassment of riches he needed.

The band barged their way through some nondescript but lively music which kept the crowd quiet and gave his girls time to ply their special trade, but still William was nervous. He chewed harder on his unlit cigar. Pieces of it fell off, leaving a trail on the floor. His inner voice told him to again check the time. He gave into it and pulled out his watch, opened the lid. The hands seemed to reach out, screaming to him that the show should have started twenty minutes ago. He heard what sounded like horses pounding the ground coming from beyond the curtains as the patrons stomped their feet in unison, as if that would somehow start the show.

He knew he had to face the audience and stall for more time. He looked behind him. A large prop table stood there, loaded with several cards, hats, flowers, and boxes. Behind and to the left of center was another smaller table with a tin funnel lying on it. A sturdy chair stood next to this table. All was ready, except for the Swami, that damned gypsy, and Cumberland.

William touched the curtain, seeking the seam to walk through. A cloud of dust rose off it, making it more difficult to find. Finally, success. He peeled apart the curtain, sneezed, and entered the front of the stage, the curtains closing behind him.

When the band saw William enter, the conductor switched from playing the ribald, *Oh How Ye Protest,* to *Rule Britannia!* The crowd immediately began singing the words:

Rule, Britannia! Britannia rule the waves!
Britons never, never, never shall be slaves.

Along with the singing, the crowd continued stomping their feet. William raised his hand. The band stopped playing, except for a clarinet that let out a few lingering sour notes which underscored the catcalls erupting from the crowd. They did not perturb him.

"Ladies and gentlemen, welcome to our grand palace and to a night to be remembered." The crowd started to cheer. Whistles cut through the din. William glanced up to the royal box, but still no Cumberland. "Because of the mystical event that will transpire tonight, I must ask for your indulgence a few minutes more as we make our final preparations. . ." Boos started to ring out. "I know how eager you all are for the show. Maestro, please play something delightful for our patrons."

The conductor turned to his band, gave a hand signal for song number four and they began playing, the ditty, *Oyster Nan.* The patrons clapped to the beat of the fast-paced melody.

William stuck his head through the curtain seam and saw a stagehand placing more props on the main table. "Where is the Swami?" he shouted as he went backstage.

The stagehand looked up and pointed to the wings. The Swami stood ready, dressed in his long flowing robe, his huge turban, adorned with a large ostrich feather, askew on his head and dangling down as he wobbled toward the prop table, dropping a few wooden balls to the floor. Luckily, the boisterous crowd muffled the sound.

My god, thought William, *He's drunk as a skunk! And where is that accursed gypsy?*

Suddenly, the noise beyond the curtain ceased. Confused, William turned to go back on stage when the band began to play *Rule Britannia!* again. Looking through the gap in the curtains, he saw a group of well-dressed patrons walking in step to the music, like a military parade, as they headed up to the royal boxes. Lucy brought up the end of the procession, her arm linked with that of Lord Cumberland.

William scowled at the drunk Swami. "Where's that bloody gypsy?"

The Swami tripped on his robe. He swayed but was able to keep himself upright. The blank look on his face told William all he needed to know.

"The Duke of Cumberland has arrived, and the show must begin. Get ready, you blunderbuss!" William stormed out front of the curtains.

The crowd booed when he appeared on stage. He saw how large the crowd had grown and, more importantly, saw Cumberland being escorted to his seat in the royal box.

"Ladies and Gentlemen, may I once again have your attention," he announced.

The crowd erupted noisily as the band played a fanfare. Cumberland entered the royal box, Lucinda guiding him to his seat. He remained standing while the band played and waved to the audience. Lucinda saw his dagger nestled in a small leather dagger-frog. As he turned to wave to those at the back of the theatre, she tried to snag the jeweled knife, but he turned back quickly. All she caught was the tail of his jacket. Cumberland felt her hands on his jacket and gave her a wink. He squeezed himself into his seat. She stood beside him in the aisle, her eye on the dagger.

As the crowd quieted, William continued his speech. "Tonight, marks an auspicious occasion and not simply because we are honored to have His Grace the Duke of Cumberland in attendance." He gestured to the royal box and applause broke out, mostly coming from Cumberland's perfumed entourage.

Cumberland struggled to stand once more to wave. Lucinda glimpsed the dagger, but again, he sat before she could strike. She did notice that the leather straps which secured the dagger had become loose.

"As I was saying," William continued, "tonight you will be treated not only to the amazing Soho Swami's mind-bending illusions, but also to those of his protégé, Stefan the Gypsy Conjuror."

A man shouted from the audience, "Get on with it!"

William cleared his throat. "The young man will perform the astounding Bottle Conjuration, taught to him, of course, by the remarkable Soho Swami."

With a sweep of his hand, William stepped to the side. The velvet curtains opened. The band erupted in another fanfare. The Swami, his back to the audience, hunched over his table feverishly arranging his props. The music startled him, and he nervously turned to the audience and bowed, catching his ill-fitting turban before it fell off. He reached his hand into the air, made a fist, blew on it and tossed butterflies into the air. Unfortunately, the prop malfunctioned; paper butterflies fell in a lump to the floor. The audience whistled and laughed, some booed.

The Swami walked to the front of the stage, holding a newspaper. He folded the paper into a funnel, reached in and pulled out some flowers. The crowd was not impressed. He was becoming more disheveled. He stood at the lip of the stage. The oil lamps on the stage highlighted his features in a warm yellow glow. The low angle of the lights made deep shadows on his face. As he pulled out a deck of cards from within his robe, the traitorous turban slipped over his eyes, causing the cards to fly off into the audience.

Lord Cumberland bellowed a hardy guffaw and looked at Lucinda. "This is far more entertaining than I was expecting, my lass!"

Composing himself, the Swami said, "My dear friends, this comedy is all part of my act to bring levity and joy to you before you experience the dark magic of my young protégé. I have travelled the four corners of this earth. I have seen many mystical feats. I caution those of you with a weak disposition, his feat may make you squeamish. You will see our young conjuror contorting his body, see his skin stretching, hear the painful sounds of breaking bones as he slips into a common wine bottle."

He pointed to the back table. A stagehand quickly turned one of the oil lights on it, revealing the table to be empty except for a tin funnel. "Oh. Uh, I shall conjure the bottle soon! Again, I warn those with weak hearts to leave this theatre before the gypsy attempts this momentous event."

The crowd became still.

The Swami looked to the wings and saw William nervously chomping on his cigar, making furious hand motions, and shaking his head. The Swami turned back to the audience. "Yes, yes, please let me introduce Stefan the gypsy conjuror!"

The band struck up another fanfare. The crowd cheered.

William, wide-eyed, shook his head and yelled out to the Swami, "He's not here, you dunce! Get back and start your act! Now!"

The Swami did not budge from the lip of the stage, confusion drawn over his face. "Stefan, oh mystical child, show yourself, lad. No reason to be shy. Stefan?"

William came out from the wing. The crowd, as usual, booed his entrance. He grabbed the Swami's arm and whispered into his ear, "You need to perform while I look for Stefan, you nitwit."

The Swami's eyes showed fear. His breath smelled of gin. "I can't go on without my assistants. I need more time to arrange my props. It's all a mess . . ."

William pinched the Swami's arm tighter. "Listen, you idiot, stall for time until I can find the kid!" The impatient crowd shouted out more catcalls and a head of cabbage flew onto the stage. The Swami looked terrified. William yelled to the maestro, "Play something while I go look for that damned gypsy!"

The Maestro turned to his band. "I think he wants us to play a gypsy song."

Three fiddlers stood and started to play a favorite folk song in a quick tempo, *The Raggle Taggle Gypsy*. The joyous notes of the opening phrases filled the theatre. The crowd settled and swayed to the beat. The tone of the song changed and became melancholy as it told the story of a lady living in comfort and leisure who leaves her husband, a duke, and absconds with a gypsy. The mood in the room became somber.

William was pleased that the song had, at least momentarily, tamed the crowd. He shouted to the maestro to keep playing until he returned with the gypsy. A fourth fiddler, a stout woman with large red cheeks, stood up and started to loudly sing:

"There were three old gypsies a come to my door
And downstairs ran this lady, O!
One sang high and another sang low
And the other sang bonny, bonny, Biscay, O!"

The Swami stood and listened. William retreated through the wings and the crowd quieted. The Swami reached out his hand and guided the stout woman up to the front of the stage. She continued to sing:

"It was upstairs downstairs the lady went
Put on her suit of leather, O!
And there was a cry from around the door
She gone with the raggle taggle gypsies, O!"

The Swami bowed to her and slowly walked backward to his prop table and started to arrange a few tricks to perform. He also made the sign of the cross, hoping for the young lad to appear.

The singer raised her voice higher:

"It was late last night when my lord came home
Enquiring for his a-lady, O!
The servants said, on every hand
She's gone wif the raggle taggle gypsies, O!
O saddle to me my milk-white steed
Go and fetch me my pony, O!
That I may ride and seek me bride
Who is gone wif the raggle taggle gypsies, O!"

William had entered the back hallway of the theatre. *Where could that lad be?* he thought. He saw that the prop room door was closed. He shouted through the door, "Stefan!"

He attempted to open the door, but it was locked. Frustrated, he rattled the doorknob several times. "Stefan, STEFAN, where are you?" Upset, he turned and proceeded to the backstage door. He flung the door open and entered the alley. Still, he heard:

"O he rode high and he rode low
He rode through woods and copses too
Until he came to an open field
And there espied his a-lady, O!"

His eyes adjusted to the darkness. The only light came from the moonlight and at the far end of the alley a streetlamp illuminated the alley's entrance. At first, he saw not a soul. Then, he spied a tall man, much taller than Stefan, wearing a long cloak. From that distance it looked as if his face was covered with a mask. Definitely not Stefan. William turned and realized the stage door had closed behind him. He was locked out. He banged on the door to gain entrance, but the music inside drowned out his battering.

"What makes you leave your house and land?
What makes you leave your money, O?
What makes you leave your new wedded Duke?
To go wif the raggle taggle gypsies, O!"

Inside, the audience, familiar with the popular song, began to sing along with the stout woman, filling the house with a chorus of twelve-hundred voices.

"What care I for my house and my land?
What care I for my money, O?
What care I for my new wedded lord?
I'm off wif the raggle taggle gypsies, O!"

The tune brought out a playful side in Cumberland and he joined in with the singing. He turned to Lucinda. "Come on my lass, join in!"

She smiled, keeping her eye on his dagger, and sang with the crowd. As she sang, the story revived her anger with Montagu. She also thought of Stefan, locked in the prop room. The verses became like tiny daggers piercing her heart.

"Last night you slept on a goose-feather bed
Wif the sheet turned down so bravely, O!
And to-night you'll sleep in a cold open field
Along wif the raggle taggle gypsies, O!"

The Swami finished placing his magical bowl of fruit on the table. He saw the tin funnel but no wine bottle on the conjuror table. He danced over, doing an Irish jig, his feet amazingly spry as he kept to the beat of the music. He noticed a strange bundle wrapped in a blanket at the far end of the stage. He whisked off the blanket and found the conjuror bottle. "Oh, there you are!"

He grabbed the vessel and moved it to the small table, placing it in the center. Still in time with the music, he placed the funnel in the neck of the bottle.

"What care I for goose-feather bed?
Wif the sheet turned down so bravely, O!
For to-night I shall sleep in a cold open field
Along wif the raggle taggle gypsies, O!'

The floor lights illuminated him, creating a long shadow stretching across the stage floor. As he danced back to the front of the stage, it appeared as if his shadow and he were dancing partners. He proceeded to dance upstage to the stout woman as she was finishing her ditty.

"What care I for my house and land?
What care I for my money-O?
I'd rather have a kiss from the gypsy's lips
I'm away wif the raggle taggle gypsy-O!"

She took a bow as the audience roared its appreciation. The Swami put his hand over her ear and pulled out a beautiful red silk scarf and adorned her neck with it. The fiddlers kept playing as the stout woman danced with the Swami.

Chapter Forty

MELCHIOR DIDN'T EXACTLY blend into the crowd of people surging through the doors of the Haymarket Theatre, but his size and ominous black eye patch magically opened a path for him. There was no one willing to stop him from entering, certainly not the perfumed fops who had arrived with the Duke of Cumberland, nor the single constable who stood on the footpath far removed from the theatre, hoping his services would not be required any time before his shift was over.

It was hot inside the theatre, the air redolent with too much perfume, the stink of unbathed bodies, and the tang of grilled sausages. Pushing through the jostling crowd, Melchior made his way up to the balcony at the rear of the theatre where he stood partially concealed in a corner. From there, he had a good view of the stage and was removed far enough to protect his hearing from that god-awful band, now raucously bungling its way through some old folk song and occasionally striking the proper notes.

He looked around, trying to spot Jonah and Abel. They had separated outside to avoid looking conspicuous. He knew he could rely on Jonah and was confident he was somewhere in the throng but as for Abel, well, there was no telling where he might be. Melchior sighed, still trying to figure out how the elders had decided to make Abel a Hunter. If the man had any hidden talents, and Melchior doubted he did, Abel had yet to display them. No matter. He and Jonah could get things done without him if need be.

The band's caterwauling finally ceased and now a ridiculous clown of a magician stood on stage. He wore a long robe and an enormous turban that wobbled precariously and threatened to topple off his head with every step he took.

The Soho Swami. Clearly a blundering drunk who could not perform a simple card trick. Even as Melchior thought this, the Swami clumsily tried to shuffle a deck of cards and ended up shooting them out over the audience. He deserved the cabbage hurled at him.

But where was the Bottle Conjuror? The gypsy named Stefan?

The Swami had introduced the conjuror and called him to the stage, but no one had appeared. The crowd was growing restive, shouting out for the conjuration, throwing rotten fruits and vegetables at the Swami.

Scanning the crowd below him, Melchior saw Jonah closer to the stage. The Hunter looked up, caught Melchior's eye, and shrugged, hands out, indicating he had no idea where the gypsy was either.

Now the Swami was performing a jig, which looked more like he was stricken with palsy, as he danced across the stage. *The man's an ass,* Melchior thought. But then, after dancing into the wing, the Swami returned carrying a magnum wine bottle.

The conjuration bottle!

Melchior moved closer to the rail, rudely pushing aside another man. He watched intently as the Swami set the bottle on a table that already held a funnel. Down below, Melchior saw Abel shouldering his way through the mob, moving closer to the stage. *Any minute now and that gypsy will appear.*

If Stefan could perform the conjuration, the Bloodstone would have to be produced to break him from the bottle and if the gypsy had the stone, then he also had to possess *The Book of Shadows.* That was what Melchior wanted. His heart pounded. They were so close!

As he turned and headed for the stairs to get closer to the stage, he caught a glimpse of Abel down below, busily shoveling a meat pie into his mouth.

Useless!

Chapter Forty-One

CURSE MY SOUL *for the awful state of affairs I find myself in,* William thought, still locked out of his theatre. In the dark alley he heard the music and singing coming from inside. He turned back to see if the tall man still lurked under the streetlamp. He was gone. William walked down the alley to Market Lane where he could go around the block to Bell Inn Street, a seldomly used lane, really nothing more than a long alley, then a short right onto Haymarket and to the theatre.

Even though he could not make out the figure under the lamppost, his gut told him it was his shylock, Plunkett. William had been aware that there was a dark side to the chemist who was known to employ a henchman when needed. Ah, no doubt, Plunkett's henchman was the lurking figure he had spied in the alley.

He picked up his pace. The money sitting in the box office could easily pay off his debt with interest and he'd have some to spare. But first, he had to get back and find that gypsy, or his house of cards could collapse.

He turned right onto Bell Inn Street and re-lit his cigar. The cigar provided the only illumination in the dark street, however meager it was. No matter, he thought, as it was only fifty-paces from there to the main thoroughfare of Haymarket Street.

Suddenly, a gentleman's walking cane thrust out of the darkness, slamming across his knees. He howled in pain and tumbled to the ground. He could make out the figure of a tall man in the dark, a man in a long black cape that covered his legs. What William saw clearly was the white Venetian mask. He rolled over and attempted to stand but his legs were limp with pain. He put his arms around his head in a feeble attempt to protect himself.

"If you intend to rob me, I have no money on me!" he cried out to his assailant.

The tall figure stood quietly and reached out his walking cane for William to grab as an aid to pull himself up. As he did so, he noticed a silver wolf's head adorned the top of it.

Once William was on his feet the stranger spoke. "Haymarket, is it?"

"What do you want? And who in the blazes are you?" William said, frightened.

The tall figure laughed. "My apologies, Mr. Haymarket. My name is Macleane, James Macleane, which is of no consequence to you, but we have a mutual acquaintance. I do hope that you are feeling sprightly after your fall. From what I can see, nothing is broken, maybe a few bruises. And for that you are in luck as our mutual friend is a chemist who, no doubt. has what ails you."

William adjusted his coat and glanced around for his cigar. "Why did you strike me?"

Macleane brushed off William's shoulders like a valet with a whisk, but when he finished, he took hold of the back of William's jacket with a vise-like grip. His fingers pulled up on the jacket, lifting William off the ground. Macleane's strength surprised William. He dangled above the ground, feet kicking, striking nothing but air. "I consider myself a gentleman and I hope you will understand that this is the last warning to you. Your debt is a fortnight past due."

"Put me down! I get your message clearly. Just put me down!"

Macleane emitted a hollow laugh beneath the mask and set him back on his feet. "Now that I have delivered my message to you, do you have a reply that I could return to our mutual friend?"

"Bugger off!"

Macleane raised his cane, but before he could strike, William pleaded. "Wait, wait! If you would give our mutual friend this message."

Macleane lowered his cane and said in a friendly tone, "Please go on, I truly mean you no harm."

"Tell Plunkett that I have his money, including interest. I can pay him after the performance tonight. The house is sold-out with the finest in London. Probably most of his clients are in my theatre. If he likes, I can settle up in the morning at his apothecary." Macleane stood quietly still, and the silence seemed like an eternity to William. Finally, he spoke. "Mr. Haymarket, I am delighted to convey your message."

"Good," said William. "Now, I must get back to my theatre, the main performance will be starting soon."

"Ah, yes, the gypsy who will contort himself into a bottle. It has been the talk of the town."

"Yes, it has, now if you don't mind." He started to walk away, limping slightly from the whack Macleane had administered with his cane.

"William!"

He turned.

"Just another reminder for you," said Macleane, "if you don't pay off the debt by the morning not only will *your* bones be contorted, I think something else more important to you will be ruined."

William stopped in his track. "If you try to harm my wife . . ."

"My dear William, I told you I'm a gentleman. I have no reason to harm your wife. I said the most *important* thing to you . . ."

William stood with a blank look. "Your theatre, my friend."

Macleane turned and melted into the darkness.

Chapter Forty-Two

THE FAT LADY continued to sing. The audience caterwauled along with her. Montagu knew the crowd would soon grow ugly if Stefan didn't show up to perform. It didn't shock him to think Stefan would back out. He must have come to his senses and realized his so-called Bottle Conjuration could be performed only in his head. Rather than risk the wrath of the mob when he failed, he simply decided not to appear.

But whether Stefan performed it or not made no difference to the duke. The proceeds from the tickets were still in the office and Lucinda would soon have Cumberland's dagger. All was going smoothly. Although, time was running out. *Where was Sophia?* She should have been there by now. Without her his plan would fail.

The fat lady had ended her song and was about to get off the stage, but the crowd became belligerent. The maestro, seeing that William had disappeared, leaving him to deal with the audience, immediately had the band strike up another tune. Like a child listening to a lullaby, the crowd calmed down, but how long would that last?

He couldn't wait any longer. Montagu started threading his way through the crowd, casually moving toward the office. He glanced up at the royal box. Cumberland was distracted and having the time of his life, singing at the top of his lungs while attempting to paw Lucinda. The duke quickly turned a corner and found himself at the rear of the theatre, just outside the office door. There was no one around. He tried the door and found it locked.

"Bloody hell!"

Someone clamped a hand on his shoulder. He whirled around, expecting the worst, but found Sophia standing there. Anger welled up in him. He shoved her against the wall.

"Sophia! Where in God's name have you been!"

"Stop it, Monty, you're hurting me!" She pushed him away. "It wasn't easy getting through this crowd. I can still feel their hands groping and squeezing my body."

"You should be accustomed to that," he said. "Alright, enough. Let's get this done. Do you have it?"

"Of course." She smiled as she withdrew a slim piece of metal from her bodice. "A good lockpick never fails to have her tools upon her at all times."

"And you're one of the best, no doubt about that."

"*The* best, Monty," she said, as she bent to her task with the lock.

He stood guard, shielding her from view with his body. Suddenly, he grabbed her wrist. "Wait! What was that?"

She froze. "What?"

"*That*," he said, cocking his head toward the prop room. "That banging noise. Do you hear it? There, again!"

She nodded. "Yes," she whispered.

"What is that?"

Sophia shrugged. "I don't know. Maybe it's coming from inside the theatre. Who knows what's going on in there?"

"Never mind, we must move quickly. I don't know where that fool Stefan is, but it sounds like the crowd is about to revolt. We've no time to waste, so, back at it!"

In less than a minute, he heard the *click!* of the lock springing open. They slipped inside the office and silently closed the door behind them. Montagu took a quick look around and spotted the large wooden box containing the night's receipts sitting on the desk.

"I guess William trusted that flimsy door lock," he said, taking hold of the box.

Sophia had hiked up her petticoats and was withdrawing several cloth bags from beneath them. She caught him ogling her blue-stockinged leg and laughed.

"You've seen much more of me than that, Monty."

He ignored her comment and, picking up the bags, began stuffing them full of the money from the box.

"Here, you take these," he said, handing her three full bags. "Go and get the horses. I'll bring the rest." He continued to shovel money into an empty bag.

The music stopped again. The audience began to shout angrily.

"Be quick about it!" Montagu said.

Sophia started for the door but stopped and turned. "What about the dagger?"

"Don't worry about the dagger. I'll get it from Lucinda and meet you in the alley. Now, go!"

She hurried out.

Montagu stuffed the last bag full and scooped the remaining bills and coins into his pockets. He peeked his head out the door to make sure there was no one around, then crept toward the backstage door, the bag in hand.

None too soon! The crowd was getting ugly.

STEFAN WAS ADRIFT in darkness. Faint sounds began to wake him, but his eyes remained shut. He felt as if he was afloat on a dead sea surrounded by a cold fog. He tried to call out but could not muster a word. Faint sounds became louder, *what is it?* First music danced on the sea, then cheering, and finally what seemed like the thunder of hoofbeats troubled the water. Nothing made sense. He saw a shoreline and began to drift towards the bank. When the fog lifted, his eyes opened, and he found himself not floating on a cold sea but lying on a hard wooden floor. He turned his head and scanned the room but could not see his walking stick. The fog in his brain cleared. He realized he was in the prop room. He recalled the tussle he had had with Lucinda. *Where is she?*

Carefully, he rose and used the nearby table to steady himself as he hobbled, searching for his walking stick. He tried the door and found it locked. He remembered Lucinda's anger and how she insisted that he not perform his conjuration tonight.

But why not?

More memories rushed up. Lucinda had made a sacred vow to Cassandra.

What did that mean?

Maybe he could find a tool to break open the door. He glanced at the high shelving against the far wall. It was filled with wigs, masks, hats, fake beards, boxes. Nothing useful. He spied a wooden tray with carpentry tools on the top shelf. He saw a try plane, a gimlet, froe, and a hammer. Things were looking up. He hobbled over to the shelf. It was too high for him to reach and there was no ladder in the room.

The table!

He turned and started pulling the oak table over to the shelf, carefully balancing himself as he pulled.

He gingerly hoisted himself up onto the table and reached for the carpenter's tools. The table shimmied, then lurched backwards. His fingers grabbed the tray when his balance gave way and he tumbled off the table onto the floor, the heavy table falling on top of him, the tools raining down on him, narrowly missing his head. He heard a loud *crack!* looked up and saw the prop shelf tilt and come crashing down.

He was conscious but helplessly pinned beneath the rubble.

Chapter Forty-Three

· ·

THE SOHO SWAMI knew he must start his act soon, before the crowd grew weary of the songs and stormed the stage, not an unheard-of event in London theatres. But Stefan still had not shown himself. He removed a handkerchief from the sleeve of his voluminous robe and wiped the sweat from his brow. The giant turban wobbled on his head. He returned the cloth to his sleeve, threw back his shoulders and resolutely strode out from the wing to center stage. When he appeared, the crowd went silent in expectation. The Swami stood nervously on stage, surveying the faces in the crowd trying to gauge their emotions. *Quiet now~good~but how long would that last?*

He turned. Behind him stood a table with nothing on it but a wine bottle and a tin funnel. A chair stood close beside the table. Still, one thing was missing~Stefan! He took out the handkerchief again and mopped the sweat dripping into his eyes.

Get ahold of yourself, man! You're the great Soho Swami!

He took a deep breath and turned back to the audience. "Ladies and gentlemen, thank you for your patience. My young protege is shy and a little nervous, as you all can well imagine. After all, he will be taking his very life in his hands! Please, I ask your forbearance for just a few minutes more as he prepares himself for this ultimate performance."

He gestured to the wine bottle behind him, wishing desperately he had imbibed even more gin. "In the meantime," he continued, trying desperately to stall for time, "I will regale you with some wondrous magic of my own."

Scattered catcalls and insults rose from the audience.

"Yes, well . . .for my feats, I require the aid of an assistant." He scanned the audience, looking up to the royal box where he spotted Lucinda sitting next to Lord Cumberland.

"Ah, there she is, my lovely assistant, Lucy. With Lord Cumberland's permission, of course, would you come down to help me?"

On hearing his name, Cumberland stood, acknowledging polite applause from the crowd, and made a show of sending Lucinda off, as if he were her father offering her hand in marriage to some eligible gentleman.

Lucinda stood and was about to step into the aisle when suddenly, her skirts snagged on the railing before the box, jerking her back. She twisted around and was about to pitch over the rail, when Cumberland leaped to her side and grabbed her around the waist, pulling her close and preventing her fall.

The crowd broke into wild applause and cheers. "Good show, Cumberland!" someone shouted.

Lucinda seemed to faint in Cumberland's arms but as he held her close, her fingers busily worked inside his coat and deftly lifted the jeweled dagger. She carefully slipped the dagger beneath her corset and then magically recovered her senses. She looked deeply into his eyes and breathed huskily, "Thank you, m'lord! I owe you my life!"

Amazingly, he blushed. Still holding her close, he said, "It was my pleasure, my dear."

She disengaged herself from his embrace, stepped back into the aisle and curtseyed deeply to him. The crowd continued its enthusiastic applause as she made her way down to the stage to join the Swami.

Chapter Forty-Four

· ·

THE SWAMI'S KEEN instincts told him that tonight was a one-way passage to Hell, and he wanted off the ship. If it hadn't been for the unruly crowd's endearment to the stout woman's musical talents, they may have erupted in a riot. He had to admit, the gypsy lad had fooled him. The passion he saw in Stefan was weaker than he thought. Talented or not, by running away the lad showed his true spirit. *No matter now.* The great Swami must use his theatrical skills to calm the storm.

He saw Lucinda heading toward the stage. How lucky, he thought that she didn't tumble over the rail. He trotted to the front, reaching out his hand to pull her up onto the stage. At the same time, he waved to the maestro to play yet another fanfare.

"Lords, ladies and gentlemen," said the Swami in a deep tone. "The musical portion of our show is over. We shall now turn to the mystical wizardry that I have gleaned from my many journeys to the Far East. Prepare to be astounded!"

A few boos came up from the crowd. A tossed cabbage fell near him and rolled away. "Oh, I say!"

"We want the conjuror! Get on with it!" someone yelled.

The Swami took Lucinda's hand and together they moved to center stage. "As I was saying, now that I have my talented and lovely assistant, Lucy, the real show will begin."

He took a step back so she could be front and center, a shield to protect him from further projectiles. He whispered to her, "Take a long, deep bow. We must calm these jackals."

Smiling, made a long low curtsey that pleased the crowd. At least the male portion of the crowd.

"Lucy will help me perform the mystical candle legerdemain." In a low voice the Swami said to her, "Fetch me the large clear goblet and a candle."

As she collected the items, the Swami walked to the front of the stage.

"On my journey to Kathmandu, I ventured into an alabaster temple. Sunlight reflecting off its golden dome made it seem as if it were ablaze. Inside, the majestic hall glowed with ten thousand candles. I have brought back one of them. Lucy, bring the candle forward."

She came forward, holding the candle and goblet and displayed them for the audience to see. They applauded and she immediately took another bow.

The Swami picked up a pitcher of water from the table. "Inside the temple, I was welcomed by a member of its sangha. As a respectful gesture, he taught me how to light a ceremonial candle not with fire . . . but with . . . water."

The crowd quieted, although the Swami noticed a few blokes stood in the aisle holding various vegetables ready to fling at his head if his act faltered. Perhaps, even if it didn't.

William had entered the theatre. He felt tension rising like heat from the audience. He knew the Swami could only perform so long before the crowd would wreak havoc if they didn't have the conjuration. He should never have trusted Montagu. He would deal with him later. Right now, he needed to inform the audience that after the Swami finished the night was over; that devil of a gypsy had run-off. One of the few solaces of the night was the profitable pickings his girls were doing among the wealthy audience members.

The Swami made a sweeping gesture with his hands, his robe falling away from his arms. "Lucy, take the candle and light the wick from the stage lantern."

She dipped the candle into the stage light, igniting it. She cupped the flame with her hand to protect it from blowing out as she walked back to him.

"Hold up the lit candle for all to see. Now, take the goblet from the table. Show it to the audience. As you can see, this ornate glass is void of any contents. In a moment, I will have Lucy place the candle into the goblet." Turning to her, he said, "But, first my dear, blow out the flame."

A tiny wisp of smoke curled upwards, the stage lights making it incandescent, like a lost spirit, and faded out.

"Excellent. Now place the candle in the goblet."

The Swami held up a pitcher. "In this vessel I have sweet spring water."

He dipped his hand into the water and droplets fell from his fingers back into the pitcher.

"Lucy, hold the goblet firmly as I shall pour the water into it, which through my wizardly powers will light the candle inside!"

Lucinda had practiced this act several times with him, but now it seemed that the thin layer of phosphorus the Swami had smeared inside the goblet was more than what they had used in practice.

The Swami slowly poured the water so the audience could watch the level rise in the goblet. A yellow flash appeared, and a spark lit the candle. The Swami grabbed the goblet from her and held it high for the cheering audience to see. Suddenly, the excess phosphorous burst into flame, creating a ball of fire that exploded out of the goblet, landing on the wooden floor. The dry old planks immediately caught fire. The Swami screamed. He dropped the goblet. It shattered on the floor, shooting flames everywhere.

Lucinda grabbed the water pitcher from the stunned Swami and dowsed the flames, smoke like a flock of spirits drifting upward. The crowd booed. Vegetables flew. The Swami ducked backwards batting away a cabbage.

William rushed up the steps to the stage. He held up his hands to the angry crowd. "Gentlemen, ladies, please! Calm yourselves!"

A tomato flew and splattered against his leg. William looked down at the mess and frowned. "Just lovely. Please, I beg of you, be calm."

Louder catcalls and the stomping of feet rang out.

William yelled, "QUIET!"

His tone got even the Swami's attention. Lord Cumberland leaned forward to hear him.

"It seems that scoundrel of a gypsy will not show his face," William said. He felt the agitation in the audience like a calm before a violent storm. "I humbly apologize for his rudeness." He glanced up and saw Cumberland talking to a large man seated in the box beside his. "But I will make it up to each of you and present everyone with a voucher for free admission to our next show!"

The outraged audience hissed and screamed. "To hell with your bloody voucher!" someone said. "Give us back our money!"

William raised his hands. "Be reasonable, you've seen a grand show tonight with music and the Great Swami!"

A woman dressed in a vermillion mantua holding a small parasol rose to speak. Her husband attempted to pull her back to her seat, but with a quick thrust of her parasol he let her be. She shouted, "We've been waiting for this so-called conjuror, and we want to see him climb into that there bottle. I told my mister he's daft to believe such lunacy."

Further back a man wearing fine silk threads stood. "I've got money riding on the gypsy lad, and I aim to collect when he succeeds. So, there will be more than hell to pay if he doesn't show."

Throughout the room, cries of "Here! Here!" grew louder.

People were standing and flinging rotten vegetables. William and the Swami were literally dancing to avoid being hit. Lucinda had slunk to the rear of the stage, fearful of the angry crowd.

William saw that the large man beside Lord Cumberland was now standing. He recognized the man as Cumberland's new protégé, Jack Broughton, England's bare-knuckles champion. Broughton started pulling on his seat, feverishly rocking it until the iron nails that held it to the floor ripped free. He lifted the chair and flung it down, crashing onto the stage, nearly hitting William.

As the threatening crowd rose to its feet, William shouted, "Alright then, full refunds!"

From the second row a man rose and shouted, "Show us the money, you thief! Now!"

"Of course, I will. I'll fetch it immediately!"

William, keeping a wary eye on Broughton, jumped off the stage. He knew it would be faster to get to the box office if he ran down the main theatre aisle and he did so at a thoroughbred's pace.

An audience member turned to his friend and said, "Think he'll come back?"

His friend watched the manager run past them. His eyes widened. "Good lord! He's going to abscond with the money!" He jumped to his feet and shouted, "Grab him! Don't let him get away!"

Chapter Forty-Five

ALONE ON STAGE before a sold-out audience. Every actor's dream thought the Swami, but this one was more a nightmare. He turned, looking for Lucy, but alas, she too had deserted him. The band members all sat motionless, wondering what should the great Swami do? The one blessing was that vegetables were no longer being flung to the stage. Glancing back at the table with the wine bottle, the Swami pleaded, *gypsy lad, please appear.* But the Swami's magic was not strong enough to conjure him up. The crowd had become eerily silent, all eyes focused on him. Slowly, he took a step to the side, his eyes glancing to the wings while his face smiled at the audience. Maybe he could dash away through the wing and out the stage door. The crowd was quiet, like dawn in a church graveyard. Another step to the wing. *Could he make it?*

"WE'VE BEEN ROBBED!" shouted William, racing from the wing onto the stage, pushing the Swami aside. His voice echoed throughout the theatre. "The box-office has been broken into! A thief is on the loose!"

The audience was stunned. Someone shouted, "Fraud!"

William walked to the front of the stage, "I beg of you, if there are any constables in the audience, come to my rescue."

Another audience member screamed, "Rescue? You'd better rescue our money, you bloody cheat."

"Swindler!"

The crowd had turned ugly.

"I will offer a substantial reward for anyone who knows who looted the theatre!"

"You're a liar and you've robbed us!"

"Get him!"

The crowd exploded in anger. Out of control. William pushed the Swami to the floor, jumped off the stage, and ran for his life but the mob immediately swallowed him up.

The Swami sat on the floor collecting himself when several audience members leaped onto the stage. They ignored him and started tipping over his props table, smashing everything. Others in the theatre started ripping up the seats, throwing whatever came to hand.

A skinny man reached down and picked the Swami up from the floor. Thanking the man with a smile, the Swami noted the rage upon his face. He reached into his inner vest pocket and pulled out a small coin purse and handed the man a quid.

"Please take this pittance for your troubles," he said.

Then he leapt off the stage and ran toward the exit. His turban swayed and fell to the ground. A small bottle of gin rolled out of it. He stopped to retrieve it but seeing the battle royale unfolding in the room, bolted for the front door.

The crowd observed his flight and fell silent. The front door slammed shut, breaking the silence. Then, shouts and curses bounced off the theatre walls. The stage was a disaster, props and vegetables strewn everywhere. At the back of the stage the small conjuror table stood untouched by the mob. Like a lonely gravestone, the funnel remained in the neck of the bottle.

A riot broke out. Anything that was not tied down was usable ammunition to be hurled onto the stage. A chair flew and knocked over a stage lantern. Another floor lamp near the curtains crashed to the floor. Yellow flames leaped out and grabbed hold of the fringed curtain. In seconds, the curtain flared up in fire and smoke. Flames spread, people screamed and stampeded to the exit. The Haymarket had quickly become a tinderbox.

The band struck up, 'Rule, Britannia!' which did not drown out the panic. The maestro, seeing his efforts were fruitless, dropped his baton, and ran out with the crowd.

The royal boxes were designed for comfort and wondrous views of the stage, but those balcony seats had no exits. The only way in or out was through a narrow staircase that led to the first floor. Lord Cumberland struggled to escape his seat, screaming as flames crawled up the walls and smoke billowed everywhere. His terrified bodyguards ran off. As he watched them flee, Cumberland pushed himself up. He reached for his dagger but, adding to his despair, found it missing! Shaking his fist, he cursed the mob and shouted, "Run ye jackals, the hangman's noose will reward your cowardice!"

Jack Broughton jumped from his seat into Cumberland's box. He bent down and reached around Cumberland's legs with his long arms, hoisting him over his shoulders like a sack of grain. Cumberland stopped screaming. Broughton pushed his way past terrorized patrons as he headed to the stairs.

Slung over the boxer's shoulders, Cumberland shouted, "Fraud! Monty will pay for this!"

Chapter Forty-Six

IT WAS AS though Hell had pushed up from the depths to swallow the theatre in its flaming maw. Smoke billowed into the hall where Lucinda frantically searched her pockets for the key to the prop room.

Dear God! Where is it? Where's that damned key?

She looked up and saw flames licking the stage curtains. It wouldn't be long before they reached her. People were yelling, running to escape. All was pandemonium.

Where was that key!

A spectral figure suddenly emerged from the smoke and grabbed her by the arm.

"Lucinda!" Montagu said, "I've been looking for you. Give me Cumberland's dagger! Quickly! This place is going to burn down around our ears."

He tried to drag her out of the building, but she resisted.

"No!"

"No? Are you mad?"

"I can't go," she said, breaking free of his grasp. She noticed the bulging cloth bag the duke carried but whatever he was up to wasn't her concern. "Stefan is locked in the prop room! I can't find the key!"

"Who cares?"

She stared at him, as if struck. "What? You don't understand. He'll die! Help me get him out!"

Flames crackled in the hall as the fire crept closer. The smoke grew dense.

"You're crazy," Montagu said, "He's not here. He never showed up for his performance." Smoke began to swirl around them. His eyes watered. "Give me the dagger, we have to go!" He tried to grab her, but she backed away.

"Stefan *is* here," she said. "I'm the one who locked him in. Help me free him and I'll give you the dagger!"

He saw the determination on her face and knew he was running out of time. "Alright, I'll do it. But . . ." A sudden fit of coughing interrupted him. "But you better not be lying to me!"

They ran to the prop room. Lucinda pounded on the door. "Stefan! Stefan, can you hear me?"

"No time for this," Montagu said, dropping the bag and pushing her out of the way. "Stand aside!"

He took a step back then hurled himself against the door. It shook in its frame but held fast. "Blast!" He kicked it once, twice, and it finally flew open, slamming against the wall. He stood away, breathing hard. "There! Now the dagger."

She ignored him when she saw Stefan lying beneath a pile of rubble. "Oh, God!" She rushed into the room. She didn't know if he still breathed, but then his eyelids fluttered, and his eyes opened.

"Lucinda! Help me, I'm trapped!"

Smoke was drifting into the room, the walls growing hot. She fell to her knees and started throwing off the debris that held Stefan fast. The hot air was like a steam bath, and she sweated as she struggled to free him.

"The dagger!" Montagu said, from outside the room.

She turned to him. "Help me, John, or I swear you'll never see the dagger!"

"Get this thing off me," Stefan said, squirming beneath the shelf. "We'll be burned alive!"

"John!" she said.

"Oh, for the love of God!"

He entered the room and squatting beside her, grabbed hold of the heavy shelf. Together, they managed to lift it up enough for Stefan to crawl out from under it.

"Now, for the last time, give me the bloody dagger!" Montagu said.

"Here, take it" She pulled the knife from under her corset and handed it to him.

"That's where you hid it?" He laughed. "I could have just taken it. No matter," he said, picking up the cloth bag, "I've got what I want."

Nodding toward Stefan, he said to her, "And I suppose you do as well. *Merci*, Lucinda, and *adieu*."

She didn't notice when he ran off as she helped Stefan up. The smoke was thick now, reducing their visibility. Flames were shooting up in the hall. There was no time to look for his walking stick.

"Lean on me!" she said, one arm around him. They staggered out of the room and down the hall to the exit. It was slow going. The fire roared.

The stage curtains were a sheet of fire. Ceiling timbers had crashed to the floor and partially blocked the aisle.

"It's no good, I'm slowing you down!" said Stefan. "Run! Save yourself!"

She found a way around the fallen timbers, tearing her dress on the splintered wood, and dragged him with her. "Never! Not without you!"

Chapter Forty-Seven

IN A MOMENT, all was lost.

Fire!

He didn't know how it happened. One minute he was muscling through the crowd, trying to reach Jonah so they could find the gypsy and the next, the stage curtains were a wall of flames shooting out in all directions. Thick smoke billowed into the theatre and Melchior lost sight of the conjuration bottle that had been on the stage, his one good eye tearing from the smoke.

The gypsy had never shown up but surely, he would not have left the bottle. Then again, it was the book of spells that was the prize, not the bottle. Stefan must have the book, but was he even in the theatre? They had to find him.

"Jonah!" he called, catching a glimpse of him in the panicked crowd.

People were screaming, pushing, and shoving their way to the exit. Melchior saw several people knocked over and bowled to the floor as the mob rolled over them. A man large as a horse plowed a path through the crowd, carrying another man slung over his shoulder like a squealing pig in a poke.

"Jonah!" he called again. This time, the Hunter saw him. "Where's Abel?"

Before Jonah could answer, a jagged chunk of the proscenium broke loose with a loud *crack!*

Melchior yelled, "Watch out!"

Jonah jumped out of the way at the last second, the chunk smashing to the floor in a thousand pieces.

They couldn't remain there. The theatre had turned into an inferno. Smoke choked them, making it almost impossible to breathe. The heat was intense. Paint blistered off the walls. The fire roared through the building, fiery tongues voraciously licking the old, dry wood. There was no way the gypsy could still be there.

"Come on, Jonah! We have to run!"

"But Abel . . ."

"Damn Abel! If he has half a brain, he'll be running, too. Now, come on!"

Jonah cast a quick look around, hoping to find his friend, but coming up empty, hurried after Melchior as he left the theatre. They emerged from the building, gasping for air. They collapsed on the footpath. All around them, people were retching, coughing, staggering away from the burning building.

Jonah propped himself up on one elbow. "Do you . . . do you think he's still inside?" he gasped.

"The gypsy?"

Jonah shook his head. "No. Abel."

He ignored the question he thought did not have a positive answer. Melchior stood and grabbed Jonah by the arm, helping him up.

"Come on," he said, "we have to get away from here."

Chapter Forty-Eight

WITH THE CLOTH bag in hand, Montagu struggled to reach the back door where Sophia would be waiting. A moving ridge of black smoke stung his eyes. With his free hand, he brought his monogrammed silk kerchief to his face. The hallway was familiar to him, but now he was confused. The leaping flames and the fallen timbers created a maze of fire which he would have to navigate to save his hide. Even with the kerchief held tightly to his face, every breath he took burned in his chest. His eyes watered. He began to doubt if he could escape with his life.

Suddenly, as if angels had arrived, the exit door flew open. The fire illuminated a figure standing in the doorway. He squinted through the smoke.

"Sophia! Is that you? Thank the gods, you are my saving grace!"

"Toss me the bag, the horses are getting spooked!"

At first, he was hesitant, but maybe he could run faster without holding the bag. He rocked it behind him, then forward, letting it spring from his hand. She bent down and quickly retrieved it, turned, and ran to the horses. The exit door swayed then closed before Montagu could reach it.

"Nooo!"

His scream echoed in the hallway, sounding like a banshee's cry. He reached for the door and grabbed the handle, which was red hot iron, burning his hand as he opened the door.

Sophia was stuffing the money into her saddle bags when he exited the theatre and stood on the loading dock gasping for air. She leaped upon her mare, grabbing the reins. As he staggered forward, she saw that Montagu was hurt. He held up his burnt hand, tears streaming from his face, his silk kerchief flying away. He started down the steps toward her.

Flames erupted from the open door. A cloud of smoke and heat flew at them. Sophia's horse reared and she struggled to control the frightened mare. Montagu's terrified horse bolted down the courtyard.

He watched his horse flee down the street. He shouted to Sophia,

"Make room, I'll leap onto your horse!" He continued down the landing but stumbled and fell the last three steps. He heard a snap as his left leg bent backwards. Pain knifed through him. He heard a loud hissing sound as he tried to stand. His thoughts were jumbled from his fear and the pain of his burnt hand and injured leg.

Was it broken?

Then he saw it. A large black snake with diamond-like scales slithered between him and Sophia's horse, blocking his way. Her horse reared again as its eyes focused on the terror at its feet. Sophia almost slipped off but regained her balance. She pulled tightly on the reins.

"What the blazes is this?" Montagu cried out, his useless leg slowing him down as he tried to elude the snake. He was too slow. The serpent, its yellow eyes glowing, struck, sending him to the ground. He tried to roll away from the demon. Like a boa constrictor, it wrapped itself around his legs and squeezed. He swung his arms wildly at the snake, screaming at it to release him. The snake kept a tighter grip, squeezing the breath out of him.

"Sophia, help me!"

She kicked her horse, turned to flee the courtyard, and laughingly said, "Don't you mean, *Madam?*"

She gave the mare the reins, calling out, "Not a chance, Monty!" as she rode off.

Chapter Forty-Nine

BROUGHTON CARRIED CUMBERLAND through the fleeing crowd and set him on his feet in the middle of the street where his cowardly guards surrounded him as though they had never left his side, never left him to roast in the theatre like so much mutton.

"A fine group of heroes, you lot are!" he bawled, his face red, eyes wild. "I could have been burnt to a crisp were it not for Jack, here."

The guards shifted uneasily; no one met his eye.

He angrily brushed off the soot from his coat. "Why are you standing there like fools? Go!" he said. "Find the performers and that tallywag owner, whatever his name is!"

The guards quickly moved off, only too happy to escape their lordship's ire. No one wanted to cross the "Butcher of Culloden."

"And above all, find my dagger!" he yelled after them.

He turned to the theatre, looking now more like an immense Hindu funeral pyre than a place of entertainment and merriment. He spotted a disheveled William threading his way through the crowd.

"Wait! Yonder stands the reprobate," said Cumberland. "Arrest him!"

Two Bow Street Runners shoved their way through the crowd, grabbed hold of William and hauled him before Cumberland, with William protesting, "I've done nothing wrong!"

A Bow Street Runner discovered Stefan and Lucinda at the edge of the crowd. He raised the alarm and was answered by two other runners and one of Cumberland's men, who encircled the besmudged and bedraggled couple. Before they could comprehend what was happening, they too, found themselves alongside the theatre manager, standing before the Duke of Cumberland.

"Arrest them as well," Cumberland said, a smug smile upon his face.

"Your Grace . . ." began Lucinda, but Stefan, looking out to the crowd and believing he saw Cassandra, hushed her.

"Shhh, it's alright," he whispered. "Don't say a word that could be used against us."

Cumberland was satisfied that the perpetrators had been apprehended but his dagger remained lost. He called out loud enough for all to hear, "Where is my dagger? Five hundred pounds sterling to the man who can bring it to me!"

Cassandra heard his pledge even from where she stood at the perimeter of the crowd. She could also see that Stefan and Lucinda were uninjured. *Thank the Fates!* That was a relief but there was something perhaps even more important–the conjuror bottle. *Where was it?* She made her way against the tide of people flooding out of the theatre. Fire or no, she had to find that bottle!

Melchior and Jonah stood at the periphery of the crowd gathered in the street, trying to regain their breath. Melchior raised his head. As if drawn by a magnet, his attention focused on a woman cautiously making her way *toward* the burning building. He couldn't see her face, but her clothing clearly identified her as Romani. *Who was she? Where was she going?*

He nudged Jonah. "Stay here," he said, "and pay attention."

Melchior slipped through the crowd, following the woman at a distance.

Cassandra shouldered her way through the people fleeing the burning theatre, ignoring their alarmed expressions and their cries to her: *Go back!* They didn't understand. How could they? The bottle must still be in the theatre. She had to get it back.

The heat of the fire rolled over her like a flaming wave as she drew closer to the theatre. Flames shot out from the windows. Black smoke billowed above the roof, rising to the night sky like a burnt offering, blotting out the stars. The doors were open and, covering her mouth and nose with a kerchief she withdrew from her skirt pocket, she slipped inside.

Melchior saw her enter the theatre. *Impossible! What was she thinking?*

But there was no help for it; he had to follow her. He pulled his shirt up over his nose and mouth as a makeshift mask and plunged into the building.

Dense smoke filled the theatre, swirling around Cassandra. Flames crackled and roared as they devoured the seats, the boxes, the curtains, and tapestries, but a simple wave of her hand kept the flames at bay.

Melchior could barely see her through the smoke and flames but suddenly they parted, seemingly at her command! *The woman must be a conjuror!*

She hurried down the aisle, stumbling on debris hidden in the smoke, but finally made it to the stage. Melchior tried to follow her but as soon as he reached the spot where she had been, the flames closed rank and shot up again, beating him back.

The conjuror bottle! She saw it sitting on the table at the rear of the stage, a ring of flames around it, threatening it, but unable to get any closer. The bottle's magic was powerful. She clambered up the steps and once again gesturing with her hand, parted an opening in the wall of flame. The heat nearly overcame her as she pushed through and took hold of the bottle. It was warm to the touch but otherwise undamaged.

Melchior stumbled into the smoke-filled theatre, trying to find a way through the flames. He could no longer see the woman. His breathing labored, sweat pouring off him, Melchior staggered backwards and stepped on something that nearly tripped him. He looked down and saw an arm attached to a body crushed beneath a heavy beam. Through the charred sleeve of the shirt, he saw the serpent and book tattoo.

Abel!

He paused, shocked, until a wave of searing heat blasted him, and he knew he had to get out. Like a blind man, he groped his way through the smoke, flames, and debris until he once again emerged outside.

Cassandra cradled the bottle in her arms as though it was as precious as a baby and, perhaps it was. She hurried up the aisle and exited the theatre, only too glad to be out in the night air again.

Chapter Fifty

JOHN GRAY HAD just stoked the embers in his fireplace one last time as he finished his glass of port and was about to retire early to his warm featherbed. Like most days, he had put in long hours and looked forward to a quiet night.

Then came the banging. A loud knock followed by several poundings that rocked his apartment. He heard someone shouting, "Master Gray, come quick! London's on fire! We are on fire!"

He threw open his door to find Samuel Marbray and a crowd on his stoop, a larger group assembled on the street. "Sorry to disturb you Master Gray, but there's a large fire on Haymarket Street," Marbray said. "The theatre is burning. I fear it's out of control!"

Marbray was not a man to panic, so his tone and look concerned Gray. "Calm down Samuel. Have you alerted the crews?"

"Aye, we have sir, but this is bad sir. Real bad. It might be another big one, like the Great Fire of London, I reckon."

"I'll get dressed and be there shortly!"

From his porch he saw the night sky illuminated brightly as a Viking funeral pyre. It worried him. He ran to his bedroom to change. He pulled on his boots and reflected that men like Marbray were well-trained on advanced techniques to control these blazes. Gray's fire office was one of the first in London to employ flexible leather hoses with brass fittings attached to hand-pumped, horse-drawn fire engines. Yet, it was disturbing to hear the dismay in Marbray's voice. He gathered his hat and gloves and hurried the ten blocks to the fire.

He saw the Duke of Cumberland standing in the middle of the cobble-stone street. He had been Cumberland's guest at several gambling parties where they had played cards. A small crowd surrounded him, some of them among London's finest. *Could that person being detained by constables be Haymarket? Why?*

"Lord Cumberland, were you in attendance at the theatre tonight? Are you alright?" Gray said.

Cumberland did not respond to him at first, his eyes darting around the scene. He finally turned to Gray and said, "Yes, indeed! A night to be remembered for sure, as I rescued as many patrons as I could. I see that your men are up to the task and are fighting a brave fight."

"Rest assured they will not allow the fire to spread," Gray said.

Gray spoke to William and said, "William, I would need a word with you."

"That reprobate has been arrested and will soon be on his way to New-gate," Cumberland said, "and if I have my way he will be sleeping in chains by midnight!"

Gray was unhappy to hear that, for surely it meant Haymarket would be unable to pay his insurance. "Well, Your Grace, I am pleased that the angels have spared you and I commend you on your bravery, but I must attend to my men. I would advise you that we will be making a fire break of this theatre and trust you stay far afield of the upcoming explosion."

He bowed and as he turned to go, three Bow Street Runners arrived almost knocking him down. They dragged a struggling Montagu between them and eagerly presented their catch to Cumberland.

"We've got 'im, your Grace!" said a barrel-chested Runner. "The crazy bloke said he was attacked by a giant snake!"

The second Runner, a short man with a long stubbled face added, "But do we see a snake? No, we don't see a snake. We don't see nothing. Just 'im rolling around on the ground behind the theatre screaming, 'Get it off me! Get it off!' I say to 'im, this 'ere's London, you daft puppy, not the bloody Amazon!"

A third Runner, carrying a heavy club in one hand, held Montagu by the ragged collar of his coat. He said, "We found him in this foul-smell-ing condition, burnt flesh and a broken limb. Mind you, I would have enjoyed making those marks on this scallywag myself! Claims he's a duke of some sort."

The three Runners broke out in laughter.

Cumberland hardly heard their report as he looked at Montagu, hum-bled before him. Clothes ripped, soot covering his face and his leg crook-ed. Obviously, the duke was in pain. Cumberland almost shed a tear of sympathy for his old acquaintance, but as the sound of the fire and screams of the crowd echoed through the street, his pity died quickly as a spent candle.

"Arrest him! Clap him in irons! To Newgate with them all!"

Montagu pleaded, "But Your Grace, I'm innocent!" He freed his arms and cupped his burnt hands, as if to plead for mercy before God.

William interjected, "That's a lie! You stole all the money from the box office. You deserve the gallows!"

Montagu was startled. "Seems a trifle harsh, William." He turned back to Cumberland. "But, Your Grace, you know me. You know I'm no thief!"

"You're worse than a thief! This whole night has been an embarrassment to the royal house, my friends, and all of London. You've humiliated us all!" said Cumberland.

Lucinda cried out, "But he *is* a thief!"

She pushed herself away from her guards and came forward, turning to Cumberland. "M'lord, I think this shag-bag has something of value to you." She deftly reached into Montagu's coat and pulled out Cumberland's jeweled dagger. "I believe this belongs to you."

Cumberland's eyes grew wide, his brows raised, and joy filled his soul as he grabbed the dagger from her hand. He raised it high over his head for all to see.

Deep in the crowd, Cassandra carried the conjuror bottle she had taken from the theatre. As Cumberland waved his dagger, she recognized the large red stone in the hilt. *The Bloodstone!*

Cumberland drew down his dagger and yelled to the waiting constables and Runners, "Get chains for that rogue, and the theatre owner!"

To Lucinda he said, "As for you, my dear. . ." He took a step closer to her, smiling. "You are free to go, as is your lame friend."

The constables wrapped chains around William and Montagu and pulled them to an empty coal cart they commandeered to haul the prisoners to Newgate Prison. William screamed his innocence while Montagu screamed in pain as they dragged him and his twisted leg over the cobblestones to the cart.

Cumberland raised his chin, and with a half-grin turned his attention to Lucinda. With a quiet eloquence, he took her hand and lifted it to his lips, gently kissing it.

"I can never repay you, but I can invite you to the royal tea at my country estate. It is the social event of the year, and you will be my guest of honor."

Stefan came forward. He bowed politely before Cumberland. "Your Grace, did you not declare a five-hundred-pound sterling reward for the return of your dagger?"

Cumberland froze, his eyes burned as red as the night sky but remained silent. Lucinda disrupted the awkward moment as she met Cumberland's eyes and politely replied, "It will be my pleasure to attend, Your Grace."

He nodded, delighted by her answer, but hurled a scowl at Stefan, and walked towards his coach. He stopped and turned back to her. "My attendant will contact you and provide you with the proper dress to wear. It's the least I can do. 'Till then."

The coachmen set down the stepping stool to ease Cumberland's entry into the coach. Broughton, who had been standing quietly aside but alert to any danger to Cumberland, started to enter the coach with him, but Cumberland waved him off.

"It's been a dreadful night. I suggest you call for a hackney and get some rest, as you need to prepare for your next bout," Cumberland said, closing the door. He thumped the roof with the hilt of his dagger and the coach took off.

In all the commotion, Broughton knew he would not easily find a hackney and prepared himself for a twelve-mile walk. The crowd was as thick as the smoke billowing from the fire, as Broughton weaved his way through them, occasionally stopping to watch the fire brigade attack the blaze. The crowds began to thin as he walked down Haymarket where he spotted a hackney. He rushed over to the carriage at the same time as a tall, disheveled man approached it. Broughton got there first and grabbed the door handle. Recognition flashed between the two men.

"You!" they said, simultaneously.

Surprise turned to fear when the Swami realized he was face to face with Jack Broughton, bare-knuckle champion. The man who had hurled a chair at him. "Please, kind sir," he pleaded, "don't hurt me. This evening was not my doing, but I'm afraid it might now turn out to be my undoing."

Broughton did not respond to the rumpled man who he recognized as the "great" Swami but held firmly to the handle.

"Please, I need to flee this street as I fear this enraged crowd may find me, although I am blameless for what has transpired."

"And I have a twelve-mile walk ahead of me to Oxford Lane so, I too, need this carriage," replied Broughton.

"Oxford Lane is near where I am headed! Can I persuade you to share? It will be my honor to pay the driver."

Broughton heard his mum's soft voice reading the Good Book to him: *"show hospitality to strangers, for thereby some have entertained angels unawares."* He opened the door and stepped back so the Swami could enter.

The Swami didn't hesitate. He stumbled as he leaned into the cab and grasped Broughton's shoulder. "My, you are a strong beast," he said. Bumping his head on the door frame, he bumbled his way to a seat.

Broughton called up to the driver, "To Oxford Lane!"

Chapter Fifty-One

THE STREETLIGHTS HAD been extinguished as a precaution, making the street pitch-dark, except for the area in front of the theatre, illuminated by the dancing flames. The darkness hampered Stefan's attempt to find his walking stick. He assumed it had been burned in the theatre. He tried to walk but faltered. Lucinda quickly supported him.

"Not sure how far I can walk without my stick."

"No matter, Stefan. Lean on me, that's all you need."

He took a firmer hold on her. His lean turned into an embrace. She looked into his eyes. She was about to speak, but he placed two fingers on her lips to forestall her and gave her a lingering kiss.

He whispered to her, "You lead the way."

Cassandra stood waiting by the cart, carefully holding the conjuror bottle in her arms. She placed it on the seat and removed a horse blanket from the cart. She was about to wrap the bottle in the blanket, but something attracted her attention. She froze, gazing intently at the bottle, the blanket in her hands. She dropped the blanket and moved closer to the bottle. She gently placed her hand against the glass. Warmth seemed to radiate from inside it. Something was becoming visible in the depths of the bottle, gradually becoming more visible, like a fish swimming up to the surface.

Could it be?

The shape took the appearance of a hand and floated up to match her hand through the glass. A tear slid down her face as she looked upon the two hands touching, but not touching. "Soon you shall be free," she whispered.

Then, picking up the blanket, she carefully wrapped it around the bottle and placed it in the cart. She wiped away her tears just as Stefan and Lucinda appeared. She smiled as she took Lucinda's hand and said, "A guest at the royal tea, are ye?"

She remembered how the fire had illuminated Cumberland's jewel-encrusted dagger and the Bloodstone embedded in the hilt. She looked deeply into Lucinda's eyes. "My sweet, the Fates tell me there is one more task yet at hand for you," she said.

Lucinda smiled as she climbed into the cart with Cassandra. Stefan cracked the reins, and they began the journey back to camp, the conjuror bottle gently rocking, *The Book of Shadows* safely hidden inside Stefan's coat.

None of them noticed Melchior hiding in the shadows but he watched them with keen eyes. So, the gypsy yet lived. The Hunter nodded grimly. Good. The book had not yet eluded him.

Indeed, the pursuit had only just begun.

The End
 Or is it?

Want to read more of *The Bottle Conjuror*? The saga continues in:
The Bottle Conjuror, Book 2—The Bloodstone
Here's a preview:

Prologue

· · · · · · · · · · · · ·

FOG LAY THICK in the forest, its tentacles floating around trees
whose ghostly figures were barely discernible yet ominously palpable.
Melchior knew there were forest entities one should have enough sense
to fear, ancient creatures who would not be cowed by even his immense
stature and muscular brawn. As he stepped from deep shadows into pools
of silvered moonlight and into shadow again, he kept his one good eye
trained on the mist, the skeletal branches arching overhead, the gnarled
thickets on all sides. Danger could come from anywhere.

Had he not been summoned he would be asleep in his tiny room in
London, overlooking the abandoned cemetery. He lived alone, a Hunter,
feared by all Romani, but fearing nothing or no one in return except for
this one thing. A summons from Kali could not be ignored.

The damp mist clung to his clothes, pearled in his beard, settling on
him like a shroud. There was no path through the forest and though he
had never been there before his feet seemed to have a mind of their own,
carrying him purposely deeper into the woods. He trusted that mystical
guidance as the handiwork of Kali.

Razor-edged brambles scored his hands as he pushed them out of the
way. Bony branches plucked at his clothes, slowing his progress. Somewhere far off, perhaps not too far off, a wolf howled. The cry stopped him
only for a moment before he pushed on through the mist.

After what seemed like an eternity of walking, Melchior saw that the
fog had taken on a pale, yellow hue. He was drawing closer. He felt his
heart quicken. The night chill began to dissipate, replaced by some un-
earthly warmth as the color deepened. The trees and bushes thinned, and
he found himself on the edge of a clearing. In the center roared a large
fire. Flames leapt into the sky, throwing up cinders that floated skyward
like black ghosts. The fire was so bright that it took Melchior a few moments to discern the figure silhouetted against the flames.

Kali.

He could not distinguish any details as she held her back to him, staring into the fire. She was merely a black figure. But he knew her stance was more like a serpent risen up ready to strike. He stopped at the edge of the clearing, fearful.

He stood silently, sweat breaking upon his face in the heat. He did not speak. It was not his place.

"You've come," she said, without turning to him. Her voice was low and sibilant, yet it resounded in his ears like a pistol shot.

"Yes, my queen."

She sighed and the breeze in the forest sighed with her, briefly fanning the flames into a swirling whirlwind.

"Do you know why you've been summoned, Melchior?" He was slow to answer, and she repeated more sternly, "Do you?"

Glowing embers floated down around him. "The Book of Shadows, my queen?"

"At least you know that much," Kali said.

She moved, perhaps turning to him but he could not be certain with the bright flames stabbing his one good eye. He took a step back.

"The book, aye," she said, "but there is more. The Bloodstone. Without that, the book is worthless. And unless we have the stone, we Shaitaan are in great danger."

"Danger?"

She chuckled and the sound chilled his bones. "More to the point, we are dead."

Acknowledgements

THE AUTHORS WISH to thank the following people for their wonderful assistance as beta readers and editors: Debbie Felton, Aparajita Hazra, Terri Gagliardo, Constance Kirker, Mary Newman, Alice Dunn, Lisa Cunningham, Tammy Vande Vusse, Stephen Gagliardo, Susan Milrod and Kathy Lorenz.

Thanks to AgencyAxis for interior formatting and for our great cover designs.

Special thanks to the folks at Beck and Branch Publishers for their support and encouragement.

About the Authors

JOHN KACHUBA is the award-winning author of twelve books and is a frequent speaker on radio, podcasts, TV and at universities, libraries, and conferences. His website is: johnkachuba.com

JACK GAGLIARDO is an award-winning writer, producer, and director of, TV commercials, documentaries, and corporate videos. The Bottle Conjuror is Jack's first novel.

9 798986 606989